I0534866

THE
LADY
OF THE
LIGHTHOUSE

TERRI GREENING

This is a work of fiction. Names, characters, places, and incidents are products of the author's imagination or are used fictitiously and are not to be construed as real. Any resemblance to actual events, locations, organizations, or persons, living or dead, is entirely coincidental.

World Castle Publishing, LLC
Pensacola, Florida
Copyright © Terri Greening 2023
Hardback ISBN: 9798385875740
Paperback ISBN: 9781960076403
eBook ISBN: 9781960076410
First Edition World Castle Publishing, LLC, March 20, 2023
http://www.worldcastlepublishing.com

Licensing Notes
All rights reserved. No part of this book may be used or reproduced in any manner whatsoever without written permission, except in the case of brief quotations embodied in articles and reviews.
Cover: Karen Fuller
Editor: Maxine Bringenberg

This fictional novel is based on the little known fact that the Soo Locks in the Great Lakes region was under military protection during WWII due to fears of sabotage.

ACKNOWLEDGEMENTS

I would like to thank the teachers, students, editors, writers, and poets who generously shared their time and advice online and elsewhere to help make this novel possible. I would also like to thank the librarians, booksellers and book marketers for their insights and reading recommendations, the online writing groups for their community and inspiration and my publisher for this opportunity.

Cast your heart to the sea, Loralei.
Your Captain will return for you soon.

Let the light shine
In the window at night.
He will sail by the light of the moon.

Keep your heart open.
Let your light shine.
Your love will come back to you soon.

CHAPTER 1

Summer 1942

The evening sun set against the magenta and orange background of the sky as Loralei Lancaster watched the dark silhouette of a freighter float on the horizon. She sighed with delight at the artistry of the scene. She was in the only place she knew where she could look north over the lake and watch both gorgeous sunsets in the west and brilliant sunrises in the east. She felt blessed to live in a place so wild and untamed in its wilderness and natural beauty that it took her breath away.

Her life and her family's life had revolved around the lighthouse and the lake for as long as she could remember. Even now, she was waiting for her husband, Devon, to return home from a long voyage on the Great Lakes — or the inland seas, as some people called them. He was a shipping captain on one of the iron ore freighters that shipped cargo through Lake Huron to Detroit to bolster the war effort. She hoped the freighter she saw was Devon's and that he would be home soon, even though he was sometimes harsh to her when he returned. It was hard for him to be on land. He preferred his command and the order and structure of his "boat."

She finished pulling open the curtains she drew during the day to protect the prismatic Fresnel lens of the beacon from the sunlight and turned to look back over the rippling, indigo-blue waves from her vantage point high in the lighthouse. She perused the sky for warplanes, one of the new duties asked of every Portstown resident after rumors of a possible attack by the Germans had surfaced in a nearby town. She was relieved to see no sign of them. Rumors had been rampant in the area since the beginning of the war, and she didn't listen to many of them. But she listened to this one because she feared for the safety of her country.

She turned to see her grandfather, Edmund Clairmont, looking at her from the top step of the spiral staircase. His white hair and mustache set off the dark tan of his craggy, sun-wizened face, and he looked careworn when he gave her a small grin.

"Are you looking for Devon?" he asked.

"Yes, actually, I am. I hope that's his freighter out there," she replied.

Edmund walked to her side and gazed out the wide, tall windows of the lantern room. "It could be. It's time he was home."

"Yes, it's been a long wait this time," Loralei said quietly, feeling the loneliness that overtook her whenever Devon was sailing his freighter on a voyage. She missed her husband when he was gone, and she wanted to see him again.

"I came up to tell you I brought water up from the barrels in the basement and poured some in the sink to do the dinner dishes. It was a wonderful meal, as always," Edmund said.

"Thank you. That was Grandmama's recipe for apple cake with sauce for dessert. Do you remember?" she asked.

"How could I forget? It's legendary." Edmund's pale grey eyes twinkled at her.

Loralei smiled at her grandfather, grateful, not for the first time, that he lived in a cottage down the beach and came by to help with keeping the lighthouse. Her grandfather was the one person she could always count on to be there for her. Before he retired, he had been a shipping captain like his son, Loralei's father, who had been lost in a shipwreck when his freighter went down in the deadly Armistice Day storm on the Great Lakes two years ago.

She swallowed hard as she remembered the full extent of the losses that day. Devon's father, who had been part of the crew, and many friends and family members of the townspeople were lost as well. The shock of the disaster had irrevocably changed her, Devon, her grandfather, and everyone she knew in the town. Devon stopped talking to her, except to grumble, after his father's funeral. He had no other family in the area, and he spent a lot of time drinking by himself. And she needed him. She needed his touch. Sometimes she wondered if she or her marriage would ever recover.

"I'm going into town in the morning with Misha to see if the *Manitoulin* is in port. I want to be the first person Devon sees when he gets off," Loralei said.

"Do you want me to go with you? I've heard rumors that Jake Calico is back in town, and I don't want anything to happen to you. I'm sure he knows you're the lighthouse keeper, and there are rumors that he is sabotaging lighthouse beacons along the coastline so he can raid the cargo from the ships that crash on the rocks as a result," Edmund said.

Loralei glanced at Edmund and looked quickly away. She didn't want him to see the fear in her eyes. "I hadn't heard that. You can come if you'd like."

She tried to control her feelings. Hearing that Jake was around again upset her. She lived alone in the lighthouse with Misha most of the time, and she didn't want to have to fight off a notorious pirate by herself. She hoped she would never have to.

"Where's Misha?" she asked, changing the subject.

"He's asleep. I read him a story and put him to bed. He'll

be glad to see his father tomorrow. He told me he misses him," Edmund said.

"Yes, I know he does," Loralei said.

She looked back out over the lake. They stood together, watching as the amber sun sank into the water, taking the fiery colors of the sky with it and leaving a dusky twilight. The scene had been so beautiful she wondered if she could remember it and capture it in one of her paintings.

"I miss Devon. I get so lonely when he's gone," she said as the light waned.

She turned to brush away a tear. She tried so hard to be strong and responsible, and she didn't want anyone to see her cry.

"I know," Edmund said. "I miss him, too. But the lake is his life, as it was mine. And his country needs him now to sail the seas and support the war. He will return."

Loralei relaxed upon hearing the compassion in Edmund's gravelly voice. He was a strong, hardened seaman but a kind man, too, especially where she was concerned. He had shared so many losses with her—the loss of her mother and father, the loss that came with the sinking of ships, and the thousand tiny deaths of losing someone to the call of the sea. She felt he was the only person who understood her pain and grief. It seemed strange to her that grief could bring some people together and push others apart. When cancer had taken her mother from her as it had her grandmother before that, Devon had been there for her. But now, something kept him from her, and he didn't comfort her in her grief over her father's death. Nor did he allow her to comfort him. She didn't know why, and she didn't know if he would ever tell her. She missed his love and touch, and sometimes she missed her parents so much that she felt a physical ache. Having her grandfather around was the only thing that saw her through.

She felt him pat her on her arm. "I'll stay over tonight. We'll take the Jeep into town in the morning," he said.

"Thanks, Grandpapa," she said, glad he would spend the night again as he sometimes did.

She watched Edmund disappear down the staircase and went over to complete her nightly inspection of the beacon. She checked to make sure it was rotating properly to flash its bright light out across the lake to the ships that watched for its guiding beam. She carefully polished the surrounding brassworks, as she had done that morning when she polished the two-foot-four-inch tall, faceted glass lens. Prisms of light cast an eerie glow in the lantern room, and for a moment, she let her thoughts wander as she was transported to another time.

In the gleam of the freshly polished brass, she saw a young Devon from ten years earlier, before they were married, beckoning to her and smiling.

"Loralei, run to me. I can't wait a moment longer to have you in my arms," he said.

She ran toward him across the sand. "Devon, you've come for me for the graduation dance. I was afraid you'd forgotten."

"How could I forget my lovely girl?" he asked.

She reached him and threw her arms around him in a deep embrace, breathing in the strong, woodsy scent of him and feeling his muscular arms tighten about her. She felt his lips brush her hair and sighed blissfully. Devon stepped back and held out a bouquet of wildflowers.

"I brought these for you. I know how you love them," he said.

"Flowers. How lovely," she said.

She smiled as she took them from him and paused for a moment to breathe deeply of their fresh scent before looking back up at him. "Did the naval academy let you leave?"

"To see my best girl? Of course. I have a two-week pass," he answered.

She skipped next to him and held out her free hand as she tossed her long, blonde hair back behind her in the early-summer breeze. "Come with me back to the lighthouse. I'll put these in water right away. Does my father know you're here?"

"Yes, he told me where you were on the beach," he said.

He took her hand, and they walked up the sand back toward the lighthouse together.

Loralei startled back to the present as Devon's face faded away, leaving only the smooth glow of the brass in its wake. She shook her head to bring herself out of her reverie and wondered what had happened to her. Sometimes, lately, she found herself lost in thought for no reason. She and Devon had been so happy then. She missed that. But there was no use lingering on it, she decided. There was nothing she could do to change things back to the way they were.

She continued her work. She wiped the lantern room windows clean to make sure the light was clear and visible. When she was finished, she entered the time she had turned on the beacon, what the weather had been like that day and the number of vessels she had recently seen pass the lighthouse in the logbook. She turned to take one last look out over the slumbering lake before heading down the staircase herself.

She knew how important it was to keep the beacon going. It was what she and her family lived for and had always lived for—to bring the ships in safely, to guide them through the channel, and to save lives. Loralei was proud of her family of origin and of their French heritage. She was committed to raising a happy, healthy child who could carry on the family legacy, despite the hardships she might have to endure to do so. They were the Clairmonts of Portstown, Michigan. Her grandfather, Edmund Clairmont, had moved to the United States from France with his parents as a child, and they still had family there. Loralei had never met any of them, but she had seen grainy pictures of her grandfather's brother, Maurice, who was an art curator in Paris. He'd sent a letter that he intended to visit them soon, and Loralei hoped she might find in him a kindred spirit in the love of painting since no one else she knew, other than her mother, who had been a wildlife painter, was very interested in art.

She went to check on Misha and found him snugly tucked in under the quilt with his teddy, Bear-bear, next to him. Her heart welled up when she saw his cherubic face and slightly flushed cheeks in the glow of the nightlight. She bent to kiss him on his forehead and touched the silky curls of his long, blond hair that was so like hers. She would do anything for him, and she knew Devon felt the same way, despite his grumpiness when he was home. Misha was a lovely child, and she thanked God for him every day. She made the sign for goodnight to him, even though he was already asleep. They'd been working on sign language to deal with his progressive hearing loss, which would eventually leave him deaf. A tutor came to the lighthouse once in a while, bringing staples from town, and it made her feel connected to Misha to use sign language. She smoothed his hair back, and when he stirred at her touch, she smiled and left the room.

Later, as the full moon took its place in the night sky, Loralei left the lighthouse after making sure she was the only one still awake. She strolled to the lake and scrunched her toes in the sand as she stepped onto the cool beach. The night air was filled with the trill of a thousand crickets and the hum of a thousand more. She was meeting him again, her midnight lover. They met on calm summer nights when the moon cast sparkles of silver on the indigo waves that lapped quietly to shore. He was her secret passion, her guilty pleasure. She walked along the beach, gazing across the water, until after a while, she saw him in his birch bark canoe, gliding toward her in the distance. He was wild. His smooth, waist-length black hair blew behind him in the gentle night breeze. She shivered as he neared the shore and beached his canoe near her. His sinewy body moved stealthily, like the stalk of a cougar, as he walked toward her, shadowed in the light of the moon. When he reached her, he pulled her to him and kissed her with the passion of a wild spirit. She moaned with pleasure, her pent-up emotions releasing into his desire, and fell with him onto the sand. They didn't talk. They seldom did at first. They made love for hours on the desolate beach in the moonlight, wrapped in each other's arms. When the breeze cooled them and the night air began to chill, Loralei murmured words of love and moved to go.

"Fly away home, little dove, until we meet again. I will wait for you here with the moon and the stars a fortnight from now, and if you are here, we will love each other again on the shores of the Gitche Gumee," he said.

Loralei pressed her lips to his one more time and felt the warmth of his ardent kiss before standing and walking back down the beach toward the lighthouse.

***

The morning dawned bright and sunny. Devon Lancaster could see the pale, cerulean blue of the sky through the small circle of his porthole when he awoke on the freighter. They had docked the night before, and he was ready to dismiss his crew and hand over his command of the *Manitoulin* to another captain. It had been a long but productive voyage, and he was proud of his crew. They had sailed to Detroit and delivered their cargo of iron ore on schedule. It would be used in the steel mills to build weaponry to send to Europe for the war effort, which he was glad to be a part of for his country. He had a two-week break until his next voyage, and he wanted to take advantage of his time ashore, even though shore leave wasn't his favorite thing. He'd much rather be out on the lake, where his authority was clear and unchallenged. A ship captain inspired respect. On land, he was sought after by women who found his occupation and his air of command exciting, but he had no real control. And he needed that control to forget how powerless he had been over the storm that took his father from him. The lake was his life, and he only felt whole and real on the water.

Devon swung his legs off his berth and kicked the empty

rum bottle under the bed. It wasn't his favorite liquor, but whiskey was rationed during the war. He'd make sure to hide the bottle in his duffel bag later. Drinking while in command wasn't taken lightly by the shipping corporation. One nice thing about being onshore was the taverns. He could hide in them for hours with other sailors, swapping sailing stories and yarns. He could forget about all the people he'd lost in shipwrecks and gales and the family he'd once had.

It didn't take long for him to sign out and carry his duffel down the walkway to the dock. When he stepped on the dock, he felt a familiar pang of sadness at leaving the *Manitoulin* behind, but it was tempered with the anticipation of finding a drink.

As he walked down the dock and into Portstown, he realized it had changed in the time he'd been gone. There were guardsmen stationed around the port, and the whole atmosphere of the small town seemed hushed and different. The shops lining Main Street seemed empty and cold, and he shivered with the sudden realization of the change the war had brought to his hometown.

When he'd disembarked for a time in the Sault Ste. Marie at the Soo Locks, he'd seen soldiers stationed in doorways and on corners. There had been soldiers before, but not as many. Devon had felt a twinge of unease at seeing them and the guns they held staunchly by their sides. He hadn't realized the front of the war was so close to home, and he wondered what they were doing there. Had the Nazis infiltrated the country while he was gone? That hardly seemed possible.

He headed for the Blue Lake Tavern and breathed a sigh of relief when he entered the cool, dim tavern room with its creaky wood floor. The polished, golden wood of the counter glowed in the low light. He sat on a barstool and dropped his duffel bag next to him.

"Well, if it isn't Captain Devon. You're back. This one's on the house." Devon's brother-in-law, Finn, drew a draft and set it in front of him.

"Thanks," Devon said. He took a long swig of the cold, frothy beer and sighed, relaxing and enjoying the tang of the ale on his tongue. "What's with all the soldiers at the Soo? I saw them when we were sailing through. There weren't that many when I left," Devon said.

Finn's eyes shifted to the left and back.

"Word is they're protecting the locks. Looks like those Nazi bastards want to bomb it and stop the shipping," he said.

Devon tightened his grip on his beer mug. It wasn't the kind of news he wanted to hear, knowing his buddies were still out on the lakes. He'd be sailing again in a few weeks, and the news made him feel protective of his crew, too.

"Man, we gotta stop these guys. They're bad news," he said.

"Yeah," Finn said, nodding. "Keep an eye out for suspicious strangers, too. We're looking for spies." He paused for a moment before continuing. "Speaking of suspicious strangers, I heard Jake Calico's back around these parts. Word is he raided a fishing boat up north that crashed in a storm. Thought you'd want to know. Maybe keep an eye out."

"Appreciate it," Devon replied. "I'll do that."

He took another swig of his beer and glanced around the tavern. Sailors from his own freighter and other freighters were laughing and drinking beers at the thick polished-wood tables, along with some old friends from the town high school. He remembered the good times they'd had before the hurricane-like snowstorm of 1913 took the lives of their fathers, grandfathers, sons, uncles, and brothers in a few days of terror and loss from an unimaginable number of shipwrecks. It was a storm rivaled, in his mind, only by the one a few years ago that had taken the life of his own father and Loralei's as well. The storms had changed all their lives, and he knew the threat of loss was still with them all, especially in these dark days of war. He shook his head to clear it and raised his beer mug in greeting. Before anyone came over to talk to him, he felt a tap on his shoulder.

He turned around. "Loralei," he said, looking at her in surprise, "I didn't expect to see you here." He was stunned at how lovely she looked as she blushed and tossed her windswept, wavy blonde hair back behind her. The months away had made him hungry for a woman's touch, but he hadn't expected to want that touch to be his wife's.

"I know. You never do, but I came to get you. I'm glad you're home. Misha and Grandpapa are waiting outside in the Jeep," she said.

Devon set his beer down and tried not to look exasperated. He had been looking forward to the morning in the tavern. He looked at Finn, who gave him a shrug and bent to retrieve his duffel bag. He'd leave with Loralei if only to keep the peace between Finn and Loralei's sister, Marie, who sided with Loralei when it came to him. That was one of the reasons he felt like his authority was challenged on land. That, and the fact that it was hard to talk to other women with Finn and Marie around. That led him to frequent other taverns as well.

He took a last swallow of beer, nodded to Finn, and followed Loralei out of the tavern. They walked down the street to the Jeep.

"Good to see you, Devon," Edmund said. Edmund stepped down from the driver's side and shook Devon's hand. "How was the trip?" he asked.

"Edmund. Good to see you, too. The trip was good. No complaints," Devon answered.

He found it easy to talk to Edmund since they shared a common love of the lakes and a common bond in their careers as freighter captains, although Edmund was now retired.

"Misha." Devon dropped his duffel and held out his arms to his son, who jumped out of the Jeep into them. "How's my boy?"

"Papa," Misha said, signing the word for hello.

Devon buried his face in Misha's hair and hugged him tightly. He was pleased to see how happy his son was to see him and longed for the day he would be old enough to sail with him on the *Manitoulin*. They held each other for a long moment before Devon put him in the back seat and tossed his duffel on the floor.

***

Loralei watched her grandfather sit in the Jeep next to Misha, then climbed into the front seat next to Devon, relieved she didn't have to miss him anymore. Devon pulled away from the curb, and they drove together in companionable silence.

"There's a rumor that Hitler plans to bomb the Soo Locks," Devon said as they rounded a curve.

"What?" Loralei looked at Devon with horror. "The locks? Why?" she asked.

"To stop the shipping operation. If we can't use the locks to raise and lower the freighters between the lake levels on Lake Superior and Lake Huron, we can't sail between the lakes. It will stop the transportation of the iron ore from the ore mines here to the factories in Detroit and destroy the war effort. All the captains and crew know about it," he said.

"I heard that, too," Edmund said from the back seat.

"If the Germans stop the production of the tanks and ships and planes for the arsenal, we won't have anything to fight them with. We need to be on the lookout for spies and anyone who might try to sabotage the locks," Devon continued.

Loralei didn't know what to say. Now she understood why she had to watch for warplanes. The lighthouse kept her isolated, and she wasn't always apprised of the details of everything that was going on. The evil of the plot left her speechless, and she wondered how their country would survive if the plot succeeded. She shivered and rubbed her arms to warm them.

She was glad he'd told her, but she was hurt that he only wanted to talk about news and wasn't more expressive with her when he got home. She supposed she should be used to it by now, knowing how hard it was for him to adjust to being on land and how much he missed his father. She wished she could have thrown her arms around him and hugged him when she saw him. And she was drawn to the way he looked with his tousled, sandy blond hair and vibrant, cornflower blue eyes. But she sensed he didn't want that from her. She swallowed her disappointment and tried to content herself with the fact that at least he was home, and she would no longer have to yearn for him.

"Jake Calico is back around, too. Keep an eye out and lock the doors. We don't want him sabotaging the beacon," Devon said.

"No, we don't. I'll make sure to do that," she said, feeling the hair stand up on the nape of her neck as she realized, again, the danger she could be in.

They drove in silence for a while. Loralei looked back to see Misha asleep with his head resting on Edmund's arm. She smiled and turned back around to talk to Devon.

"Misha missed you. I did, too," she said.

"Well, I'm back now," he said shortly.

Loralei felt tears sting her eyes and looked away.

Devon pulled up in the back of the lighthouse, and Loralei got out and took Misha in her arms.

"We're home, Misha," she said when he opened his eyes. "And Papa's home, too."

Loralei glanced around at the woods behind her and shivered again before following Edmund and Devon into the warmth of the lighthouse with Misha. She was glad they were all safe at home...at least safe for now.

CHAPTER 2

Andre Sorrento tapped his foot impatiently on the expertly polished, golden-wood parquet floor of the Chateau de Chambord in France and perused a priceless painting on the wall as he waited for his friend, Jacques Boudrais, to meet with him in the lobby. At Jacques's request, he had hurried to the chateau as quickly as he could the day after the murder of their mutual friend and colleague, Monsieur Didier. He wasn't sure why Jacques wanted to see him, but Andre hoped to smooth over any questions or suspicions his art curator friend might have about the death of their peer — if that was, indeed, the reason for the meeting.

As far as Andre knew, no one suspected him of being responsible for Monsieur Didier's death, but one could never be sure. His training as a deep-cover agent in Italy had taught him that. If someone did suspect him and found out that he had, in fact, murdered Monsieur Didier for discovering that he was a spy, his life and the lives of his countrymen would be in grave danger, and possibly over if the spy network Andre worked for was discovered and destroyed, and the Allies got the upper hand in the war. Andre could not let that happen. He had devoted his whole life as a deep-cover agent working as an art curator in

France to keeping Italy safe from enemies, and he wasn't going to give that up now if he could help it.

He looked more closely at the brushstrokes on the canvas in front of him. French Impressionism was his passion, and the rare Monet he was looking at was truly lovely. He was pleased that it had been saved from the Louvre and hidden by him and his group of French curators in the chateau. They had moved thousands of priceless paintings and masterpieces to the opulent Chateau de Chambord in the Loire Valley in France to keep them out of the hands of the German soldiers. He knew he was taking a chance by hiding the paintings from the Germans, but his love for art transcended the politics of war and overcame his fear of discovery. He was pleased to see the masterpiece safely displayed in front of him.

Andre loved beautiful things, and he enjoyed collecting them. He had a small chateau of his own in the French countryside, filled with paintings and sculptures and works of art that he hoped to keep secret from the Germans, as well. He was extremely proud to have acquired a *Mother and Child* by Mary Cassatt for his personal art collection. He loved it for its exquisite use of light and color on a muted blue/green background. Something about it touched him deep in his soul, and he never tired of looking at it. The fact that he had been able to acquire it for himself was a great pleasure to him.

So far, he had had no problems with raids or theft, although he had heard that other curators had lost their private art collections to such things. Andre hoped to return to Italy someday with his collection and set up a home in Tuscany. But for now, he kept the artwork in his chateau a secret, as did so many others during the German occupation of France.

"Andre, I see you have found the Monet," Jacques said.

"Yes, you have placed it in an excellent location. I couldn't have asked for more. I trust you are continuing to regulate the temperature and humidity of the storage areas within the chateau to maintain the health of the paintings," Andre said.

"Yes, yes, of course. Would you care to follow me? I will show you more of what we have done," Jacques said.

"Yes. Show me the way," Andre said.

"We're looking into ways to continue to keep the paintings secure. I'm sure you've heard by now that Monsieur Didier was found deceased in his bed this morning. I believe he was smothered," Jacques said as he walked briskly through the chateau.

Jacques turned his head and glanced back at him, and Andre tried not to show his dismay. He hadn't heard from anyone else that Monsieur Didier had been smothered, but the fact that he was, according to Jacques, put him in a difficult position.

"Yes, yes, it's very unfortunate that that happened. We must be careful," Andre responded, keeping his thoughts to himself.

"Yes," Jacques replied, picking up the pace until Andre found himself sprinting after him. "Are you fearful, as I am, that the Germans may have a lead on where the paintings are?"

Jacques looked back at him over his shoulder, and Andre nodded. He would rather have Jacques think the Germans were responsible for Monsieur Didier's death than that he was.

"I'm sure you know that Monsieur Didier was not well liked by them," Jacques continued, "and they were well aware that he was an expert in the field of art restoration. If they are looking for the paintings, they may have gone to Monsieur Didier to find out where they are hidden and killed him in the process. We are on the lookout for spies. Perhaps they tried to find out from him where the paintings are."

"Perhaps," Andre said.

He wasn't sure yet why it was that Jacques wanted to see him. Jacques didn't appear to have suspicions about him in regard to Monsieur Didier's death, but Andre suspected he must have some reason for calling him to the chateau so soon after his death. He tried to catch up with Jacques to see his face, but he seemed intent on moving quickly through the chateau. When he suddenly stopped outside the doorway of a large room filled with paintings, Andre almost ran into him.

"Before I show you where the paintings are stored, I think I should tell you why I have asked you here," Jacques said.

"Yes?" Andre said, trying not to sound annoyed.

"Monsieur Clairmont is quite concerned about Monsieur Didier's death. He is afraid the Germans may have killed him while trying to find out where the paintings are hidden. He would like to discuss traveling to the United States to work with some art museums there, specifically the Detroit Institute of the Arts in Michigan, in regards to transporting the artwork to the United States if further security for them becomes necessary. He could go, or perhaps you could, although he has family in the area. Both of you speak excellent English. Would you, perhaps, be amenable to that?" Jacques asked.

Jacques paused for a moment, appearing to wait for him to respond. Andre caught his breath and shifted his gaze to a gold-framed Renoir mounted on the red and gold damask wallpaper of the hallway they had entered. He paused, considering his answer. He had been approached by his spy network several times in the past year about traveling to the United States on a mission, and he didn't want Jacques to realize he was familiar with the request. Traveling to the United States himself was uppermost in his mind.

"I would be amenable to discussing it, yes," Andre said evasively.

"Fine. Here we are," Jacques said, leading Andre into the room filled with paintings. "This is the storage area we are using to catalog many of the paintings. You can see they are in excellent shape, and many of them are ready to be moved to other areas as well to benefit from a climate rotation."

"Yes, very good," Andre agreed. "It is important to keep

them in a comfortable atmosphere."

He found himself less interested in talking with Jacques and more interested in the presence of the beautiful young woman with long dark hair, marking file folders at a desk in the corner.

Jacques noticed his interest. "This is Alma. She keeps track of the dates the paintings arrive and where they are placed. She's very good at what she does. Alma, this is Monsieur Sorrento."

Alma blushed and looked up.

"Yes. I'm sure she is. You appear to be very competent," Andre said, smiling at the girl.

She blushed again and looked down.

"Could you bring tea into the parlor? Monsieur Clairmont and I have something to discuss with Monsieur Sorrento," Jacques said to Alma, motioning to Andre to leave the room with him.

Before she could answer, Jacques left the room with Andre and walked across the hallway. They entered a large room wallpapered with silver stripes and accented with dark mahogany wainscoting. There were deep blue tapestries at the windows and antique mahogany tables placed strategically around sofas upholstered in pale blue silk.

"Please, have a seat. Monsieur Clairmont should be here shortly," Jacques said.

Andre walked toward the sofa, but before he could sit down, Jacques announced the entrance of the curator in charge of the chateau.

"Ah, here he is. Monsieur Sorrento, Monsieur Clairmont has arrived. Monsieur Clairmont, Monsieur Sorrento."

"Andre, how nice to see you. It's been a while," Monsieur Clairmont said.

"Yes, it has. How have you been, Maurice?" Andre asked, turning and walking over to shake his hand.

"As well as can be expected during these times," he answered.

"Yes, of course," Andre said, surprised to find that Maurice's usual firm handshake was weak and that his silvery-white hair appeared to be thin and wispy about his face. "I'm sorry. Have you been unwell?"

Maurice waved his hand. "Nothing to be concerned about. Shall we sit down?"

As they sat on the sofas, Alma walked in with the tea and set it on the Queen Anne coffee table in front of them. She poured them each a cup. When she handed a cup to Andre, they exchanged an intimate glance, and he was pleased to find that she remembered him. He had found her to be extremely accommodating the last time he had visited the chateau, and he made a note to get her alone again soon. She smiled at him as she placed some tea cakes on the table and left with the silver platter.

"Andre, I'm sure you know by now about the plans for a trip to the United States to explore further security for the art," Maurice said, after taking a sip of tea. "It has become even more imperative that we go soon, given what has happened to Monsieur Didier and the possibility that the Germans could be actively looking for the paintings. I had been planning to go to Michigan and also visit my brother, who takes care of a lighthouse there. But I haven't been my usual self lately. I hope you might consider traveling in my place. The Detroit Institute of the Arts is expecting me, but there's no one I'd rather have represent us than you. Would you consider going?"

"I'd be honored," Andre replied, making a special note to himself that Maurice had family in Michigan. He had heard of Michigan before from his spy network.

"Good. I'll let them know to expect you, and I'll be in touch about the travel arrangements. You'll need to take a ship across. It could be dangerous. There are German U-boats, you know, trying to sink the ships," Maurice said.

"Of course. I will still go," Andre said.

"Good," Maurice said, appearing to be relieved. "There

is one other thing. I don't know if you've heard this, but there has been talk that the Germans want to take out the shipping operation on the Great Lakes in the United States. It's possible that they may send spies and saboteurs to the United States to infiltrate the region. If you travel to Michigan, you may need to know this information to remain safe."

"I will keep that in mind," Andre responded.

They finished their tea in good spirits, and Andre agreed to stay for a small, catered dinner party later in the evening for some of the curators. He was pleased to accept when Jacques invited him, and Jacques seemed happy as well. Andre shook hands with Maurice and Jacques and agreed to see them later before going across the hall to see some more paintings. Alma was still cataloging in the corner.

"I see you're as lovely as ever," Andre said, walking up behind her.

She stood from her bent position and turned around to embrace him.

"It's been so long," she said softly, bringing her lips to his.

Andre was surprised and pleased that she was so responsive. He gripped her arms and kissed her before leading her into a small alcove on the side of the room. They embraced passionately, and Andre groaned as he pulled her to the floor.

Suddenly, an air raid siren blared in the distance. Alma jumped up and smoothed her hair.

"We must go. We must hurry for cover," she said, grabbing his arm.

They ran through the room out into the hallway and followed Maurice, Jacques, and a few others down to the lower levels to wait for the all-clear. The filtered light of the lower levels became dark as evening descended on the chateau. They waited in the dark, knowing they could not turn on the lights until the all-clear sounded. When it did, they ambled back upstairs slowly, reorienting after having been confronted again with the harsh reality of the war.

Alma touched Andre on the arm and told him she hoped she'd see him again before leaving for the day.

The dinner party went on as planned later in the evening, and Andre enjoyed himself despite the many things he had on his mind. He was pleased with the choice of wine being served and was having pleasant conversations with several of the curators. They were gathered around a table enjoying a wonderful dinner of roast duck and rice pilaf when the lights flickered and went out.

"What is it? What could have happened?" Jacques asked.

There was a general commotion as people pushed back their chairs and stood to determine what was going on. The only light remaining was from the pale flickers of the tapers on the table.

"I'll check the fuse box," Andre said, standing to leave the room.

Jacques asked if he needed help, but Andre declined. He knew where to go, having been at the chateau before. The others nodded as he stood. Andre was usually in charge of electronics wherever he went. He had a natural affinity for knowing where to go and what to do in the field of electronics. He always had, even as a young boy in Italy. He had often rewired electrical circuits in the small art museum in Florence curated by his parents and in the home in which he had grown up and honed his taste for beautiful paintings.

Andre picked up a candle and walked through the room to the kitchen. The caterers were standing around, murmuring to each other. One of them approached him as he walked through the kitchen with the candle casting a pale glow to light his way.

"Andre? Could that be you?" Andre heard someone say.

He peered through the darkness to see the face of a lovely young girl peering back at him. "Yes. And who do I have the pleasure of speaking with?" he asked.

"It's Sofia from Florence. You remember. I was friends with your sister, Isabella, when we were children."

Andre looked at the girl more closely and found that he recognized her. "Yes, of course. How nice to see you," he said, raising his hand and blinking as a circle of light stabbed his eyes. "A flashlight. Could I borrow that, please?" Andre asked the apron-clad boy holding it.

He secured the flashlight and a fuse from the pantry and headed to the basement with Sofia following him.

"I hope you don't mind if I go with you," she said as she caught up to him. "But it's so nice to see someone from Italy. The last time I was there, your sister was onstage playing the piano at the Teatro Carlo Felice. You look like her, you know."

Andre turned to see Sofia regarding him intimately before looking away.

"She's very good," Sofia said.

"Yes, she is," he agreed, walking down the stairs.

He was briefly reminded of his younger sister Isabella's thick, wavy brown tresses, dark brown eyes, and lovely music. She was an angel to him—a beautiful gift given to protect and care for. He had grown up with her in a world of art and music, and they shared a love for beautiful things.

He walked through the basement and found the room with the fuse box. He spent time investigating the problem, with Sofia holding the flashlight for him. He found the problem and replaced the fuse. When the lights came on, Sofia clapped with delight and touched his arm.

"How wonderful. You've fixed it," she said.

"Yes," Andre said, smiling at her.

He was surprised at the beauty of Sofia in the new light. The last time he had seen her, she had been thin and gangly. She was now a lovely young woman with smooth, black hair and porcelain skin. He wondered, momentarily, if he should take advantage of the situation but thought better of it, considering that she was Isabella's childhood friend.

"Shall we head back?" he asked.

"Yes," Sofia said, smiling.

When they got back to the kitchen, everyone was milling about and serving the food. Andre said goodbye to Sofia and headed back to the dinner party. The other curators clapped lightly and goodheartedly when he entered the room.

"Thank you," he said, giving a slight, amiable bow.

They finished the dinner without incident and talked for a while before people began leaving and saying their goodbyes. Soon, only Jacques, Maurice and Andre were left talking together at the table. Maurice pushed his chair back.

"I'm afraid it's time for me to say goodnight. It's been a wonderful evening, but I fear I'm not up to staying awake anymore. Good luck on your trip, Andre. It was nice to see you again," Maurice said, turning and leaving the room.

Andre turned to Jacques after Maurice left.

"There's something I'd like to discuss with you," he said quietly, leaning toward him. "I'm sure we're alone, but I'd like it to be more private. Would you follow me, please? I'd like to make sure no one can hear us."

"Yes, of course," Jacques said, gazing back at him for a long moment with what Andre took to be curiosity.

They pushed their chairs back from the table, stood, and left the room together. The evening was warm, and the slight breeze that blew across the lantern tower of the chateau was a welcome relief to Andre after climbing all the stairs, using a flashlight, to the top. He could see that Jacques appeared to feel the same way. He headed toward the overlook to get a view of the expansive grounds at night, dimly lit and mysterious in its way.

"What is it that you want to discuss?" Jacques asked, whispering, although his low voice hardly seemed necessary given that there was no one around. "It has to do with Monsieur

Didier, does it not? Perhaps you wonder what happened to him?"

"Perhaps," Andre said, quietly.

They stood in companionable silence for a moment, absorbing the night air.

"Do you see the sliver of the moon? It reminds me of a VanGogh," Andre said, gazing into the night sky, and moving closer to Jacques.

"Yes. It's lovely," Jacques replied.

Andre stepped quietly towards him. When he got to the stone railing next to him, he grabbed Jacques's arm and twisted it behind him.

"What are you doing?" Jacques shrieked, struggling to free himself from Andre's grasp.

"I'm sorry, Jacques. This is just the way it has to be," Andre said, grimacing. "I wish you didn't know about Monsieur Didier. He, unfortunately, overheard a conversation he was not supposed to hear, and he could not be allowed to repeat it. I had hoped it would appear that he passed away quietly in his sleep. I'm sure it appeared that way to most people, although apparently not to you."

He tightened his grip on Jacques's neck. "Italy needs me now, and Germany as well. I am going to the United States, but not only because of the art. I think you deserve to know the reason before I kill you. I need to answer the call of my country at war."

For a split second, Andre was sorry. Jacques was a good curator, and the art world would miss him, and perhaps, he would, too. Andre exhaled forcefully as he twisted Jacques sideways and expertly broke his neck before lifting him onto the railing and pushing him over the side. He heard, after a moment, an almost imperceptible thud before racing down the dark back stairs and leaving the chateau undetected.

CHAPTER 3

Loralei ripped open the letter as she stepped out the door of the post office and read it quickly. It was short and to the point, from her Great Uncle Maurice in France. He was canceling his trip to the United States because he wasn't feeling well and didn't want to make the long voyage across the ocean. He had been planning to visit them while on a business trip to the Detroit Institute of Arts but had cancelled his plans and sent someone else to the institute instead. Loralei frowned and read the closing paragraph, wishing them health and safety, before sighing and putting the letter back in the envelope. She understood but was disappointed, as she was sure her grandfather would be, too. They seldom received visitors at the lighthouse, and she had been looking forward to having a guest, especially her great-uncle, whom she had only seen in old, grainy photos. She had wanted to meet Edmund's brother and find out more details about her ancestry which, at the moment, was confined to knowing that Edmund's older brother, Maurice, had stayed in Paris to attend art school when his family immigrated to the United States many years ago.

Loralei ignored her disappointment and went to find Devon and Misha. At least she still had the evening to look forward to. She and Devon were in town for a dance to raise money for the war effort, and Loralei was excited to attend the social occasion. Edmund was watching the lighthouse.

"Loralei, what's wrong?"

She found Devon standing in front of a storefront with Misha in tow. He was in his captain's dress best, a navy uniform with gold buttons and a white, visored hat, and Loralei thought he looked very handsome.

"Nothing. We got a letter from Great Uncle Maurice is all. He's not coming to visit after all. He's not well," she replied.

"I'm sorry. I know you were looking forward to it," Devon said.

She was surprised by Devon's kind words. He had been so aloof and disagreeable with her since he returned from his trip. He walked on the beach for hours and stood alone, looking out over the lake. He seemed restless and uneasy, and it bothered her to think that he would probably rather be aboard the *Manitoulin* than home with her. But now, he seemed more relaxed. She gave him a slight smile, hoping he might be pleasant for the evening after all.

They strolled together with Misha down the main street of the town, watching seagulls sail by the fishing boats docked in the harbor and breathing the cool, early-evening air, fresh with the smell of the lake water. When they got to the outskirts of the business district, they walked down a dirt lane and headed for a small cottage fronted by a white wooden gate. They waved to an older woman with grey hair in a loose bun, tending a garden.

"Mrs. Petrova, we've brought Misha," Loralei said, making a sign to Misha's sign language teacher as they approached so that Misha would know what she said.

"Babushka," Misha said, running to Mrs. Petrova and making the sign for grandmother.

Mrs. Petrova had told Loralei Misha could call her that if he wanted to after Loralei had told her that her own mother and her grandmother had died years before, each of cancer and Misha's other grandmother lived far away.

"Hello, dear," Mrs. Petrova said, straightening from her gardening and signing back. She smiled and greeted them all. "Just the fellow I wanted to see. You two have a good time now. Mishka and I will stay here and plant some flowers. Right, Mishka?"

Mrs. Petrova always called Misha, Mishka. She said it was the way they pronounced it in her country. He was named after Loralei's late maternal grandfather, who had emigrated from Russia.

"We'll add to the beauty of God's green earth," she said.

Misha smiled and dropped down onto the dirt next to her. Loralei thanked her, and she and Devon waved to them and headed back to town for the dance.

The fundraising dance for the war was outdoors on a raised wooden dais in the town square near the lake. As Loralei and Devon neared the dais, a small band of flutes and horns struck up "Stars and Stripes Forever," and Loralei stopped and tapped her foot in time with the music. She hoped the dancing would begin soon. She turned to see Annie Paxton, an old friend of hers from high school, who was the daughter of the mayor of Portstown, walking toward her and sipping lemonade.

"Loralei, you're in town. It's great to see you," Annie said.

"You, too. It's nice to be in town and away from the lighthouse for a while," she said, smiling.

Annie looked at her closely. "Is everything all right out at the lighthouse? Is your grandfather okay? Forgive me, but you look a little pale to me."

"We're fine," Loralei said, trying not to let Annie see the pain in her face or the sudden welling up of emotion she felt at having her friend ask about her feelings. It had been so long since someone had asked her if she was okay, but she didn't want to have a deep conversation with Annie right then.

"Grandpapa's watching the lighthouse tonight, and I'm just busy, that's all. As always."

"Well, if you're sure."

"I'm sure," Loralei said.

As she continued her conversation with Annie, she saw Devon from the corner of her eye walking toward the other side of the dais. She didn't think much of it until she saw him talking to a woman with lustrous, wavy, dark hair and ruby-red, lipsticked lips. She recognized her as Carlotta Pomodoro, the daughter of a shipping captain they had known before he was lost in a storm several years ago. She was very beautiful, more beautiful than Loralei had remembered, and she felt a pang of jealousy. Carlotta had a reputation for being wild, and Loralei didn't like the idea that Devon was talking to her.

Loralei knew Devon wasn't faithful to her, but she didn't know what to do about it other than to look the other way. She wanted their marriage to be different, and she wanted them to be only with each other, as they had promised when they married years ago. She had been so in love with him before the cares of the world had torn them apart. But she realized she had to accept the reality of her situation. Grief over the deaths of their fathers had ripped them apart, and reconciliation seemed only a distant dream. She blinked her eyes, which had become blurry for some reason, and looked away. She, herself, had strayed when Devon was gone, and that made her feel she didn't have the right to judge him. But she lost a little piece of her heart any time she saw him with another woman.

"That's Carlotta, isn't it?" Annie asked, taking another sip of lemonade.

Loralei felt mortified to realize her feelings must be obvious to Annie, who seemed to have noticed her looking at Devon.

"She's after all the captains. That's just the way she is. Everybody knows it. You'd better go get him. The dance will be starting soon." Annie patted Loralei on the arm and walked away.

Loralei felt her cheeks warm with embarrassment. She didn't want pity from her friends. She turned and walked toward Devon, determined to reclaim her husband and have an enjoyable evening.

When she reached them, Carlotta turned to talk to her. "Loralei, how nice to see you. It's been a while. Devon was just telling me he's on shore for a few weeks. I was saying how hard it must be for him to be out on the lake by himself without a woman to talk to. I'm sure you must think that, too."

She smiled at Loralei and turned and batted her eyelashes at Devon. It was all Loralei could do to keep her composure.

"I'm sure I can think what I want to, Carlotta. I don't need you to tell me about my husband," she said.

"No, I'm sure you don't. I didn't mean —" Carlotta said, taking a step back.

"Loralei," Devon said, sternly.

"Devon, could we get something to eat?" Loralei asked, taking his arm and leading him away from Carlotta toward a fish fry that had started on the other side of the dais.

The air was smothered with the heady smells of pan-fried lake trout and onions and french fried potatoes. Loralei felt her mouth water and realized she was hungrier than she'd thought. She supposed the pregnancy had something to do with it. When she had been carrying Misha, she'd been hungry all the time, and it seemed this time would be no different.

"You were very rude, don't you think?" Devon asked as they headed toward the fish fry.

"Oh, I was rude? You left me alone to go talk to another woman. I think that's rude," she answered.

Loralei felt her cheeks get warm, and she took a deep breath to keep from saying any more. She was glad Devon didn't say any more, either. She nipped her lip as she thought about her plans to tell him about the baby this evening. She would have to wait for the right time, perhaps when he was more relaxed and in a happier mood. She hoped the dance would do that for him and that she would know when the moment was right. Most of all, she hoped he wouldn't ask too many questions about the timing and that her worry that the baby might not be his would remain concealed. Devon had been suspicious, lately, of what she was doing while he was gone, and she didn't want him to suspect anything was wrong.

They took their time going through a short line and loading their plates with food before sitting at a long table covered with a red gingham tablecloth, set up on the grass nearby. Loralei was pleased to see her sister, Marie, and her husband, Finn, walking over to join them.

She always looked forward to spending time with her sister. They shared a common history and knew each other so well. Loralei and her brothers and sister had grown up in the lighthouse and helped care for it. Her brothers were gone now to other states, and only her sister was left. Marie lived in town with Finn and worked at his tavern.

Sometimes Loralei would bring Misha with her and visit them at their wooden clapboard home near the dock in town. Misha loved to walk with her along the dirt path through the woods by the lake, using his hands to sign the names of trees, flowers, and birds along the way. He knew the path by heart by now and was always excited to go into town. Finn and Marie didn't often come out to the lighthouse because they had put their car up on blocks when gas rationing had begun several months before and no longer used it. Marie occasionally walked out to the lakeshore to visit her and Misha at the lighthouse and their grandfather at his cottage.

"Nice night for a dance," Finn said, sitting next to Devon. "I'm glad it didn't rain. I thought it might earlier. Looks like we're safe for now."

"Yes, I predict a red sky at sunset tonight. It's that type of weather," Devon said.

"I hope it doesn't rain. I've been looking forward to the dance. Finn's always been pretty good at doing the jitterbug," Marie said, sitting next to Loralei.

Marie gave Finn an affectionate smile, which he returned before turning to talk to Devon. The exchange seemed so casual and yet so loving, and Loralei felt a moment of wistfulness as she wished she had that type of relationship with Devon.

As the men talked, Marie leaned in closer to her and whispered, "Did you tell Devon yet?"

Loralei knew Marie was talking about the baby. She had told her about the pregnancy after she saw Doc Bailey a few weeks ago.

"Not yet. I'm waiting for the right time," she whispered back.

"Well, don't wait too long. It's going to be obvious soon. I'm surprised it isn't yet. Your dress hides it well," Marie said.

"I know. I'll tell him." Loralei glanced over at Devon and saw him deep in a conversation with Finn. She turned back to Marie. "Grandpapa said Jake Calico might be around again. Do you know anything?"

Marie looked at her for a long moment. "You really don't know, do you?" she asked.

"Know what? Where he is?" Loralei asked.

"No. Who he is," Marie said.

"What do you mean?" Loralei asked.

"Nothing. I have something to tell you later," Marie said. "Anyway, Finn said Jake was canoeing in the harbor last week, but no one's seen him since. I'm sure he's returned to the deep forests of the wilderness by now. He knows he's not welcome here." Marie paused for a moment. "Is there anything you want to tell me? I mean, about the baby?"

"Such as?" Loralei asked, averting her eyes.

She hadn't told Marie about her fears that another man

could be the baby's father and that she was afraid the baby might look like him with his dark hair and black eyes, and everyone would know. But she realized, when she heard Marie's worried tone of voice, that she probably had her suspicions about it. One time, when Marie made the trek out to the lighthouse, she had stumbled upon them together and knew that something was going on. She had left quickly and never mentioned it again.

"If you think of something, you can tell me later if you want. I want you to know that Finn and I will be there for you, no matter what," Marie said.

"Thanks," Loralei said, taking a sip of lemonade and trying to calm her nerves.

They ate in silence for a while and listened to the band playing "In the Mood," one of Loralei's favorite songs. She loved the Glenn Miller orchestra she had heard playing on the radio. As Devon talked with Finn and Marie, Loralei relaxed and enjoyed the evening. She didn't feel like talking, but it did her heart good to see Devon relaxing and enjoying himself. It wasn't something she was used to seeing, and it made her feel happy to think the dance might improve his temperament and change his treatment of her.

"I hear they have silver sausages at the Sault Ste. Marie," Finn said after a while.

"Silver sausages? What in the world are those?" Marie asked.

Loralei looked up, puzzled as well.

"They're hydrogen balloons floating over the Soo Locks. Steel cables hang down from them to keep aircraft from flying through the airspace. They don't want German paratroopers finding a way to take out the locks by coming in by ship or sub through Canada's Hudson Bay, or down the St. Lawrence River or some other way. It's too far to fly planes over from Europe. Instead, they'd need to sail close enough to the Soo with paratroopers and saboteurs and find a way to purloin a plane.

It's not clear how close they could get through the St. Lawrence because of the change in water levels and the falls on the river between the Atlantic Ocean and the Great Lakes. They're still afraid they could find a way to bomb the Soo Locks. There's pretty tight security around there," Finn said.

"I've seen the balloons. There were a lot of them when I came back through the locks this time," Devon said.

Loralei nodded, trying to take in what she was hearing. The war front seemed to be getting closer and closer to home, and it frightened her. Things were already bad enough, and the thought that the Germans could be so close upset her. She was afraid for her unborn baby, her family, her town, and the lighthouse. What would happen to all of them if the Germans invaded? If their town and livelihoods were destroyed?

They continued talking as they finished their dinner and listened to the soft music of the band. The sky reddened slowly as the sun set, then grew dark. Lanterns were lit on the dais.

Loralei bent over to pick up a napkin that blew off the table. When she looked back up, she saw Devon gazing across the dais at Carlotta, who was laughing and shaking her hair back as she talked with another ship captain. Loralei felt a warm flush rising in her cheeks as she realized Devon was staring at them and scowling as though he was jealous. She tried to think of something to say to distract him.

"I've been doing some more painting," she said hesitantly.

Devon hadn't been very supportive of her work in the past, but Loralei couldn't think of anything else to say.

"I could show you some of my seascapes when we get home." She glanced toward Marie in desperation.

From the way Marie looked back at her, Loralei could tell she had also noticed Devon's interest in Carlotta.

"That's nice," Devon said, shifting his gaze back to her.

"Yes, Loralei is very gifted," Marie offered, smiling at Loralei as she said it. "She could have her artwork in galleries if she wanted to. They're that good."

Marie looked back and forth between Devon's scowling face and hers.

"If you don't mind, Devon, I'd like to talk to Loralei alone for a moment. We'll be right back," Marie said, touching Loralei's arm.

Loralei didn't know what Marie wanted but was relieved to be rescued from the conversation. She stood and followed her away from the table and sat with her on the grass under a large maple tree, out of earshot of the men.

"I need to tell you something," Marie said. "I don't know how, but I have to."

The music played softly in the distance, and the night breeze rustled the leaves in the tree.

"What is it?" Loralei asked, feeling perplexed at Marie's obvious discomfort. She was obviously keeping something from her. "You're frightening me."

"I guess I'll just say it. The man you're seeing, the man I saw you with at the lighthouse…."

"Yes?"

"It's Jake Calico. The man you were with is Jake Calico, the pirate."

Loralei sucked in a breath and stared at Marie. She couldn't believe what she'd said. "You're mistaken. His name's Grayson. He lives on the other side of the peninsula."

"No. His name's Jake. I know. I've seen him before, canoeing the harbor. You're in danger, Loralei," Marie said.

"It can't be," Loralei said, letting out a breath. "It just can't."

She didn't know what to do. *How could Grayson possibly be Jake?* She touched the bodice of her high-necked dress, underneath which she wore the mourning dove feather Grayson had given her on a leather cord around her neck. What would this mean for their future together?

"I'm sorry," Marie said, patting her arm. "Let me know if you need to talk sometime. We have to get back before the men wonder what we're talking about."

Loralei stood, dazed, and walked back to the table with Marie. The men were still talking about the war and seemed unaware of them when they sat back down.

"Why don't you and Loralei dance together? It's a beautiful night, and the music is lovely," Marie said, breaking in on the conversation.

Loralei flinched, wishing Marie had asked her first before making the suggestion. She didn't feel much like dancing after the shock of hearing about Jake and especially not after the way Devon had flirted with Carlotta. On the other hand, she was still hoping for a nice evening. She had worn the floral dress she saved for special occasions and had pulled her hair back at the sides with tortoiseshell combs, letting it flow freely down her back. She had hoped to capture and keep Devon's attention that evening and had been bitterly disappointed before to think that she wouldn't be able to do so. She held her breath, waiting for him to say something.

"Yes, all right. Shall we dance?" Devon asked.

She blinked away tears and nodded as he took her hand and led her over to the dais. They walked together up the stairs and out onto the dance floor. Even though her heart felt swollen and sore at the moment, she was thrilled with how handsome Devon was and proud that he was her husband. She melted into his strong arms as they glided across the floor to the tune of "String of Pearls." The smooth tone and laid-back beat lifted her spirits slightly, and she sighed, enjoying the nearness of Devon, the only man she had ever given her heart to. She could see other old friends and townspeople she had known since childhood milling about the square and casually vying for space on the dance floor. She warmed with emotion at the feeling it gave her of being connected to the people of her town and her country.

The light from the lanterns, strung from the railing of the dais, cast an amber glow in the deepening darkness of the impending evening.

She leaned her head gently on Devon's shoulder as they moved to the music and tried to imagine that they were the way they used to be long ago, so in love and looking forward to their future together. She closed her eyes and remembered dancing with him at their wedding years before. He had been so handsome and so in charge of everything after having graduated top in his class from the Great Lakes naval training center and starting on the career track toward becoming a captain of his own freighter. They had been happy then, and he had been admired by everyone in the town. She smiled as she remembered the joy she had seen in his eyes when she walked down the aisle toward him and the love she had felt for him then. But that was a long time ago. It had been a long time since she had seen joy like that in Devon's eyes.

When she opened her eyes, she realized the music had stopped, and the dance was over. She looked up at Devon, hoping he might want to dance another, but as she did so, she noticed someone standing off to the side, dimly illuminated by the glow of a lantern. Her heart fluttered with apprehension. It was Grayson. But it couldn't be him if he was really Jake. Jake wasn't welcome at town social occasions. She looked more closely at the shadowy figure. It was him, she realized when the flame from the lantern flickered in the evening breeze. He was watching her. She nipped her lip as she returned his unwavering gaze. She glanced at Devon, but he was looking in the other direction.

When she looked back over Devon's shoulder, she saw Jake raise his hand toward her and grin before disappearing down the stairs into the darkness of the evening. She shivered as Devon released her from the warmth of his embrace into the cool air of the evening.

"Shall we take our seats?" He took her arm and led her

back down the stairs to their table.

"If you don't mind, there's something I need to talk to you about," Loralei said, trembling as she made a sudden decision.

She was going to tell Devon about the baby now. Seeing Jake had rekindled her desire for him, but it had frightened her, too, knowing what she now knew about him, and she didn't want to wait for another time. Devon was starting another voyage the day after tomorrow, and she wanted to make sure she talked to him about the baby before he left.

"Could we go down to the beach and talk?" she asked.

Devon turned and looked at her quizzically. "Of course, if you'd like."

They walked together past the dais, down the street toward the beach, in awkward silence. When they stepped onto the sand, Loralei bent and took her shoes off and breathed a sigh of relief. Dancing had made her feet swell. She pressed her bare toes into the cool sand and tried to control her trembling. She looked out over the dark surface of the lake, the crests of its low-rolling waves reflecting the twinkling stars and the half-moon in the clear sky.

"I have something to tell you," she said softly.

Devon turned to look at her, and she stared down at the sand, feeling suddenly shy. She looked back up at him and swallowed hard as she tried to think of the words to say.

"What is it?" he asked in the pause that followed.

She took a deep breath and let it out slowly. "I'm pregnant."

She heard the waves lapping at the shore and the muted beats of the music in the distance, where she knew the dance continued without them. But most of all, she heard his silence.

After what seemed like an eternity, he asked with a cracked voice, "How? When?"

Loralei looked up to see Devon watching her, his face scrunched in thought, and she jumped to say something. "In the spring. Remember? Before you shipped out for the new season. I didn't tell you until now because you've been gone, and I wasn't sure until a little while ago."

A cold rivulet of sweat ran down her back as she waited for his reaction. When she saw him nod, she sighed with relief.

"I remember," he said.

"You're not angry, are you?" Loralei wasn't sure she should ask the question, but she wanted to know.

"It's not the best time," he answered, shaking his head and looking out over the lake. "The war makes it wrong for all of us." He rubbed his chin and appeared to be pondering the situation before dropping his hand and turning to her. "We'll have to make do. Did you see Doc Bailey?"

"Yes. A few weeks ago. That's how I know."

"All right," he said.

She watched Devon's face for any sign of emotion or love for her, but she didn't find it. She swallowed hard and looked out over the dark water at the few boat lights she saw glimmering in the distance before looking away and turning to go.

"Loralei?" Devon said.

"Yes?" She turned back to look at him and saw a glimmer of emotion in his expression, but she wasn't sure what it was — sadness, maybe, or nostalgia. The last time she had told him she was pregnant, they had been so happy.

"Nothing," he said, looking away after a moment. "Shall we go get Misha? It's getting late."

"Yes," she replied quietly.

They walked in silence to Mrs. Petrova's cottage, where they retrieved a sleeping Misha. Devon carried him back down the lane to where they had parked the Jeep, and Loralei held him in her lap as Devon drove down the winding road toward the lighthouse and home.

CHAPTER 4

Andre Sorrento made sure the porter had his trunk safely in tow before heading up the gangplank to board the *Queen Elizabeth* ocean liner in Cherbourg, France. It was a beautiful day for a sail. The mid-afternoon sun sparkled off the clear blue water of the harbor and glistened on the tall, sleek sides of the ship, but Andre didn't pay much attention. He had other things on his mind. He was crossing the Atlantic from Cherbourg to New York City to fulfill his obligation to Maurice Clairmont. When Maurice asked him to go to the Detroit Institute of the Arts, he seized the opportunity. He had already been asked by his spy network to travel to the United States, and traveling on business as an art curator fit in nicely with his plans.

Andre had agreed to help Maurice find a secret place for the paintings he and the other art curators from the Louvre had hidden in the opulent Chateau de Chambord three years earlier to keep them safe from the Germans, should it become necessary to move them again. The Nazis had plundered the great art of countries they had invaded for Hitler, who wanted it for Germany and his own art collections, and Andre and the other art curators intended to keep that from happening to the

art from the Louvre. The Germans knew he worked undercover
as an art curator but did not know that he knew about the hidden
art and was on a covert mission to save it. It was dangerous to
withhold the information, but he cared more about the paintings
and saving them for the art world than he did about his own
safety. To him, art was beauty, and beauty, art. Both were to be
protected. He felt that deep in his soul.

He handed his passport and ticket to the boarding official
and waited for his papers to be validated. He adjusted a cufflink
that had gotten caught on the sleeve of his suit coat and glanced
around the ship, looking for a familiar face, but found none. His
trip was ostensibly a business trip to meet art curators in the
United States. But his ultimate mission was known only to him
and the few people who had relayed it to him through deep-
cover channels in France and Italy. He was to find out about the
shipping operation on the Great Lakes, especially in the area of the
Soo Locks in northern Michigan, as it related to the production of
weaponry used in the war. He was then to relay that information
to his spy network in the hopes of subverting the operation. His
trip was conveniently twofold—to find a place to relocate the
hidden paintings in France and save them for the art world, if it
should become necessary, and to secure information about the
Great Lakes shipping operation for his spy network that could be
vital to winning the war.

The boarding official stamped Andre's passport and
waved him through to the ship's main deck, where page boys,
wearing grey uniforms studded with gold buttons and sporting
jaunty, visored hats strapped to their chins, directed passengers
to their cabins. Before Andre turned to go, the ship's captain,
who had been standing next to the boarding official and listening
to their conversation, addressed him.

"Monsieur Sorrento, we are honored to have you on
board," he said, extending his hand. "I am Captain Lamont, the
captain of the *Queen Elizabeth* ocean liner. Monsieur Clairmont of

the French Fine Art Administration has made arrangements for your trip. It isn't every day that we have a former curator of the Louvre as a passenger. You are quite welcome here. Please let me or my crew know if we can do anything to make your voyage more enjoyable."

"Thank you," Andre replied, shaking the captain's hand.

He was surprised that his arrival had been announced but pleased that his cover as an art curator was secure. Maurice Clairmont and the other curators from the Chateau had been devastated over the loss of Jacques Boudrais, their friend and colleague from the Louvre. Maurice had told him that they had found Jacques dead on the grounds in the back of the Chateau on the morning after Andre had been there for a catered dinner, and they had attributed it to a terrible accident. But, he said, he wanted Andre to be especially careful on his trip in case Jacques' death had been more than an accident. They were suspicious of foul play, Maurice continued, especially in this time of war. Andre had commiserated with him and assured him that he would take precautions.

It was unfortunate, Andre mused now, that Jacques had questioned what happened to Monsieur Didier, their friend and colleague found dead in his bed a few days earlier by the local police, and put Andre in such a difficult position. Andre could not allow such questioning to continue. He had hoped it would appear that their older colleague, Monsieur Didier, who had overheard a phone conversation of Andre's that he should not have overheard, had died in his sleep of natural causes, not that he had been smothered, as Jacques surmised. Andre had had some reservations about killing Jacques, but his training as a spy left him with no other choice. The consequences of discovery, if his position as a spy was revealed and the spying operation was shut down, could change the course of the war, and Andre could not let that happen.

He followed the page boy, who directed him down a long,

luxuriously carpeted hallway dotted with wood-inlaid marquetry panels. Andre tipped the boy and settled into his sumptuously decorated room to await the arrival of his trunk. He planned to dress for dinner and find some entertainment. He was sure that he could find a woman or two who would share his interests on a ship of this size, but he had to have the right clothes. One thing he had always prided himself on was knowing how to properly present himself.

The phone by the bedside rang. Andre picked it up and hesitated for a moment, wondering who knew he was there. "Hello." He heard a static silence. "Hello," he said again.

"Yes, ship to shore communication. A message has been left for Signor Sorrento. Is this Signor Sorrento?"

"Yes," Andre answered.

"The message asks you to arrive at the Veranda Grill at eight for dinner with a friend. There is no signature. But it does say that the weather on deck is cold this time of year."

"Thank you," Andre said before hanging up.

He recognized the traveling code phrase of his spy network in the message and pondered for a moment, wondering who the message could be from or about. He assumed that the dinner meeting was related to his mission for the war effort and that he would receive further information on his assignment. He had been informed before he left that other agents from his network would be traveling with him. That was one of the reasons he felt confident that the German U-boats would not try to sink the ship as it made its way across the Atlantic. His mission and the mission of the deep-cover network were too important.

When his trunk arrived a short time later, Andre unpacked and readied the room for his stay, after which he took a short nap. He awoke later to the sound of three intermittent horn blasts as the ship was leaving the dock. He prepared for the evening, giving himself enough time to determine where the Veranda Grill was. He not only prided himself on his well-tailored, pressed black tuxedo and crisp, white shirt with a black bowtie but on being punctual, as well.

When he arrived at the Grill, it was exactly eight. Andre approached the maitre d' and looked around the large room of the dimly lit restaurant at the tables covered with white linen. The cloths glowed with the flicker of miniature hurricane-lamp centerpieces.

"May I help you, sir?" the maitre d' asked when Andre approached the podium.

The maitre d' glanced at his attire as he addressed him in a seemingly deferential manner.

"Yes, I am to meet someone here. Perhaps they've already arrived? My name is Andre Sorrento," he said.

The maitre d' looked down at his podium before looking back up and gesturing with a wave of his hand for Andre to follow him. "Yes, of course, sir. Right this way," he said.

Andre followed him to a table near the back of the room. He had been expecting to see an art curator or someone he knew. Instead, he was pleased to find a beautiful young woman wearing a stunning aubergine evening gown sipping a glass of white wine. Her green eyes twinkled as she set the wineglass down, and the maitre d' turned to go.

"My. Signor Sorrento, I presume," she said, smiling.

She smiled more widely as he nodded.

"Your reputation precedes you, sir. I was expecting to meet a charming gentleman, and I must say, it's more than a pleasure to meet you in person," she said.

Andre was extremely aware of the way she flipped her deep-auburn hair back when she spoke to him. He determined that he could be in for a very pleasant evening.

"And who do I have the pleasure of meeting?" he asked, returning her smile and pulling his chair out to sit down.

"I'm Angelina Rossi from the United States Embassy in Rome. I had heard you were traveling to the United States, and I hoped I could be of service in some way in orienting you to your new surroundings."

"How nice of you," Andre said.

"Yes. I'm sure you know that the diplomatic relationship between our two countries is on hold at the moment, and the embassy is closed. Still, I had hoped that I could make your trip more enjoyable," Angelina said.

"Yes, I'm sure you can," Andre replied, adjusting his tie and gazing deep into her eyes.

When she gazed back without hesitation, he decided that she could be another beautiful woman he added to his collection of broken hearts. They ordered more wine, a very good Bordeaux that Andre had suggested, and made light conversation as they waited for the dinners they ordered to arrive. Andre enjoyed himself immensely as he listened to the entertaining stories of his dinner companion. He was extremely flattered to find her looking at him closely over the top of her wineglass more than once.

"Have you been back to Italy lately? It has changed with the war," Angelina said.

"I'm sure it has. I have not been back, but I hope to return someday," Andre said.

When their meals arrived, they paused in their conversation. Andre was pleased with the beef medallions and roasted red potatoes that they both had ordered with green beans almondine and was glad the chef that evening was evidently one of the better ones. Andre, himself, was known to prepare gourmet meals for dinner guests in his home, and he appreciated a properly prepared dish. They ate with relish and laughed at each other's jokes.

"Would you care for some more wine?" he asked, reaching for the carafe after the waiter had cleared their plates.

"Yes, perhaps a touch. It is very good," Angelina said.

"I'm glad you like it."

Andre refilled her glass and his own. As he set the carafe down, he could see Angelina looking at him with some seriousness. She took a sip of wine and leaned toward him.

"There are some things I need to tell you that are best said in person and not over the phone on such a 'cold' day," she said, lowering her voice.

Andre felt momentarily disappointed at the reminder that this beautiful woman was not here simply to enjoy a meal with him.

"Yes. It is very cold today," he said, using the network code phrase.

"I'm going to be very clear," Angelina said. "I have been asked by Il Capo to relay some information to you."

Andre leaned forward and looked at Angelina even more intently. Very few people knew about or had access to Il Capo, their name for a secret agent high up in the military intelligence branch of the Royal Italian Army.

"Yes, please continue," he said as she paused.

"There is a man in Detroit named Giorgio Bartoli who has some information for you. You can meet him Thursday evening after you arrive in the United States at Merchant's Wharf on the Detroit River in Detroit. He will be by the number forty-seven slip at midnight. It is very important that you receive this information and that no one ever knows where it came from. Do you understand what I'm saying?" she asked.

Andre stiffened slightly. He was well aware of what she was saying. Giorgio Bartoli was to be an unfortunate messenger, and Andre was to be the source of his misfortune. But Andre kept his reaction to himself.

"I understand," he said.

He made a note in his mind about this business necessity and put it behind him. He didn't want to talk about business at the moment. He had other things on his mind. Andre took a sip of wine and considered that Angelin was truly lovely with her dark, half-lidded eyes and flushed cheeks.

"Would you care to see some of the artwork on the other side of the ship near my room? It's truly something to see. It's an opportunity, I assure you, that you don't want to pass up." He gave her a charming smile and touched her hand where it lay on the table.

She looked at him for a moment before taking his hand and running her forefinger over his palm. "I'd love that," she said.

"Good," he said.

Andre pulled Angelina's chair out for her, and they left the restaurant to return to his room together. He held the door open for her when they arrived back at his cabin and stepped aside as she rustled through in her taffeta gown. He caught a whiff of an enticing, sweet scent wafting from the thick waves of her dark auburn hair as she brushed past him and found himself briefly stunned. He shook his head to clear it and closed the door behind them.

"I must say, I'm quite happy with the way the evening has turned out," Angelina said, smiling and turning to look at Andre. "This is such a nice interlude to such an endless war. It's not often that I meet such an intriguing gentleman and such a handsome one."

Andre gazed back at her, appraising her slightly flushed cheeks and half-lidded eyes, glinting with desire or cleverness. He couldn't tell which. "And it is not often that I meet such an intriguing woman. You are bellissima. Be with me, and together, we will make the cares of the world go away."

He moved toward her and pulled her roughly to him. He felt her tremble as he smoothed his fingers through her hair and brought his lips to hers. Her lips were warm and tasted of wine. He felt his need for her rush through him. He hadn't had a woman in a long time. Angelina pulled away for a moment.

"How do I know I can trust you?" she asked, placing her

hand lightly on his chest as though to push him away.

"There is no war tonight," Andre whispered, pulling her with him toward the bed. "There is no enemy here. There is only you and me and the way we feel about each other."

Her eyes softened as she allowed him to pull her to him. "Yes," she said as they fell on the bed together. "We will be safe in each other's arms."

CHAPTER 5

The morning dawned bright and pleasant. Loralei opened her eyes to the rays of sunshine beaming through the window. She sighed and took a deep breath of the fresh lake air wafting through the bedroom and stretched her arms.

It was another day at the lighthouse, and she smiled when she remembered that Devon was home to share it with her. His seemingly unhappy reaction to finding out about the baby wasn't the excited response she had secretly hoped for, but at least he hadn't questioned her much about the timing and didn't appear to be suspicious. He had been agreeable to her for the rest of the evening, and she hoped he might be the same way today. She turned to watch him sleeping next to her, his light breathing slightly stirring the covers. She caught her breath as she watched him slumber and realized again what an attractive man he was with his sandy blond hair and chiseled features. His slight stubble of beard made her feel even more attracted to him. He looked so strong and handsome. She wished things were different between them and that she could snuggle up next to him and whisper, 'Good morning,' the way she did when they were first married. But that wasn't the way their relationship was right now. Loralei nipped her lip and sighed.

"Mama," Loralei heard Misha say. She smiled as he came running into the bedroom and jumped on the bed with them.

"Good morning, sweetheart," Loralei said, signing to him.

She was pleased that he signed back. Loralei sat up and put Misha in her lap as Devon turned over next to her.

"Papa," Misha said, patting him on the arm.

"Good morning, Misha. How's my sailor?" Devon asked, yawning while he talked and running his fingers through his hair.

Misha signed good morning to him but didn't answer his question. Loralei knew it was because he hadn't heard or understood what Devon had said. Devon didn't seem to mind. He had told Loralei he would learn sign language when he had the time. He pulled Misha to him and hugged him.

Loralei wanted Devon to learn sign language so he and Misha could better communicate, but Devon wasn't home enough to take lessons right now. Loralei took them herself with Misha. Doc Bailey had told her that Misha's hearing loss was most likely due to the fact that he had been born a premature baby and that it would get progressively worse until he would eventually be unable to hear at all. Loralei had been devastated by the diagnosis, but Doc Bailey had said the best thing they could do was to accept it and learn to deal with it. He had suggested a sign language tutor, and Loralei had agreed to find one. She was relieved she had found Mrs. Petrova, who seemed very good at teaching and whom Misha seemed to like.

"What shall we do today?" Loralei asked. "How about fishing? We could get Grandpapa, and you could go fishing with him this afternoon. Would you like that?" Loralei signed to Misha.

Misha jumped up and clapped his hands.

"Okay. That's what we'll do then," Loralei said, laughing. She swung her legs out of bed and took Misha into the other room to dress him. She made sure he brushed his teeth and started making his bed before returning to her room to get ready for the day.

Devon was already dressed and heading for the stairwell. "I'm going to check on the beacon. I hope the coffee's ready when I'm done."

Loralei nodded and hurried to finish getting dressed. She wanted the day to go well, and she wanted to get the coffee going and make a nice breakfast for Devon and Misha. She also hoped to get started putting up cherries in her mason jars to store in the fruit cellar. She had bought some, which were grown at Hanson's orchard when she was in town. She might be able to do that while Devon, Misha, and Edmund went fishing.

When she got to the kitchen, she started the coffee and looked out the window at the lake. She could tell by the way the sun sparkled off the water that it was going to be a beautiful day. She heard a knock on the door and went to open it just as Misha came running into the kitchen.

"Hi, Misha," Edmund said, scooping him into his arms and walking over to sit at the table with him.

Later, when Devon came back down the staircase, they all had eggs, bacon and coffee together and talked about fishing off the layered rocks near the bluff's base nearby. It was one of the best places for fishing. The rocks were flat and jutted out into the lake, allowing for a smooth surface to fish off of.

When they finished breakfast, Loralei shooed them out the door and went about cleaning the lighthouse and preparing to jar her cherries. She filled out her log entry on the beacon and polished the brass in the lantern room until it shone. They never knew when a coast guard inspector might show up, and it was important that the lighthouse met all the standards laid out by the officials. Some of the other lighthouses on the Great Lakes had been decommissioned or had their beacons replaced with automated lights when the coast guard took over their operation a few years ago at the beginning of the war. Loralei felt even more obligated to keep the Portstown lighthouse running smoothly since she remained in charge of its operation, albeit under coast guard authority. She wanted to make sure the lighthouse and the beacon were always prepared to bring the ships in safely.

When she was through with the lantern room, she went back to the kitchen and swept the floor and got her mason jars ready. She put up sweet cherries in the summer and applesauce in the fall.

Later in the day, when the men returned, Loralei made dinner, then put Misha to bed. Edmund and Devon talked late into the night about the war and how the Allies, France, Great Britain, the United States, and China could fend off the Axis Powers of Germany, Italy, and Japan. And they talked of the ships and storms of the past on the Great Lakes when Edmund had been sailing the lakes as a ship's captain, which he had done for a great part of his seventy years. Loralei had heard it all before, but she listened and let them talk. The legends of the Great Lakes and the stories of the shipwrecks and gales had been passed down through generations before them, and Loralei supposed they would be passed down for generations to come. It bothered her sometimes to hear about the storms because they brought up such sad memories, but she didn't want to forget about the people they'd lost in them, either.

When it got late, Edmund said he would stay over and drive Devon into town in the morning to leave on his voyage before heading to the scullery quarters off the kitchen to sleep in a bunk there.

Loralei finished washing a few pans in the kitchen before walking to the bedroom to join Devon and get ready for bed. She put on a lighter gown than she usually wore and slipped into bed next to him, where he was curled under the blankets. Loralei watched him for a moment before reaching over and caressing his arm. He was warm, and his hair smelled of the woods and the water of the lake.

"I'll miss you when you leave again," Loralei said, trying to control the trembling of her voice as she felt her desire for him rush through her.

"I know," he responded, turning over.

She lay back and stared at the ceiling, trying not to cry. It hurt her so much that Devon was so cold to her. And what was worse was that she didn't understand why he was like that or how to change it.

"What is it, Devon? Why won't you talk to me anymore? Is it because of the sea or because of me, or because of your grief? Please talk to me. I need to know why," she said.

She put her hand to mouth and tried to stifle a sob. She didn't want to make Devon even more upset by crying. She waited in the pause that followed her words for him to say something.

"It's the way things are, that's all," he said.

"But why?" she asked. "Why won't you ever talk to me, and why won't you let me cry about my father's death and your father's death? Why don't you cry about it? I don't understand. How can we ever get through this if we don't talk about our feelings?" Loralei was frightened that she was being so open about her feelings but was unable to stop herself.

When Devon was quiet again, Loralei began to weep.

"Stop. I can't stand it. I can't stand to hear you cry," Devon said.

"Devon, please. I need to. Tell me why I can't," she said, trying to talk through her sobs.

She waited through another pause and realized that the only sound in the room was the sound of her crying.

"It was my fault, Loralei. It was my fault they died," Devon said gruffly after a moment.

"What do you mean? It wasn't you. There was a storm on the lake. There was nothing anyone could do about that," she said.

"I told them to go," he said quietly. "I told your father and my father that the storms would hold off, and they could make the circuit before the weather got bad. I was such a fool. I thought I was so smart after graduating with honors from the naval center and becoming a new ship captain. I thought I knew everything. I didn't know that it would take them longer than they thought to sail the circuit and that the gales of November would come early. I thought I knew it all, Loralei. And I didn't know anything. It was my fault they sailed in the storm. It was my fault they drowned. Oh, God. I'm so sorry."

"No. It wasn't you," Loralei said, horrified that Devon blamed himself for the death of their fathers. "It wasn't your fault. Storms come up so fast on the lakes. Don't blame yourself. You can't blame yourself. My father was the captain of the freighter. He made the decision to sail, not you. I don't blame you. I don't blame anyone. It was an act of God. Please, don't do this to yourself."

"I'm tired," Devon said, turning away from her. "I need to go to sleep now. We'll talk another time." He rolled over on his side and turned away from her.

Even after everything he had said, Devon didn't cry. She lay next to him for hours, weeping into her pillow. It took her a long time to go to sleep.

In the early morning of the following day, Loralei tried to smile as she waved to Devon when Edmund drove away with him in the Jeep. She watched the Jeep head down the gravel path toward the road, then went back into the lighthouse. She slowly climbed the staircase with Misha to the lantern room and looked out over the lake as she began to wait again for Devon's freighter to return.

**

Andre stepped off the train in Detroit and looked around to get his bearings. It had been a long trip from New York, and he was tired, even though he had been in a sleeper car. Something about sleeping on a train didn't agree with him. He hailed a taxi and headed for the Statler Hotel, where he knew arrangements had been made for his stay. His trunk was to be sent over later. He was a day late arriving in Detroit because the train wasn't running on schedule. His Wednesday meeting at the Detroit Institute of the Arts had been rescheduled for Thursday afternoon. It was Thursday morning. Andre knew he had a full day ahead, meeting with the art curators at the institute in the afternoon and meeting with the undercover agent Angelina Rossi had alerted him to at Merchant's Wharf at midnight. He told the cab driver he'd double his fare if he got him to the hotel quickly. He wanted to check in and get a bite to eat. It was important for him to be registered at the hotel, whether he stayed there or not. He needed to have a contact address to maintain his legitimacy with the institute as an art curator, and he needed a place to stow his things. He settled into his seat to watch the sights of the city fly past as the cab picked up speed.

Andre had been sorry to leave Angelina in New York. He had to admit that she was one of the more beautiful and charming members of his spy network. They had had a wonderful ocean cruise together, and he wanted to spend more time with her, although not in any serious way. But Angelina had told him that Il Capo had given her her own mission to complete in the United States, and she didn't know if her and Andre's assignments would intersect. Andre had expressed his disappointment at their parting and said he hoped to see her again at some point. They had parted amiably and agreed to meet each other again after the war was over. He didn't know if that would happen, but he wasn't opposed to the possibility.

"Here we are, sir," the cab driver said as he pulled up to the hotel.

A bellboy hurried over, and Andre tipped the driver handsomely before stepping out of the cab and following the bellboy into the hotel. Andre walked to the registration desk and tapped a bell on the counter for service. After a moment, a small, bespectacled man with short, scruffy brown hair appeared from below the counter, where he had evidently been filing something, and stood to address Andre.

"May I help you, sir?" he asked.

Andre thought the man's voice sounded high and shrill.

"I am Andre Sorrento. I believe arrangements have been made for my stay," Andre said.

Andre waited as the man flipped open a leather register and looked through it.

"Yes, here it is. Your room is ready and available for as long as you wish. I will have your trunk delivered to your room if you'd like," he said.

"Yes, thank you," Andre replied.

The man reached for a key hanging on a board with many others on the wall behind the counter. "Here you are, sir," he said, handing the key to Andre with one hand and adjusting his spectacles with the other. "I hope the room is to your liking. If it is too cold, please let me know," he said.

Andre made eye contact with the desk clerk and nodded. He realized at that point, when the clerk used the code word of "cold," that he was also part of the deep-cover network, and Andre was amazed at how widespread the spy network was.

"Of course," Andre said, taking the key from him and walking away.

Andre walked around the hotel and, while waiting for his trunk to arrive, he found a restaurant that had a brunch buffet with coffee. After he ate, he went to his room, where he found his trunk near the bed, dressed and went back to the lobby, where the bellboy hailed another cab.

Andre took the cab to the Detroit Institute of the Arts, where he met with several art curators, many of whom were very familiar with Maurice Clairmont. They agreed that the institute could be a repository for the hidden art of the Chateau de Chambord if it became necessary. They were quite adamant that protecting the art was of the utmost importance to them, as it was to him, and that they would do anything to help. They asked him to keep in touch. Andre shook hands and left, feeling very relieved that the meeting had gone so well.

After returning to the hotel and having dinner, he dressed in baggy cotton twill pants and a poplin shirt. He pulled on a denim jacket and work boots he'd bought in New York in anticipation of visiting Merchant's Wharf. He took the elevator to the lobby and headed out onto the street. He didn't take a cab this time. He wanted to walk. It took him a while to get to the wharf. He walked down the lighted streets of the city and on through the dark streets and back alleys he encountered as he neared the river. He heard the gurgling of the water moving in its current before he actually saw the blackness of the river before him. It smelled fresh and fishy. Lights twinkled on ships navigating the river as they passed by in the distance in front of him. He looked around and behind him to make sure no one was following him before walking to the wharf and heading for slip forty-seven, as Angelina had directed.

Andre brought his wrist close to his face and twisted it back and forth as he tried to garner what light he could to look at his watch. It was too dark on the dock to see anything, but he was sure it was close to midnight. He stopped by slip forty-seven next to a wooden post hung with a white lifesaving ring. Andre looked around but didn't see anyone in the shadows on the wharf. He didn't know what the man he was supposed to meet to receive further information about his mission looked like, but he assumed the contact knew what he looked like. He hoped the man could find him in the darkness, but he was also glad the dark hid him from easy view. His own mission, to receive the top secret information and to eliminate the messenger, was topmost in his mind.

The evening was warm, with only a slight breeze, and

Andre contemplated taking off his jacket. Before he could do so, he saw a shadowy figure slinking toward him. The figure moved slowly and appeared to be trying to hide his appearance by pulling the brim of his hat down over his face. It was hard for Andre to make out the figure's features, but he appeared to be a large man carrying a small valise. Andre waited for the man to come nearer.

"The weather is cold this time of year," the man whispered as he approached. He seemed about to walk on by.

"Si. Fa molto freddo oggi," Andre said.

The man handed Andre a valise. "You are to relay this information to your specified contact, then leave the country through the Sault Ste. Marie and French-speaking Canada, where we have undercover agents to help you escape. The secret information can only be relayed to another agent through Morse Code in ship-to-shore communication. Telephones are not to be trusted. Further orders as to the continuation of your assignment and an updated passport are in the valise. The orders involve gathering information about the operation of the Soo Locks in northern Michigan. That is all I can tell you. I must go," the man said.

The man touched his fingertips to his forehead in a casual, semi-salute before pulling the brim of his hat lower over his face and starting to move past Andre to continue down the dock.

"One more thing," Andre said, setting the valise on the dock. "I have something for you, too," he said.

As the man began to turn back around, Andre grabbed the life ring off the post and hit him on the head with it. The man grunted and bent forward. Before the man could recover himself, Andre slipped the coarse rope of the life ring around his neck and twisted it. He pulled it tighter and tighter as the man struggled and choked. Andre waited until he felt him go limp in his grasp before releasing the rope and dropping the man to the dock. He glanced around quickly to make sure no one was around before rolling the man off the wharf and into the water. Andre grabbed the valise and began to run down the wharf toward shore, but he heard muffled shouts from far down the wharf that sounded like they were coming from the shore.

"Hey, what are you doing? Get him."

Andre heard shouts and realized someone must have seen him even though the lights were dim where he was. He whipped around in mid-stride and ran back down the wharf farther out into the river, where the blackness of the night hung in a shroud around the dock. He glanced behind him as he ran faster but could see no one following him through the darkness. He saw a freighter loaded with coal at a distant slip preparing to leave the wharf and shouted to it to stop.

"I'm Andre Soren, your new cook," he yelled to the crewmen releasing the lines on the dock. "You can't leave without me. I was called at the last minute. If you want to eat, you better take me with you," he said.

Andre saw the crewmen look at each other for a moment, seeming to contemplate the situation. One shrugged and stopped pulling up a ladder he was retracting to allow Andre to board the freighter. Andre took one last look around but saw no one behind him. He jumped on the ladder, slipped his wrist through the handle of the valise, and climbed aboard.

Andre nodded his thanks as he stood in the darkness with the crewmen, smelling the fresh, fishy air and watching the freighter pull away from the dock and sail into the inky river. He knew he could pretend to be a ship's cook because he was a good cook and a great con man. And he knew large sailing vessels usually had more than one cook aboard. But he needed a moment to think. Andre took a deep breath. He stared out into the night and began to plan his next moves as he started the next leg of his journey to complete his mission, wherever it would take him.

***

Devon shouldered his duffel bag and boarded his freighter in Portstown after Edmund dropped him off at the dock and left in the Jeep. He was excited to get back on the *Manitoulin* and even more excited to think of commanding another voyage. He enjoyed sailing and the freedom and spirit of the lake. Waves of pleasure washed over him at his sudden feeling of power as he walked up the gangplank and onto the ship's deck. He was in charge again. He was the captain of all he surveyed. He walked over the deck toward the bridge. His first mate, Lanny Thompson, raised his hand in greeting from his position behind the wheel as Devon stepped into the pilothouse.

"Captain Lancaster, welcome aboard. We're getting ready to sail. The boat's loaded, and all the safety checks have been made," Lanny said.

"Great. Let's get underway," Devon said, dropping his duffel in the corner and walking over to take the wheel.

Lanny did a good job at the helm, and so did the wheelsman, but Devon wanted to steer. He wanted to be the first to guide the *Manitoulin* into its familiar circuit to Detroit and back. The freighter was loaded with heavy, red iron ore for the trip from Portstown to Detroit and would be loaded up even more with lighter-weight black coal for the trip back from Detroit to Portstown. Devon's was one of many freighters that followed the route through the Great Lakes, and he never tired of it. He felt like he was fulfilling his duty to his country by delivering the iron ore needed to make steel for the weapons, and he jumped at the chance.

"I saw you with Loralei at the dance in town. Millie said to say 'hi' to Loralei when I saw you. She said she doesn't see her around much," Lanny said, stepping away from the wheel.

"Yeah, she can't leave the lighthouse unattended, so it makes it hard for her to get out. And Misha keeps her busy," Devon said.

"He's a great kid," Lanny said.

"Yeah," Devon said.

"Chief engineer reports engine ready for use," a crewman called out as he stuck his head in the door.

"Let's go," Devon said. He could feel his heart pump as he readied the *Manitoulin* to leave. "Helm is at hand, rudder amidships, steering off the port pump," Devon said.

"Very well," Lanny replied, as per protocol.

Devon steered the freighter away from the dock and out into the harbor. The familiar view of the deep blue lake sparkling in the morning sun took his breath away. He couldn't wait to get out onto the open water.

"I saw you with Carlotta Pomodoro, too. I hear she took up with Captain Blake at the dance. Just thought you might want to know. She gets around," Lanny said.

Devon stiffened in surprise at Lanny's statement. He wasn't used to hearing idle gossip from his first mate, and he wondered if there was another reason he mentioned it. He wondered if it had to do with his wife, Millie, being friends with Loralei. He felt a flash of anger as well at the thought of Carlotta being with another captain. He cared for Loralei and his family, but when he looked at Loralei, all he could think about was how happy she used to be. Now, all he saw when he looked at her was sadness, and he couldn't deal with that, especially when he was dealing with his own feelings of loss. He didn't have time for emotions. Carlotta was wild in a way that filled something in him and made him want to be around her. She gave him relief from his problems. He had taken up with her a few times when he'd run into her at taverns in town, and he didn't like the idea that she was interested in other captains. Devon turned the wheel and concentrated on steering.

"It's not just captains, either. I heard she was with Jake Calico for a while," Lanny said.

"Enough," Devon said, feeling exasperated with Lanny's openness. "I have other things to do. Take my duffel to my cabin, would you? And tell the galley to get me some coffee," he said.

"Right away, sir," Lanny said.

Devon was relieved that Lanny assumed a professional attitude and left to carry out his orders. The conversation had made Devon uncomfortable.

Devon sailed through the early morning on Whitefish Bay in Lake Superior to the St. Mary's River and through the day to the Soo Locks. He readied the *Manitoulin* to make the precision route into the locks. He had been through here many times before but was still careful to properly steer through the approach channel in the St. Mary's River system. Once he got into the lock and the gates closed on either side, it took about nine or ten hours for gravity to let the water flow out of the lock chamber through an opened valve into the St. Mary's canal and the lower lakes. This lowered the freighter twenty-one feet from the level of Lake Superior to the level of Lake Huron so it could sail through into the lower lake.

But Devon didn't know, as he expertly navigated his freighter of iron ore through the Soo Locks and began his nearly month-long circuit through Lake Huron to Detroit to drop off the iron ore and sail back loaded with coal, that Andre Sorrento had sailed up through Lake Huron and was passing him in the locks from the other direction on a coal-bearing freighter headed for Portstown.

CHAPTER 6

Loralei walked down to the beach at midnight, a fortnight after she'd been there before, to meet Grayson, who she now knew was really Jake Calico. He'd been lying to her all along. She'd asked Edmund to stay over and take Misha into town in the morning for a tutoring session with Mrs. Petrova. She had waited until they were both asleep before venturing into the warm summer night.

The lake shimmered like smooth, clear glass under the twinkling, ebony dome of a starry sky, and she gazed across the water, looking for him. She had thought about not meeting him and letting their relationship fade away on its own, but she was afraid he would come to the lighthouse to find her, and she didn't want that. She wanted him to stay away. *Where was he?* Her heart skipped a beat when she saw the shadow of his canoe down the beach. He was here. Somewhere. She turned when she felt the warmth of him and gasped. She hadn't heard him come up behind her. He pulled her to him, and for a moment, she forgot why she was there as she melted into the pleasure of his kiss. But fear overtook her, and she pulled away.

"Grayson, no," she said, trying to control her trembling

body and hoping she could carry out her plan to break up with Jake without him knowing she knew who he really was. "I only came tonight to tell you something. I can't see you anymore." She shivered when she felt his body tense up but continued. "I'm sorry. I've decided to go back to my husband and make my marriage work. I hope you understand."

The night seemed suddenly cold and menacing, and she wanted more than anything to run back to the lighthouse. But she had to stay, and she had to tell him to stay away.

Jake pulled her to him again and ran his fingers through her hair. "Are you sure, little dove?" He looked deeply into her eyes. "I can feel you tremble. You want me."

She moaned when he brushed his fingers down her arms.

"Be with me tonight. We will take each other to the moon and the stars. You are my love," he said.

She clenched her teeth and tried to control her desire for him. "No." She moved away. "Please, Grayson. I can't see you anymore."

His black eyes pierced hers as he grabbed her arm and pulled her back toward him. "You will change your mind. I can see it in your eyes. We will meet again. You are mine."

"No. I am no ones. I'm leaving now."

She ripped her arm from his grasp, feeling suddenly terrified that she had met Jake alone after finding out who he was. She realized that the fact he didn't know she knew was the only thing that saved her from his wrath. She ran down the beach without looking back toward the relative safety of the lighthouse.

***

Loralei stepped into The Blue Lake Tavern in Portstown after dropping Misha off at Mrs. Petrova's cottage for a sign-language lesson. She had come into town for supplies while Edmund took care of the lighthouse and stopped to talk to Finn and Marie. It was a chilly morning, and she was glad to walk into the warmth and coziness of the tavern. She closed the door on the loud bustle of the street and the blaring ship horns of the harbor to the welcome quiet of the room. There weren't many people there, but she saw a few sailors sitting at the counter talking and laughing with Finn. She walked quietly over.

"What brings you in?" Finn asked, moving away from the sailors and rubbing a cloth over the polished wood counter as she approached him.

"Is Marie around? I was hoping to talk to her," she said.

"Sure. Let me get her. Be right back, guys," Finn said.

The sailors nodded as he turned and went through the doors to the kitchen.

Loralei turned away and went to sit at a table nearby. Her feet were swollen from the pregnancy, and she didn't want to stand any longer. She had to pick Misha up later and drive back to the lighthouse, and she needed to rest. She dropped her shopping bags on the floor before sitting down in the wooden chair, leaning back, and sighing. She'd spent the morning visiting shops in town for food staples and painting supplies and was pleased with her efforts. She had enough paints to last her for a while now and was looking forward to starting another project. She might paint a lake view from the lighthouse at sunset with a freighter in the distance and imagined the warm shades of color she would use as she brought the painting to life.

Marie walked over, wiping her hands on her white chef's apron. "Loralei, how nice to see you. I was just doing the dishes. Do you want me to make you something to eat?"

"No, thanks. I'm in town doing some shopping, and I came in to ask if you knew of anyone who could work on the beacon and do some maintenance around the lighthouse. It's getting to be a little much for me, and I know you run into a lot of people here. I saw the freighter come in, too, and I wondered if anyone had news about the war," Loralei said.

"I'll ask around for someone. It must be hard to keep up with Devon gone and the baby on the way. You look great, though. I can hardly tell you're pregnant," Marie said.

"Thanks. I didn't show that much with Misha, either, but I still feel pregnant," Loralei said.

"Yeah. By the way, Finn heard Jake Calico was spotted canoeing the harbor a few nights ago. You might want to be on the lookout for him again. You never know what he could be up to," Marie said.

"I know," Loralei said, looking away. She had told Marie she broke things off with Jake, but she hadn't told her how hard it was not to see him anymore and how much she had cared for him.

"I'm sorry. I didn't mean to—" Marie said.

"No, it's okay. It's important to the safety of the lighthouse that I know when he's around. Sometimes I can't believe I fell for someone like that or that I let him into my life—into Devon's and my life. I wish I could do things over and change the past. I wish things were different between Devon and me," she said.

"Give yourself a break. Marriage is hard, and you're dealing with a lot. And Jake is handsome in a wild, untamed way. Nobody's perfect," Marie said softly, touching Loralei's arm.

"Thanks," Loralei said.

Before she could say anything more, she was distracted by a commotion at the door of the tavern. She watched several men, obviously, sailors, stomp through the door singing a bawdy song, and trudge over to the counter. Finn raised a hand in greeting.

"Are you the sailors from the *American Intrepid*? I know she pulled into port this morning. What can I get you?" Finn asked.

"Yeah, we just got in," one of the sailors replied.

"Give us some beers. Rum for this guy, though. He's not much for beer, but he sure can cook," the sailor said, laughing and slapping the man next to him on the back.

"Sure can," the others agreed.

"Couldn't have made it here without him. What was that stuff? Creme brûlée? Never did have a dessert burned on top on purpose like that, but it was the best thing I ever ate. Scullery Joe liked it, too, even though I don't think he liked having you in his kitchen. But the more cooks, the better, right? You can sail with us anytime, Andre," he said.

A beautiful man with thick, wavy, dark hair turned from the counter to thank the men and looked over at her. He stared at her a moment too long, and she wondered who he was. She'd never seen a man whose face was so sculpted and well-defined. His jaw was chiseled and his chin strong, and he held himself with a regal bearing. She wondered where he'd come from. He didn't look like a sailor, and he didn't look like anyone from town, either. She shivered as she returned his gaze. His eyes were a deep, warm brown, but something about the cool glint she saw in them made her gasp.

"What is it?" Marie asked.

"Nothing. I just thought I saw something, that's all," she replied, not looking at Marie.

She did see something—something in the man's eyes that both attracted and repelled her, but she wasn't sure what it was. She tried to lower her eyes, but she couldn't. When he gave her a slow grin, she felt her cheeks warm and flush. She grimaced when he dropped her gaze and returned to his conversation with the sailors. She realized that she felt disappointed he looked away. Something about the way he looked at her made her want to go to him. It was the same pull she'd felt when she met Jake—a deep, physical reaction to something wild.

"Do you know that man?" Marie asked, following Loralei's gaze.

"No, but he reminds me of someone," Loralei replied, looking away quickly. She didn't want Marie to see her reaction to him. "Maybe I could get some hot tea, or something, while I wait for Misha to be done with his lesson. Would you mind?"

"Nope. Coming right up. I'll be back in a minute," Marie answered.

She turned and walked toward the kitchen, and Loralei shifted her gaze back to the counter where the sailors were. She tried not to be obvious about staring at the dark-haired man. Something about the way he moved touched her. He was graceful and deliberate in his movements, like a sleek, young panther stalking its prey. And yet, he seemed able to fit in with the others as though he were one of them. But he wasn't one of them. Something about him was unusual.

"Finn, Loralei needs someone to help maintain the beacon at the lighthouse. Keep an eye out, huh?" Marie called out to Finn as she came out of the kitchen with the tea.

"Sure," he answered.

The dark-haired man separated himself from the group as Marie walked by.

"I could do that," he said. "I am good with electronics, and I plan to stay in Portstown for a while."

Marie stopped for a moment and hesitated before walking toward Loralei. "Follow me."

Loralei felt her cheeks warm when she saw the man walking toward her. She didn't know what she would say to him, especially since she felt an odd connection to him that she wasn't sure she wanted to pursue.

"I am Andre Soren. At your service, ma'am," he said, introducing himself when they arrived at the table and bowing his head slightly.

"Oh, thank you," Loralei stammered. She wasn't used to someone talking to her with such formality. "I'm sure that's very nice." She sat still for a moment, trying to think of something more to say.

"Could I talk to you for a minute?" Marie asked, taking her arm and pulling her away from the table when she stood up.

"What is it?" Loralei asked when they had walked a few tables away.

"Maybe this isn't such a good idea. Is there something

going on between you two?" Marie asked.

"No, not at all. I don't even know him. I'm just feeling a little flustered from all the walking I did today, that's all. I think he'll be fine for the job. The crew from the ship seems to like him, and I need someone to start work as soon as possible," Loralei said.

"Well, if you're sure," Marie said.

"I'm sure," Loralei said, walking back to the table with Marie following her. "Could you come out to the lighthouse sometime this week?" Loralei said to Andre. "It's on the lake outside town. I'll show you what needs to be done, and we can make arrangements from there." She hoped she sounded professional, as she didn't want her obvious attraction to Andre to be a problem for Marie.

"Yes, of course. Could you suggest a place to stay in town?" he asked.

"The Pointer House," Marie said quickly, looking from Loralei to Andre. "You can stay there for a nominal room and board. It's down Main Street by the pier."

"Thank you," Andre said, tipping his head and leaving to rejoin the sailors at the bar.

"What are you thinking? Do you see the way he looks at you?" Marie asked when he was out of earshot.

"I'm thinking I need to keep the beacon maintained," Loralei said, getting up to leave. "I have to get Misha now. Thanks for the tea."

She grabbed her shopping bags and hurried past Marie and out the door, being careful not to look at Andre. She didn't want Marie or Finn to say anything to her about him. She breathed a sigh of relief when she closed the door behind her and stepped onto the sidewalk in front of the tavern. It was still chilly outside, but now she welcomed the brisk air as it cooled her warm, flushed cheeks. She walked quickly down the street and headed up the lane to Mrs. Petrova's cottage. As she neared the cottage, she saw Misha playing on the front step while Mrs. Petrova watered her flowers.

"I've come for Misha," she called out.

"Already? We had such a nice time. It just flew by," Mrs. Petrova said.

Loralei was relieved to see Mrs. Petrova's smiling face. Seeing her always made Loralei feel better. She supposed it was because she reminded her of her mother. She was such a warm, caring person, and she never felt judged by her in the way she had just felt judged by Marie. Mrs. Petrova touched Misha on the shoulder and pointed to Loralei when he looked up. Misha ran to the fence and through the gate when Loralei opened it. They signed their goodbyes, and Loralei took Misha back to the Jeep with her. She tried not to think about Andre as they got in the Jeep and drove back to the lighthouse.

***

Andre saw the lighthouse overlooking the lake as he walked up the dirt path through the woods from the road. It had taken him about half an hour to walk down the road from town. The Pointer House, where he was staying in town, barely afforded him the amount of privacy he desired, and he hoped to work at the lighthouse and move out soon.

He had locked the valise he had been given in Detroit in his room, seeing no other options until he could find a more secure place to hide it. The information contained in the valise was extremely volatile. Giorgio Bartoli hadn't stood a chance at remaining alive after delivering such vital information. It contained shipbuilding invoices with a list of locations where minesweeping ships, a new technology developed by the Allies, were being sent. It was imperative that the discovery of this new technology be relayed to his spy network as soon as possible, and if he worked at the lighthouse, he was sure he would have access to a radio there. He planned to find out what the job entailed and looked forward to seeing the beautiful young woman who had offered it to him.

He had been stunned when he first saw the woman across the room at the tavern. She wasn't the type of woman he had expected to find in the wilderness of northern Michigan. Her long, wavy hair was a rich, lustrous gold, and her cheeks were pink and flushed. Her rosy lips had pouted at him when he looked at her. He had been mesmerized. He could not look away. She was a rare, delicate beauty, the type of masterpiece he would find in a priceless painting, not in the wilds of the north country. She had been sitting all alone in a sailors' tavern, and he had been intrigued. She didn't seem to fit into the rough surroundings, and he wondered who she was. He had jumped at the chance to meet her.

Now, here he was, walking to the lighthouse to see her. He had waited until early afternoon to head out, hoping to take advantage of the sunny weather and cool breezes off the lake. It was a beautiful day, and he breathed deeply of the fresh lake air as he watched the sunshine filter through the leaves of the trees along the path. The lighthouse stood in a large clearing in the woods, flanked by a few small wooden buildings. A large vegetable garden and a smaller flower garden surrounded the base.

He approached from the back and knocked on the door. He waited a moment and knocked again. He caught his breath when the woman opened the door. She was truly lovely, with her damp, blonde hair bouncing in ringlets around her flushed, pink cheeks and her azure-blue eyes widening in surprise. She wiped her perspiring brow with the back of her hand.

"Oh, hello. Forgive me. I was scrubbing the floor and didn't hear the knock. Won't you come in?" she asked.

"Yes, thank you," Andre replied, feeling the hairs of his arm stand up as he brushed lightly past her through the open door.

He was amazed that a woman could have such an

overwhelming effect on him. He was more than a little interested in her and could sense her attraction to him. He could only anticipate what the future held for them. But he was also interested in continuing his mission of gathering information about the Great Lakes shipping operation and the Soo Locks. He expected his current location in Portstown to help with that. It wasn't far from the locks, and he had settled into the boarding house in town the previous week.

"May I offer you something to drink? I made fresh lemonade this morning. And I have some ginger cookies," she said.

"Yes, that would be nice. It was a long walk out here, and the lemonade would be refreshing," he answered.

"Have a seat," she said.

She waved her hand toward a wooden kitchen table and chairs. Andre walked carefully over the wet floor and pulled out a wooden, slat-backed chair. He sat down next to the small boy who was eating a cookie at the table.

"Hello," Andre said.

The boy looked at him but didn't answer.

"This is Misha, my son. He doesn't hear very well, so he doesn't say much," she said.

Andre watched her sign to the boy.

"Hello," Misha said, turning to him.

Andre smiled at him.

"I'm Loralei Lancaster, by the way," the woman said, setting a plate of cookies on a tray. "The lighthouse has been in my family for many years, and I'm the current keeper. I'm glad you're able to help us out. I'll give you a tour after you eat."

"I would be honored," Andre said.

She poured three glistening glasses of iced lemonade and added them to the tray. "My grandfather helps out, too, but it's harder for him to get around as he gets older. It will be nice to have another set of hands around here. Inspectors can show up at any time, and we have to be ready for inspection. We have maintenance duties that must be adhered to every day to keep in line with government regulations."

"I would imagine you do." He smiled at her when she brought the tray to the table and leaned over in front of him to set the plate of cookies down. He glimpsed her slightly rounded figure through the flimsy, sweat-dampened cotton of her blouse and reached out to touch her hand. "Allow me to take those from you."

"Yes, of course," she said.

He was charmed that her cheeks turned pink as she flinched at his touch and looked away. He took the cookies, and she set glasses of lemonade in front of him and Misha without saying anything. She stood, sipping her lemonade and watching him.

"This is very good. I needed this," Andre said as he took a sip.

The tart-sweet taste felt tangy on his tongue. He looked up to see Loralei watching him. He needed more than that, Andre thought as he returned her gaze. He needed her. And he could tell she needed him. He felt the tension between them escalate. It had been building slowly since he walked in the door.

"Do I need to talk to your husband about the job? Is he around?" Andre asked as he took another sip of lemonade.

"You can talk to me about it. My husband is the captain of a freighter on the Great Lakes. He's on a trip right now," she said. She tucked a curl behind her ear and glanced at him.

"I see. It must be difficult to take care of the lighthouse and live out here all by yourself. Are you not afraid?" he asked.

He was amazed that such a beautiful woman would be left alone to fend for herself in such a wilderness. She appeared so delicate and vulnerable to him, a precious beauty that needed to be protected. She reminded him of the woman in the *Mother and Child* rendering he had, one of many paintings by Mary Cassatt but his personal favorite. She was a beauty of rare caliber.

"Not really. I grew up here in the lighthouse with my family. It's my home. We do have to watch for pirates, though. We have to keep the lighthouse safe. The pirates raid the ships on the lakes. Sometimes they sabotage lighthouse beacons to cause shipwrecks so they can steal the cargo off the ships," she said.

"How terrible," Andre said.

"Yes, it is. Jake Calico is a pirate around here. We have to watch out for him. He caused a shipwreck up north a few years ago, and he was seen around here a few weeks ago," she said.

"If you need me to stay with you, I can," Andre said.

There was silence for a moment.

"Tell me about yourself. Where are you from? You don't seem like a sailor even though you were with the men from the ship. What do you do for a living?" she asked.

He smiled at her. "A little bit of everything. I find work where I can and stay where I find it. It is a way to live during the war. I am from everywhere and nowhere."

Loralei held his gaze for a moment and seemed to give him a tentative smile in return. She turned and set her lemonade on the counter.

"Misha, it's time for your nap," she said.

She took the boy's hand and led him into the other room, and Andre waited for her to return.

"If you'd like to follow me, I'll show you the rest of the lighthouse and what your duties will be," she said, walking back into the kitchen after a moment.

"Yes, of course," Andre said.

He followed her to a spiral staircase of painted, grey, iron stairs on the side of the room. They climbed them together, occasionally pausing to rest. He felt her nearness and caught the scent of fresh lavender from her hair. When they reached the top of the staircase, Andre followed her into the lantern room and caught his breath as he looked out the windows over the wide expanse of the lake.

"This is very beautiful," he said.

"Yes, it is. I never tire of looking at the lake. It gives me strength. It always has," she said.

He saw freighters in the distance and a seagull soaring high over the lake. A few sailboats dotted the water near the shoreline. "The view is lovely. Almost as lovely as you." He smiled when her cheeks flushed.

"Let me show you the beacon," she said, turning away. "This is the Fresnel lens. We used to use kerosene vapor lamps for the light, but they replaced them a few years ago with electricity. We keep it polished and shining. It's very important for it to be in perfect shape for the sailors to see the light at night. It is electrified, and the circuitry must be kept in pristine condition. This is what I want you to look at, among other things."

"Yes, I can see that this is quite ingenious," Andre said, inspecting the beehive-shaped lens and surrounding circuitry.

"And the exterior of the lighthouse needs to be painted. It's quite a job, but it needs to be done," she said.

"I can do that. It would be my honor," he said.

"Thank you. I'm glad you feel that way. I feel that way about taking care of the lighthouse. I feel like it's an honor to be entrusted with people's lives," Loralei said.

"It is," he said.

She looked at him thoughtfully, and he returned her gaze until she looked away and motioned to him to follow her. He was well aware of her nearness as he tried to keep his mind on the business at hand. She showed him more of the workings of the lighthouse and the duties and responsibilities of the job. As the afternoon light faded into the evening, she got Misha up from his nap and made dinner for them all. She made a light, savory stew and served it with bowls of fresh, wild raspberries he supposed she'd gotten from the bushes he'd seen on the lighthouse grounds for dessert. He was pleased to find that the stew was perfectly seasoned with fresh herbs and spices. When they were finished, she stood and gathered the plates to take them to the sink.

"Would you like some apple brandy? I have some," she asked.

"Yes, very much," he answered.

Loralei poured him a snifter and one for herself, and they took them into the living area. She sat on the sofa with Misha, and Andre stood at the fireplace, leaning against the mantel. He took a sip of his brandy and let the thick, sweet liquid sluice through and warm him.

"It must be lonely to live out here by yourself with no one to talk to and a small child to care for. How do you do it?" Andre asked.

"It is lonely, sometimes. But it's what I do. It's what my family has always done. I can't imagine living any other way. But I do miss my husband, and it's very hard to have him gone," she replied.

"I would imagine it is," he said.

They sat in companionable silence for a moment, enjoying each other's company.

"You are very good with him," Andre said, swallowing the sudden welling of emotion he felt, watching Loralei smooth her fingers over her little boy's hair and kiss him on the cheek. "He is very lucky to have you."

"Of course. I'm his mother," she said.

"Not all mothers are like you," Andre said, looking away. "Some mothers never touch their little boys."

"I can't imagine that," she said.

"No. I do not imagine that you could," he replied.

"I'd better put him to bed. I'll be back in a minute," she said.

Andre waited for her in the cozy room, looking out the window at the dark, moonlit-tipped waves of the lake rolling to shore. Silvery stars studded an amethyst sky that glowed near the horizon with an emerald light. Light wisps of gossamer clouds skimmed over the woods near the shore, adding an ethereal atmosphere to the peaceful scene. He heard Loralei pad lightly into the room behind him, and he felt his body warm with anticipation as she neared him. She paused next to him, and he saw her look across the lake at the sky.

"It's the aurora borealis, the northern lights. We see them sometimes on mostly clear nights. It's the magic of the sun at night," she said.

"It is magnifico," he said.

"Yes, it is," she said.

They stood together for a while in awed silence, sharing the beauty and allure of the fluorescent night sky. Andre felt her nearness warming him until he became helpless with a fever of desire. He turned to her.

"You are so lovely. You are a rare beauty in the wilderness that rivals the beauty of the sky. I am your servant, bella signora," he said.

She gazed at him for a moment before touching him on his arm. She was silent as he bent to kiss her on her trembling lips. For a moment, time went away for him in the pleasure of the kiss, until he heard the light patter of rain on the window.

"It's raining," she murmured.

"Yes," he said.

"I don't think you should go back to town in the rain. You could catch a cold, and you wouldn't be able to work," she said softly.

"That is true. Perhaps, I should stay...for the sake of the lighthouse," he said.

"Yes. For the sake of the lighthouse," she said.

Andre looked at her for a long moment before gently taking her hand. He walked with her to the bedroom, where she closed the door behind them.

***

Loralei padded into the fluorescent darkness of the bedroom that flickered from the raindrops dappling the window against the backdrop of a neon night sky. Andre's shadow merged with hers on the wall near the bed, and she felt the tiny hairs of her arms spark against her skin as Andre pulled her into a feverish embrace.

"I need you," she said, losing her breath as he pressed his lips to hers and crushed her hair with his fingers. "It's been so long since I've had someone love me."

"We will change that," Andre said. He moved his lips away for a moment. "A woman as beautiful as you should never be without what she needs."

She sighed and leaned into him as he returned his lips to hers. His kiss was warm and voracious, and she moaned with longing. She felt her thoughts recede and her mind relax. There was only her and Andre, lost in a pillowed cloud of desire.

"Be with me, mio splendore, mia donna rara e bella," Andre said.

She trembled at his ardent words. She understood his emotion, if not his meaning.

"Yes, I will be with you. We will be together," she said.

She followed him to the bed. The hurt, disappointment, and grief she had felt when Devon was home disappeared. There was only the glow of knowing she was desired by a handsome, desirable man.

"The night will be ours alone. We will make the cares of the world go away," Andre said.

"Yes. Together, we will make the cares of the world go away," she said, melting into his deep embrace and giving herself up to the pleasure of desire.

CHAPTER 7

Devon took a swig of rum and tried not to think about Loralei. It had bothered him lately that he wasn't home more often, especially now that she was pregnant with their second child and the war appeared to be moving closer to home. He didn't like the idea that the Soo Locks could come under attack by the Nazis. He had thought they were more protected than that in the wilderness of northern Michigan, but it appeared he could be wrong. Soldiers were everywhere, and hydrogen balloons were floating over the locks to protect them. He couldn't deny that the war was closer to home than it used to be and threatening his family. He took another pull of rum and laid back on his berth.

The lighthouse was a lot of work, and he hoped Loralei could handle it. She'd always been strong and capable in his mind, but after seeing her when he was on shore leave, he wondered if she was more vulnerable than he had thought. She had seemed sad and tired, and he wondered if the pregnancy was hard on her. He hadn't had strong feelings for her in years. The loss of his father and her father and of the crew of the freighter that went down two years ago had taken away any feelings he had. He had loved her when they were first married, and sometimes he remembered, wistfully, how happy they'd been. But now he felt numb inside and cold. It was an icy numbness, a frosty chill, more bitter than the deep cold of the winds off Lake Superior in winter. And it froze his heart.

Devon heard a knock on the door as a crewman called to him.

"Captain Lancaster. You're wanted on the bridge," he said.

"Be right there," he responded, corking his bottle and rolling out of bed.

He had been expecting to sleep through the night and morning while his first mate, Lanny, steered the *Manitoulin*. He'd gotten off duty at three a few hours ago and had been drinking to relax. He wondered what the problem could be. When he arrived on deck, he found Lanny looking out the windows of the pilothouse with his wheelsman steering the freighter.

"What are we dealing with?" Devon asked as he walked over and stood next to Lanny.

He followed Lanny's gaze out the window to the steel-gray cover of thick clouds roiling against the deep black of the night sky. The waves of the lake were tall, dark, and ominous. They thumped against the sides of the freighter as it heaved ahead through the blackness of the water and the night.

"Storms ahead, Captain," Lanny said, standing up straight.

"We have the weather report and the sighting. There's a gale warning here and on Lake Superior. It looks like we're in for a real squall. You can see the cloud line over there," he said.

Devon surveyed the sky and the lake in front of him. He knew storms could come up on the lakes and last for days at a time, especially in the fall, but it was still summer. His gut told him it was bad, but he didn't think it was anything they couldn't get through. They were in the middle of the lake, not near the shore where the rocks and shoals lurked that wrecked the ships. He had ridden out storms before on the open water and was ready to do it again. Lake Huron was known for its dangerous storms and sometimes monster, ocean-like waves, as were all the Great Lakes, but he knew her like the back of his hand. He was prepared to fight her for the safety of the *Manitoulin*, as he always had. He was going to battle the waves with speed by charging through them.

"Batten down the hatches," Devon said, taking charge. "We're going to ride this one out, mates, and we're going to do it in style. Full speed ahead," he said.

***

Loralei awoke to the flutter of the gingham curtains in the bedroom window. A cool morning breeze blew in off the lake, a remnant of the storm the night before or perhaps a harbinger of a storm to come. She took a deep breath of the rainwater-fresh air before turning over on her side to look at Andre, sleeping there next to her.

She could see the light cotton blanket raising and lowering with his slumbering breaths. He was so beautiful. His hair was a silky, wavy brown, haloing the high cheekbones of his aristocratic-looking face. A slight stubble of beard touched his cheeks and only added to the attraction she felt for him.

But, despite his looks, he wasn't angelic, not at all. He had a tough core. Something about him was dark and unbridled and mysterious. She sensed it, and it had brought her to dizzying heights of pleasure during the night. He excited her in ways she couldn't explain, and he, in turn, seemed to love her body's ripe fullness. He was wild and untamed, and she wanted more. She felt close to him, if not yet emotionally, physically, through the pleasure they shared, and she wanted to explore more pinnacles with him. Loralei reached for him, but before she could touch him, she saw Misha standing in the doorway.

"Mama?" Misha said, rubbing his eyes with his hands.

"Yes, I'm getting up," Loralei signed, sliding carefully out of bed so as not to disturb Andre.

She didn't want to wake him for no reason. Besides, she had a million things to do. She had the beacon to polish, daily logs to keep and chores to do, and she had to get herself and Misha dressed and ready for the day. And she wanted to get a weather report, too. She saw Misha looking toward Andre and hurried to sign to him to go back to his room before he came close enough to see him. She would be in later, she said, after she got dressed. She watched him turn and pad away and hoped he wouldn't ask too many questions.

Loralei heard the low rumble of thunder in the distance and walked over to the window to peek through the curtains at the sky. Clouds were forming a dark blue bank on the horizon, but she didn't see anything to worry about at the moment.

"You are incredibly beautiful in the morning, cara mia (my dear)."

Loralei heard Andre's low voice and turned to see him looking at her and smiling. The fierce glint in his eyes took her breath away.

"Come back to bed, Lori," he said.

"I can't. I have too many things to do," she answered, smiling at his tender name for her. "There could be storms coming in, and I have to prepare the lighthouse. Come with me, and I'll make you some breakfast."

Loralei wanted more than anything to go to Andre but hurried to put on her dress and shoes instead. She saw him calmly watching her.

"Grandpapa will probably come over soon. He always knows when storms are coming in, and he'll want to help with the lighthouse. I don't want him to know about us. I'll tell him I hired you as a lighthouse tender and that you're here doing some work," she said.

"Of course. I'll be out soon," Andre said.

Loralei paused and smiled at him tentatively before turning and leaving the room. She didn't know him, but in an odd way, she did know him. After the night they'd shared, she felt that she knew him on a deep level. And yet there was something about him that couldn't be reached, something dark and hidden and cold.

She called to Misha to stay in his room until she came for him before hurrying up the stairwell to the lantern room to check on the beacon. She was only required to run it from sunset to sunrise, but she left it on when she looked out the window at the dark, cloudy sky. She turned on the radio as she wiped the beacon clean and polished the surrounding brass. The weather report confirmed her fears of a line of storms entering the area, and she opened the lighthouse log and recorded the weather on its pages, along with her list of completed daily chores. She took a last look out the window at the churning lake before heading back downstairs to retrieve Misha. She brought him with her into the kitchen and sat him at the table while she made breakfast.

As she stirred flour, sugar, and oil together for the fluffy hotcakes she was known for, she thought about Devon and wondered if he was okay. The weather report had mentioned storms on Lake Huron, too. But she tried to put it out of her mind. Devon was a seasoned sailor, and he had been sailing the lakes for most of his life. She had to think he could handle a summer storm. At the moment, she was more concerned about her duties and keeping the lighthouse running for the sailors in the area.

Loralei expertly poured rounds of batter into a skillet. As she turned to set her mixing bowl on the counter, she saw Andre standing near the table. She caught her breath when he gave her a charming smile. He had shaved, but his dark hair was still pleasantly disheveled. He looked rested and casual and impossibly handsome.

"May I help you with something?" he asked.

She was surprised that he asked. Devon left all the kitchen duties to her, but then she remembered that Andre had been a cook on a freighter and realized he was probably as comfortable in a kitchen as she was.

"No, thank you. Have a seat. Everything should be ready in a moment," she said.

Andre said good morning to Misha and sat down next to him.

"I noticed some beautiful seascape paintings on the walls. Where did you get them?" he asked.

Loralei laughed lightly, feeling flattered that he thought her paintings were store-bought. "I painted those myself. It helps me relax when I have time to myself. I sometimes paint when Misha is napping, and I'm caught up on my chores. The view from the edge of the bluff is constantly changing and gives me lots of ideas," she said.

She turned around to look at him and smiled at the look of shock on his face.

"You painted those?" he asked, as though not believing his ears. "They are extraordinary."

"Do you really think they're that good?" Loralei asked.

"They are bellissimi. I know. I used to work as an art dealer before the war put an end to my post. You could show these. You could be on commission in a gallery," he said.

"No," Loralei said before turning around to flip a cake.

"Yes, you could," he said.

"Thank you. I have some similar ones on display at the Methodist church in town that my family and I attended when I was a child. I still take Misha there sometimes. That's as close as I've ever gotten to showing my art to anyone," she said.

"They should be shown to everyone," Andre said.

Loralei smiled and thanked him again as she served up the hotcakes and sat down at the table to eat with them. She was pleased to have someone appreciate her paintings. Just as they finished breakfast, Loralei heard a car. She hurried to the door and opened it to see Mrs. Petrova getting out of her gray Studebaker, carrying some books and heading for the lighthouse.

"Hello, dear," she said as she entered the kitchen. "I've brought some spelling books along with some signing books for Misha. The sooner he learns to read, the sooner he'll have another way of communicating. We'll have to get him started on these. Hello, Mishka," Mrs. Petrova said, signing good morning to him. "Oh, and who is this?" she asked, looking toward Andre.

"This is the new lighthouse tender. He's doing some work for me," Loralei said.

"Nice to meet you," Mrs. Petrova said.

Andre nodded.

"I wanted to drop off the books on my way back to town. Storms are coming in, so I won't keep you. Keep up the good work, dear. I'll see you later," Mrs. Petrova said.

And with that, she left.

Loralei spent the afternoon showing Andre what needed to be done and what needed to be painted at the lighthouse. She told him the coast guard wanted many things painted green, but the outside of the lighthouse would probably stay the same stark white. And some of the walls needed to be whitewashed. Andre nodded and agreed with what she said. As the afternoon waned, Andre went to the lantern room to further inspect the electrical wiring of the beacon.

Eventually, the rain let up, and Loralei walked to the garden in the back of the lighthouse to pull up some carrots and turnips after putting Misha down for his nap. She wanted to make stew for dinner and hoped the rain would hold off long enough for her to dig up some vegetables. As she set the basket down that she had brought with her and kneeled to dig, she saw a slight movement in the woods. It was barely noticeable, but something about it made her heart race. She looked more closely at the shadows between the trees. She didn't think it was a bear or bobcat, but she was sure something was there. She stood slowly and walked toward the trees. The leaves of the trees dripped in pattering unison from the rainstorm, and she heard a low rustling in the brush. She saw the movement again and caught her breath.

"Jake," Loralei said, gasping and putting her hand on her heart.

He stepped out from behind a tree when she said his name and grinned at her.

"What are you doing here?" Loralei asked, barely choking out the words. She felt her heart skip a beat.

"Bonjour, little dove. You do know who I am, don't you? Did you miss me?" he asked.

She shuddered when she heard his familiar greeting. She usually found his blending of the French language of his and her heritage with his Chippewa name for her alluring, but now, even though she still loved him, she found it terrifying. He stared at her with his penetrating black eyes, his straight, black hair ruffling in the breeze around the waist of his fringed suede jacket. Loralei tried to say something, but her tongue felt thick and dry. She stared back at him and shivered when he gave her an insolent smile.

"You missed me, I think. I can see it in your lovely blue eyes," he said.

Loralei stepped back when he took a step toward her. She took a quick survey of her surroundings and tried to decide what to do. She could run, but he was faster than she was, and he had a jump on her with his moccasined feet. She had on her uniform-regulation high heels, and she could never outrun him. If she could make it to the door of the lighthouse, she could call for Andre to help, but, as it was, she was too far away. She decided to play along instead.

"Yes, I did miss you," she said softly, putting her hand, damp from raindrops, to her mouth to assuage her parched lips. "Won't you come in?"

She motioned to him to follow her to the lighthouse. If she could make it there with him, Andre would help her. Jake moved toward her, and she turned to go. But before she walked toward the garden, Andre appeared at the back door of the lighthouse. Loralei raised her hand and waved, trying to appear as though nothing was wrong until she could get closer to him. She heard Jake rustling through the woods behind her and felt a stab of fear. She decided to make a run for it.

"Andre, help," she called.

She hitched up her skirt and dashed for the door.

"What is it? What is wrong?" Andre asked.

Before she could answer, he ran out the door and raced toward her. She glanced behind her as she ran faster and saw Jake standing his ground on the edge of the woods. She looked back toward Andre.

"It's Jake Calico, the pirate," she screamed, racing past him as he passed her on his way to the woods. "He's here to make trouble."

She ran all the way to the lighthouse before turning around to see what was happening behind her. Andre had reached the edge of the woods where Jake was standing.

"Get out of here. You are not welcome here," Andre yelled at Jake.

"Who the hell are you?" Jake responded.

"That is of no importance. Get out," Andre said.

Loralei shrieked when she saw Jake pull a knife out of a sheath in his jacket.

"Back off," Jake said.

Andre grabbed a thick branch from the ground and thwacked him hard on the arm. The knife went flying into the woods. Jake raised his arm to fend off another blow and punched Andre in the face. Andre fell back. Jake grabbed the branch, but it appeared that Andre had a strong hold on it. Jake grabbed a rock and hit Andre in the face before turning and running into the woods.

"I'll be back. Nobody messes with Calico," Jake yelled.

Jake disappeared into the shelter of trees.

"Andre," she called out frantically, racing back to the woods.

Andre was lying on the ground, holding his face. Loralei ran to him and knelt beside him.

"Are you all right? You saved me. You're bleeding," Loralei said. She sucked in a breath when Andre lowered his hands, and she saw a welt forming on his cheek and blood streaming from his nose. "You're hurt. Here. Let me help you. We have to get you back to the lighthouse."

She bent down and put his arm around her shoulder. She raised herself back up, lifting him gingerly as he struggled to stand.

"He surprised me with his fist. I did not expect the knife, either. I will not make that mistake again," Andre said.

"Try not to talk too much. Lean on me, and I'll get you home," Loralei said.

She was surprised that she thought of the lighthouse as Andre's home. She managed to get him into the lighthouse and seated at the table before running to the sink to run cold water over a cloth. She placed it on his forehead and told him to hold it there while she used another cloth to tend to his wounds. She jumped when she heard the kitchen door open. Edmund shuffled in on his cane. Sometimes, when the weather was bad, it was hard for him to walk. Damp weather affected his joints, and he sometimes used a cane to get around.

"Grandpapa, I'm so glad you're here. This man's been hurt. We have to help him. He's here to tend the light, and Jake Calico pulled a knife on him. Could you stay with him while I check on the beacon?" Loralei asked.

"Yes, go tend the light. Storms are coming in again fast. I saw them on the way over. I'll tend to him," Edmund said.

Edmund set his cane on the table and waved her away. "And start the foghorn. It's getting hard to see."

"Of course," Loralei said.

She hurried away to carry out her duties. When she got to the lantern room, she checked on the beacon, making sure it was rotating to cast its bright flashes of light out across the lake into the darkening sky. She looked out the windows at the lake to see the waves building and crashing into the shore. The sky was dark and turbulent. She caught her breath. No matter how many times she wrestled with the anger of the lake in a storm, it still frightened her. She checked everything before heading down the stairs and out to the side building to turn on the foghorn. The wind picked up and howled as she ran across the grounds, holding her skirt down against the wind. She entered the foghorn building and sounded the horn. The loud blast burst forth, and she made sure it was operating properly before heading back to the lighthouse. As she stepped out the door, she saw a figure leave the lighthouse and run down the path through the woods, his long, dark hair blowing in the wind.

"Jake," she screamed as she ran toward the lighthouse.

She yanked open the door to see her worst fears realized. Edmund was lying on the floor next to an unconscious Andre.

"Jake knocked me out," Edmund said, holding his head.

"Oh, no, Grandpapa," Loralei called out in concern.

"I'm okay, but I think he knocked out the beacon. Check and see. Light the old lamp if the electricity is gone. We have to maintain the beacon," he said.

"Yes. But Andre, is he all right?" Loralei asked.

"This man? He will be, I think. He was unconscious before Jake got here. I'll watch him. Go," Edmund said.

"Yes, Grandpapa," she said.

She ran up the staircase to the lantern room. The beacon was out, and she rushed to light the old kerosene lamp to replace it. She looked out the window at the lake as she ran to retrieve the can of kerosene, which she had used earlier to clean with, to use it to fill the lamp, and screamed at what she saw.

"It's a shipwreck. A fishing boat smashed on the rocks. I

can see it. We have to rescue them," she called out.

But she realized, as she swallowed her panic and hastily filled the lamp, that neither Edmund nor Andre could hear her over the blasts of the foghorn.

CHAPTER 8

Loralei finished lighting the lamp and ran for the stairwell. The foghorn blasted a long, low, tuba tone amidst the howling crescendo of the wind. She screamed again for help in the two-second pause between blasts, even though it was impossible to be heard from her height in the lighthouse. She tripped down the first step of the stairwell and swooned momentarily at seeing the immense drop to the floor below. She shook her head and grabbed the railing to steady herself before bolting down the stairs to find her grandfather. She ran to the kitchen.

"Grandpapa. There's a shipwreck. A fishing boat crashed on the rock shoal in the channel," she said, trying to catch her breath.

Edmund was holding a cloth to Andre's forehead, and she heard Andre moaning quietly.

"Ring the bell, Loralei," Edmund replied, releasing the cloth into Andre's grasp and turning toward her. "We have to summon the townspeople for help. I'll get the rescue boat."

"You're right. I'll meet you at the boat," she replied, turning quickly to go.

"I shall assist, as well." She was startled to hear Andre

offer to help as he opened his eyes.

"In a momento," he said.

Loralei nodded and grabbed her rain slicker off the hook in the kitchen before running into the backyard to ring the warning bell they only used for shipwrecks and in dire situations. The clang of the bell signaled an emergency to the townspeople, and Loralei knew they would rush to the lighthouse to help. Torrents of cold rain sluiced through her dress as she struggled to fasten her raincoat and lashed at her face as she splashed through the mud to the bell. She reached it and grabbed the long rope hanging down from it. She rang the bell three times when the foghorn paused and three times more when it paused again before running toward the path that led down to the beach to get the rescue boat. Andre shuffled out of the lighthouse wearing Devon's rain slicker and bending against the wind to run to join her. She slowed to allow him to catch up to her and motioned to him to follow her down the path.

"Your grandfather is staying with Misha. I will assist with the rescue," he shouted to her through the wailing wind and battering rain during a pause in the foghorn blasts. "Let us hurry. There is no time to waste," he said.

Loralei nodded and ran to the path through the woods. She headed for the wooden steps that led to the beach. The steps were soaked with deep puddles and wet sand, but she ran down them anyway. When she reached the last step, she glanced behind her to make sure Andre was following her. He was close behind her and jumped into the wet sand in front of her. She raced toward the rowboat they kept upside down near the water. She glanced into the distance and thought she saw the shadowy outline of the fishing boat that had crashed on the rocks, but she wasn't sure. The fog was rolling in and blanketing the dark shore with silvery billows of white fluff. Loralei leaned down to pull up the side of the boat to turn it over. It was slippery and cold and heavier than she remembered, but she gritted her teeth and lifted it slowly.

"Allow me to assist you," Andre said.

He leaned in next to her, and together they flipped the boat over and onto the sand.

"We can push it into the water together. I shall return to retrieve the oars," he said.

She nodded and waited for Andre to go around to the other side of the boat. They pushed and pulled it through the sand to the water's edge, and Loralei stood, struggling to keep her balance in the raging wind, as he ran to retrieve the oars. He ran back and threw them in the boat, and they pushed the boat into the churning waves of the shallow water.

"Jump in," he said, holding one side of the boat.

She did as he asked and grabbed an oar to put it in its oarlock as he pushed the boat farther out and jumped in himself. A white-capped wave broke over the stern, and Loralei choked on a mouthful of water. Andre grabbed the other oar and jammed it into its oarlock just as another wave tipped over the bow.

"Hold on," he yelled.

Loralei grabbed the side of the boat and tried not to swallow more water as she felt the cold slap of the wave wash over her. She shivered as she strained to hear Andre over the wind and the blare of the foghorn.

"Lean to the right," Andre said.

She did as he asked and was relieved that the boat stayed upright. She was glad he was there to row the boat. She had been through rescues before and knew how dangerous they were. But she didn't hesitate to ride the boat into the wild water of the lake. There were men's lives at stake, and the faster they got there, the more survivors they could find. And she was counting on the townspeople to show up with their boats soon to rescue more survivors. She turned around in her seat to look over the bow at the lake and squinted through the rainswept darkness and fog while Andre pulled at the oars. They rode the choppy waters to the rhythmic clicking of the oars as he thrust the boat through the waves. The rain pelted them with cold sheets of icy pinpricks as she gestured to guide Andre to the rock shoal. Eventually, she saw the rock shoal through the fog and gasped when she saw splinters of the crashed boat slamming against the black rocks and churning through the dark water as they drew closer. She saw movement on one of the rocks.

"There…." Loralei yelled through the wind at Andre and pointed to the rocks. "I see a survivor. Ahoy," she shouted to the bedraggled figure clinging to the side of a rock. "We're coming up on you on the port side."

She motioned to Andre to turn the boat. Andre pulled hard on the right ore and brought the boat around sideways to the shoal.

"Can you grab the side of the boat?" Loralei asked.

She could barely see the man through the sheets of rain, but she heard a slight sound that she took to be an affirmation. She secured her foot behind the boat seat and reached out to grab the man's arm. "Grab the side. I'll pull you in." The man pushed off the rock and grabbed for the boat. He went under and came up choking and gasping. Loralei held onto his coat sleeve until he grabbed the boat with one hand and then the other. As she pulled him, she saw the desperation on his face.

"Dan," she said, recognizing him as her friend, Annie Paxton's brother. "You have to make it. Pull on the boat and swing in. I'll lean in the other direction."

She held tightly to Dan's sleeve until he swung his leg over the side of the boat. She leaned back against the starboard side while he pulled himself into the boat with help from Andre, who was struggling to keep the boat afloat. A renegade wave crashed over the bow, soaking them with a torrent of cold water.

"Lean back toward the other side," Andre yelled, pulling on the opposite oar. "We are going over."

Loralei screamed, and she and Dan leaned sideways together just in time to keep the boat from capsizing. Another wave crashed over the side, dousing them with another torrent of water.

"We must go back," Andre shouted. "The water is too wild to stay out here anymore."

"No. We have to save the others," Loralei shouted back. "Who's left, Dan? Who else was on the boat?"

Dan coughed and choked out an answer. Loralei struggled to hear him over the wind and rain and the blast of the foghorn.

"Three others. The old gang. They were all on the boat with me. I don't see them now," Dan said.

"We must return to the lighthouse," Andre yelled, turning the boat and rowing away from the shoal.

Loralei shrieked in terror. She couldn't imagine losing more friends to the anger of the lake. And she couldn't abide losing sailors to the storm because the beacon went out. She was in charge of the beacon. It was her responsibility to keep the light shining no matter what Jake did. No one could drown on her watch.

"Turn around," she yelled to Andre.

"We cannot," Andre yelled.

"God help us. God help the sailors," Loralei shouted, hearing the sound of her desperation carried on the wind.

"Ahoy!"

Loralei heard a muted shout amidst a low rumbling. She turned to see two motorboats racing toward them on the way to the rock shoal. Someone waved to her as they passed by. She waved back as she watched the boats slow to approach the shoal and breathed a sigh of relief as she realized people from the town, and probably the harbor patrol, had arrived to help with the rescue. She hoped they would find the others and bring them to safety. Loralei sat back and turned her attention to Dan.

"Will you be all right? We'll get you back to the lighthouse and into dry clothes. I'm so glad you made it into the boat," she said.

"Yeah, me too," Dan said. He brushed the rain off his face and turned to look at her. "I don't know what happened. We were in the channel, and the light disappeared. There was nothing we could do," he said.

Loralei grimaced and looked down. "I'm so sorry, Dan. There was nothing I could do. Jake Calico put out the beacon before I knew what was happening," she said.

"Stay low," Andre yelled through the storm. "Another wave is coming over the side."

Loralei held her breath as the cold water crashed over her and rocked the boat. It drenched them all, and she fought to catch her breath after the wave receded. She grabbed a bucket and bailed water over the side. The last thing she wanted was to lose the boat and their lives after making the rescue.

"The town will get rid of Jake," Dan said. He was huddled on the floor of the boat, and his body was shaking. "They'll run him out on a rail. We can't have this kind of thing going on."

"You're right, of course," Loralei answered.

She bailed until they were in sight of the shore near the lighthouse. When they reached the beach, she and Dan jumped out and pulled the boat through the shallow water. Andre grabbed the oars and jumped out to help them pull it onto the beach and turn it over in the sand. They ran through the rain, up the steps, and down the path through the woods to the lighthouse. Loralei let out a deep breath when they closed the door on the furor of the storm and entered the warmth and quiet of the kitchen. She was glad they had made it home.

"You can change in the side room over there," she said to Dan, pointing to an alcove on the side of the kitchen. "I'll bring you some dry clothes."

Dan nodded as he pulled off his boots and coat and sloshed through the kitchen in his wet socks and dripping clothes.

"Andre, you can change in the bedroom. There are some clothes in the closet you can wear," she said, glad to be taking charge and looking around for Edmund.

She looked up to see him limping down the stairwell and grabbing his cane.

"Are you okay? You look worn out. Were there any survivors?" he asked.

"I'm all right, Grandpapa. Yes, one survivor. Dan Paxton. There are three others that the boats from the town are looking for," she said.

"Dan? I'm glad he's safe. I hope they rescue the others. I was looking out the windows of the lantern room when I heard you come in. I couldn't see you coming back in the storm. The harbor patrol was out here earlier. I told them about Jake putting out the beacon. They'll be back to investigate later in the week," Edmund said.

"I'm glad you told me," Loralei said.

"The patrol mentioned that the storms have ended on Lake Huron, although they're still going strong around here. Just thought you'd want to know, so you didn't worry anymore about Devon," he said.

"Thanks. How's Misha?" she asked.

"He's sleeping. I put him to bed hours ago, and he stayed asleep through the storm. You'd better change into dry clothes. I'll make some tea," he said.

"Thank you," she said.

Just then, Andre walked out of the bedroom wearing Devon's clothes. Loralei saw the look of shock on Edmund's face.

"I told Andre he could change into dry clothes," she said quickly, hoping to assuage the awkwardness of the situation. "He would have caught a cold if he stayed in those wet clothes. I'll be back in a minute," she said, heading for the bedroom to change. "Andre, I'll give you some clothes to take to Dan."

Loralei went to the bedroom and found some of Devon's clothes, and walked back to the kitchen to give them to Andre to take to Dan before returning to the bedroom to change. When she was done changing, she set her wet dress near the lighthouse door and went into the kitchen to drink tea with rum with the men. They talked and warmed themselves by the wood stove until it got late. She knew they were all hoping the others had been rescued, but there was nothing they could do about it now. They would find out what was going on in the morning.

"I'll sleep in a bunk in the scullery quarters, too," Edmund said, yawning when Loralei told him that Dan and Andre were sleeping in the scullery quarters that night. "I'll leave in the morning." Using his cane, he headed into the alcove where Dan was already headed. "Goodnight."

"Goodnight," Loralei said, watching him leave and standing to go retrieve her dress. "Thank you for helping me," she said to Andre as she turned to go. "You were wonderful. I could never have done it without you. And Dan is safe because of you. I can't thank you enough."

"It is nothing. I was happy to assist," Andre said.

Loralei smiled and left Andre to finish his tea and rum. She picked up her dress and went outside to shake the water out of it. She heard a twig snap and looked up from wringing out her dress at the back door of the lighthouse. She was exhausted but wanted to hang her dress up near the wood stove to dry overnight. She had gotten most of the water out of it.

"Who is it? Who's there?" she called, peering into the moon-shadowed woods.

The wind was still gusting around the lighthouse, and they were in the eye of the storm for now. There was more to come. She paused for a moment and took an unsteady breath. He was there again. She could sense it.

"Jake?" she asked.

She felt the skin on her forearms pimple with goosebumps.

"Jake, is that you?" she asked.

She should have guessed it, she thought, trying to control the shaking that started in her legs and moved up toward her shoulders. *Jake was back. He didn't want a fishing boat. There was no money in that. He wanted a cargo ship or a merchant vessel to crash on the rocks. He didn't care about fishermen. He wanted money, the money that came from looting a large ship that had shipwrecked. Jake wanted to put out the light he had sabotaged on top of the lighthouse she had restored by lighting the lamp. He had returned to finish what he had started and put the beacon out for good.*

"Jake. Go away," she called into the darkness.

"What makes you think it's me?"

Loralei jumped as she heard Jake's voice and saw him step out from behind a tree. She could see him grinning at her in the pale light of the moon that shone between the storm clouds.

"Go away," she said again.

"Not likely," he replied.

"Is that a fact?"

Loralei heard and turned to see Andre standing behind her at the lighthouse door. He stepped in front of her and walked toward Jake.

"That's a fact," Jake said.

Loralei caught her breath as she realized Jake wasn't going to run away this time. She put her hand to her mouth as Andre drew nearer to Jake. Jake looked like a wild man to her, with his long hair whipping about his face in the wind and his mouth twisted in an insolent scowl. She had been frightened of him before, but it was nothing compared to now. She screamed when she saw him pull a knife and stab it into the air in front of him.

"Andre, run," she shrieked.

She bit her knuckle as Andre continued walking toward Jake.

"Come on, pretty boy. No one messes with Calico," Jake said, stabbing the air again.

"Is that right?" Andre asked.

"That's right," Jake said.

Before Loralei comprehended what was happening,

Andre yanked a length of knotted sailing rope out of his coat and whipped it at the knife in Jake's hand, striking Jake's hand full on. Jake bellowed and grabbed his flopping hand with his other hand as the knife flew into the woods. He fell to his knees. Andre switched the rope again and caught Jake on the side of the face with it. Loralei felt a cold chill shake her body as Andre kneed a flailing Jake in the head and wrestled him to the ground.

"Andre, stop," she screamed as she saw Andre twist the rope around Jake's neck. "Stop. You're killing him," she said, throwing her dress to the ground and racing toward Andre. She felt the blood rush to her head and ran faster, gritting her teeth against the pounding in her temples. "Andre," she screamed again.

"Stay back, Lori. Stay where you are," he shouted.

Loralei stopped in mid-stride. Something about the tone of Andre's voice made her quiver. She felt her eyes glaze over as she watched him bend over Jake for what seemed like an eternity before slowly standing and turning to face her. She looked past him to see Jake's still body lying on the ground with the rope around his neck.

"No, you've killed him!" Loralei heard herself screaming, but the sound seemed to come from outside of herself. She felt like she was floating in a hazy, claustrophobic, tin tunnel of echos. "What have you done?" Her heart skipped a beat when she saw the look in Andre's eyes.

"He deserved to die, Lori. He tried to kill these fishermen, and maybe he did kill some of them. And he killed all those people on the ships he sabotaged in the past into shipwrecks, as surely as if he had done it by hand. Someone like that does not deserve to live," Andre said.

She watched, mesmerized and trembling, as he walked toward her. She couldn't accept what she had just seen. She couldn't believe that Jake was gone and Andre had killed him. She still cared about Jake, at least enough to wish he was alive.

He had saved her from her loneliness, and they had shared so much pleasure.

"I did it for you," Andre said quietly.

"What?" She felt the bile rise in her throat as she struggled to catch her breath. She choked and doubled over to spit up over and over until a welcome feeling of peace washed over her. She stayed in a crouch, taking deep breaths. When she opened her eyes, she saw the tips of Andre's shoes come into focus. She looked up and saw his dark, icy eyes staring at her. She shivered and held his gaze for a moment before she saw his eyes begin to thaw.

"I am sorry you had to see this, bella mia. It was not what I wanted. I want to protect you. You are too beautiful and vulnerable to fight the battles of the world on your own. I want to help you. I want to be there for you. I did it for you and all the people you care about in this town," he said.

"No," Loralei said, moaning.

"He needed to die to keep you and the town safe. Let me help you," Andre said softly as he stopped in front of her and held out his arms. "I did it for you. I did it for Misha." Andre leaned forward and took Loralei into his arms. "We must find a place to bury him."

"No, we can't. We have to tell someone," Loralei said, moaning.

"We cannot do that. We must dispose of the body," he said.

She shook her head and stood up slowly, letting him guide her to her feet. She felt herself shaking as she took in the true nature of her situation. Andre was a killer, but he had saved her from Jake. He had saved the lighthouse and the beacon and the lives of the future sailors who might otherwise meet a similar fate. And, with Devon gone, she had no one else to protect her. She thought for a moment and stared into the woods.

"Lori?" he said.

Loralei looked back at Andre and then at Jake's crumpled body sprawled in the woods before looking back toward the lighthouse. "I know where to bury him. We'd better get to work."

CHAPTER 9

The clear, azure-blue of the late afternoon sky was mottled with seagulls swooping and diving toward the net of a fishing boat off the starboard side of the freighter. The seagulls followed the boats sometimes, far out into the lakes, hoping to abscond with scraps of food and fish. He watched them as he gnawed on a floury corner of the slightly salty hardtack he'd swiped from the galley. The storms had ended the night before, and he was relieved and proud that he and his crew had forged through the worst the storms had to offer and come out unscathed on the other side. He'd heard about the shipwreck in Portstown, and he and his crew were relieved that the fishermen, who many of them knew as friends and relatives, were safe. Devon was proud to hear that Loralei had been part of the rescue, although he didn't know the details. The fact that Jake Calico had sabotaged the beacon weighed heavily on his mind, and he found himself worrying about Loralei, something he hadn't done much of over the last few years. It bothered him that she might not be safe at home in the lighthouse. Devon shook his head to clear it and tried to think of something else.

The air smelled crisp and clean, fresh from the rainshowers of the storms. He stood gazing across the lake for a while, enjoying the freedom of the afternoon after having been on call all night and morning and fighting the storms of the day and night before. The light waned as the sun fell lower in the sky, and he watched as hues of reds and oranges enveloped its descent on the horizon.

"Captain Lancaster, First Mate Thompson requests to see you in the navigation room."

Devon heard. He looked away from the lake and over at a crewman, who gestured to him to follow him. He walked down the deck with the crewman. He hoped Lanny didn't have too much to say to him. His stomach was grumbling, and he was looking forward to making it to the mess hall in time for dinner. He was surprised to see that Lanny didn't look up when he entered the navigation room. He was used to having sailors jump to attention when they saw him. But Lanny appeared to be deep in thought, perusing a chart on a nearby table.

"Did you need to see me about something? Make it quick. I have other things to do," Devon said.

He didn't want to spend any more time with Lanny than he had to. His conversation with him about Loralei and Carlotta when they first started the trip had made him question Lanny's loyalty to him, and he didn't want to be around him.

Lanny looked up. "Captain Lancaster," Lanny said formally. "I'm glad you made time to see me. I have some things I need to talk to you about."

Devon thought Lanny looked uncomfortable and somewhat apprehensive about something. He wondered what could be bothering him.

"Yes, what is it?" Devon said shortly.

"Captain, we've received a ship-to-shore message. It's marked 'urgent,' and I need to talk to you about it right away," Lanny said.

Devon saw Lanny look down at a piece of paper in his

hand while brushing a drop of sweat from his forehead with his other hand.

"This message is from Rear-Admiral Flynn of the United States Coast Guard. A personal watercraft reported being nearly run over by a runaway freighter in the storm last night, and they insist it was ours. I've talked to the Officer of the Deck, who was on watch at the time of the incident, and he reports that he was unaware of the incident. The rear admiral did not take lightly to hearing that information. Regardless of whether the Officer of the Deck knew it or not, the rear-admiral is holding you, as captain of the *Manitoulin*, responsible for the situation. I'm sorry, Captain, but the rear admiral has issued an order to have you relieved of your command. I've been designated to replace you until we return to Portstown," Lanny said.

Devon stared at Lanny in disbelief. He'd never heard of such a thing before.

"Relieved of command? On whose authority? Flynn doesn't have sway over me," Devon said.

"I'm afraid he does, Captain. It's authorized by the rear-admiral and the head of the shipping corporation in charge of the *Manitoulin*. Someone reported that you had been observed on the bridge at that time in an intoxicated state. The corporation is also holding you responsible," Lanny said.

Devon felt his face begin to heat up. "Someone reported me? Was that 'someone' you?" Devon asked.

Lanny looked away without giving him an answer.

"It was you, wasn't it, you two-faced bastard. Give me that," Devon said, grabbing for the paper.

Lanny thrust the paper away from him before relenting and handing it over to him. Devon stared at the orders incredulously. He threw them to the floor.

"I'm afraid you'll need to be confined to quarters if you don't comply with the orders. It's up to me now to maintain control of the *Manitoulin*," Lanny said.

"You? You'd like that, wouldn't you? You've always wanted to have your own command," Devon said. Devon was beside himself. He watched Lanny nod to the crewman standing behind him.

"Please escort Captain Lancaster to his quarters. I'm not going to confine you to quarters, Captain, but I suggest that you do as I ask and return to your cabin," Lanny said.

Lanny turned away from him and walked over to look out the window. Devon felt as though he'd been dismissed and by his own first mate. He rubbed his face with his hands and turned to look at the crewman, who was looking down at the floor. Devon scoffed in disgust and, feeling he had no other options, turned to follow the crewman back to his cabin.

***

Andre stood on the bluff's edge, looking out over the lake at the hazy, pale blue line of the horizon. Ontario, Canada, was on the other side of Lake Superior from Portstown, but he couldn't see it across the vast expanse of rippling, indigo-blue water. The fog from the night before was gone, but the lake, warming up in the early morning sun, steamed near the shore from the cold rain of the passing storms. He sipped deeply from the lukewarm cup of coffee Loralei had made for him at breakfast and let the strong, bitter liquid jolt him awake. The events of the night before had exhausted him, and he was trying to get his bearings. He took another sip of coffee and listened to the waves lapping quietly at the shore.

They had buried Jake in the fruit cellar last night after dragging his body through the woods and over the grounds of the lighthouse to its resting place on the cellar's floor. They had been careful to make sure the others were sleeping before executing their plan. Andre had dug a makeshift grave in the cool, damp alcove behind the shelves of mason jars, and he and Loralei had rolled Jake's body into it and covered it with dirt. She had said she was the only one that ever went down there, and she didn't think the grave would be discovered in its underground crypt. After looking around at the dark confines of the cellar, he had agreed with her assessment.

He shook his head and tried to clear his thinking. Loralei was his now, even though she was devastated by Jake's death. His gut told him she was his. He could see it in her lovely, clear blue eyes that had dimmed with grief the night before but were now trusting and true when she looked at him. She had forgiven him for killing Jake and perhaps even accepted it as necessary. He was glad she agreed with him. He had wanted to do it for her and for Misha. It was the first time he had killed someone because he wanted to and not because he had to for the sake of his country. He wanted Loralei, his beautiful Loralei, and he didn't want Jake coming between them.

"Is there any sign of the lighthouse inspector? I have everything in order inside," she said.

Andre turned to see Loralei walking up to the bluff to stand next to him. Her blonde hair ruffled in the breeze, and she put her hand to her cheek to push it off her face. He stood awestruck. Her exquisite beauty took his breath away.

"No, not yet," he said, gazing at her for a moment before looking back over the lake for any signs of a boat.

She had told him that the inspector was coming to inspect the beacon and to document why it failed during the storms.

"How can I know it is him?" Andre asked.

"The inspector flies an American flag on his boat with an inspector pennant underneath. The inspector pennant is white with a red outline and a blue lighthouse in the middle. That's how you can tell he's coming," she said.

"I will watch for him," Andre said, turning back to her.

"The harbor patrol radioed that it is coming out today, also to investigate the shipwreck," she said.

He saw a flash of fear in her eyes. "They want to talk about Jake, too," she said.

Andre touched her arm. "Do not worry. We will handle it. They will not find out anything. They have no reason to suspect we would know Jake's location."

"I suppose you're right." She blinked her eyes as the breeze blew fine, wispy sifts of sand over the bluff.

He wanted to kiss away the tears the sand made in her eyes, but he didn't want to risk being seen. She was so beautiful and vulnerable, and she had been traumatized by the events of the night before. But there was something more about her, something strong and indissoluble, something anchored in this time and place. He wasn't sure what it was, but he felt it when he looked at her. She was as much a part of this lonely, untamed wilderness as the lake and the lighthouse were. She was her own person, a grounded and yet free spirit, and he loved her for it.

"I'd better go back. Misha's awake, and Grandpapa is still sleeping. I only came out to tell you about the harbor patrol," she said.

Andre could sense the awkwardness between them as she turned to go. "You have been very brave. I have never met a woman like you," he said, touching her arm.

He swallowed to stem the force of his emotions at seeing her delicate profile turn away from him. She stumbled suddenly and seemed to try to steady herself, putting a hand to her ample waist. He reached out to save her and pulled her to him in a deep embrace, unable to control his feelings for her any longer.

"No, Andre. Someone will see us. Later," she said.

He sighed deeply, and after a moment, he released her. The tremulous smile she gave him seemed shy and sad and yet full of promise. "Yes, all right. You must take care of Misha, of course."

She turned and walked toward the lighthouse.

"I hear a car," she called back to him. "Someone's here. It could be the harbor patrol. Keep watch for the inspector, won't you, and I'll see who it is."

"I shall go with you," Andre said, turning away from the lake to follow her. He didn't want her to have to talk to the harbor patrol alone. "The inspector will arrive whether I am standing watch or not. I will help you handle the visitors, and we will handle the inspector when he gets here."

Loralei paused and nodded. Andre caught up to her, and they walked back to the lighthouse together.

***

Loralei walked into the kitchen through the side door of the lighthouse, afraid of who or what she might find there. She found Dan sitting at the table with Misha and two men standing nearby.

"I let them in. I didn't think you'd mind. It's Colton Fischer and Willet Hall from the harbor patrol. You remember Colton from high school, don't you, Loralei?" Dan asked.

Loralei nodded and greeted the two men. She knew they were with the harbor patrol. Colton had come out to the lighthouse many times before, and he was Devon's best friend from high school. Loralei sighed deeply. She was relieved that the investigation would be by someone familiar. She didn't think Colton would harbor any suspicions toward her.

"This is Andre. He tends the lighthouse for me," she said, gesturing toward Andre.

Colton and Willet exchange glances.

"That's quite a shiner you have there. Mind telling me how you got that?" Colton asked Andre.

"Not at all. I was overcome last night by the pirate you call Jake Calico," Andre said.

"Overcome?" Colton asked.

"Yes, I became unconscious and unaware of any further happenings last night," Andre said.

"I see," Colton said.

Colton exchanged glances with Willet again and raised his eyebrows before pulling a notepad and pen out of his coat pocket.

"You're not from around here, are you?" Colton asked.

"No. I am here doing work for the lady of the lighthouse," Andre replied.

"I see," Colton said again, writing something down on his notepad.

"Would you like some coffee?" Loralei asked, trying to take charge of the situation by playing hostess and making the men feel at home.

"No, thanks. If you don't mind, we need to ask you some questions," Colton said to Loralei, shaking his head when she gestured to him and Willet to sit at the table. "We need to ask you about Jake and about how the lighthouse beacon failed. It won't take long. Could you show us the beacon while we talk?"

"Of course," Loralei said, turning and heading toward the stairwell and motioning to Andre to sit at the table with Dan and Misha.

Andre nodded and sat down. The two men followed Loralei, and they climbed the spiral staircase to the lantern room at the top of the lighthouse.

"Here it is," Loralei said, showing them the Fresnel lens of the beacon, which was no longer lit up during the day.

The prismatic lens, which some people said looked like a large glass beehive, sparkled in the light from the morning sun. To Loralei, it looked like a precious jewel, her precious jewel that she polished and cared for with the vigilance of a gem cutter. Its failure to work during the storm affected her deeply. She felt like all her work and care had been rejected as though by a recalcitrant child snubbing its mother. But it wasn't her fault, she reminded herself, or the beacon's fault. It was Jake's doing.

Colton inspected the beacon and the electrical wiring and wrote things down on his notepad.

"It looks like Jake cut the wires and tried to smash the lens. It's scuffed. The lens looks okay, but the wiring needs repair. The inspector will look at this, I'm sure. Do you have a lighthouse tender?" Colton asked.

"Yes. It's Andre," Loralei replied.

"Good. This needs work. Now, tell us more about what happened last night. Did Jake attack you or get in somehow? What exactly happened?" he asked.

Loralei had been waiting for this question, and she swallowed as she felt herself shaking. "I was checking on the foghorn in the shed when I saw Jake run out the door of the lighthouse and into the woods. When I ran back to the lighthouse, I found Andre and my grandfather in the kitchen recovering from an attack, and I discovered that the beacon was out."

"Sounds like sabotage. We'll investigate further. Any idea where Jake could have gone?" Colton asked.

"None at all," Loralei replied.

"Okay. Thanks, Loralei. We'll get right on this," he said.

As she followed Colton and Willet to the staircase, a tall, thin man in a navy blue regimented uniform and cap appeared at the top of the stairs.

"I'm Inspector Bevins from the coast guard. I'm here to take a look at the beacon," he said to Loralei, nodding to Colton and Willet. "I understand you're in charge?"

"Yes," she said.

"Let's take a look," Inspector Bevins said.

The inspector checked the beacon and said similar things to Loralei about its needed repair and upkeep while Colton and Willet looked on.

"I'm not going to fine you or relieve you of your post because of the nature of the situation," the inspector said, finally. "But, the seriousness of this incident will be on the report."

"Of course," Loralei said, trembling.

She couldn't help but feel responsible for something she couldn't have done anything about. She tried to recover her composure as she realized that her feelings of guilt stemmed more from witnessing Jake's death and her fear of his body being discovered than from the failure of the beacon.

"You might want to consider keeping someone here at the lighthouse with you, perhaps your lighthouse tender, who is aware of the dangerous situation with Jake Calico, to prevent further incidents of this type. I'll take a look around and write up a report. I think I'm done here," Inspector Bevins said dismissively.

"We are, too," Colton said.

They all headed back down the staircase to the kitchen, where Edmund, having woken up, greeted the men and gave his version of what happened before they left, taking Dan with them. Loralei spent the rest of the day caring for Andre and Misha and following the checklist the inspector had left for her of things to do around the lighthouse. Edmund helped her with the chores before cautioning her to be careful and leaving in the late afternoon.

When the evening came, and they had finished dinner, Andre took Misha into the other room to read to him from one of the picture books Mrs. Petrova had brought over, and Loralei sat back in her chair and sighed with relief. Finally, everyone was gone, and the lighthouse could return to some semblance of order. She relaxed for a moment, thinking of Devon and hoping his trip was going well. She hadn't thought about him all day with all the other things going on, but she found herself wishing he was home. She wished she could talk to him and pour out all her feelings about what was happening in the way she used to early in their marriage. She sighed as she remembered that things were different between them. Devon would never sit still long enough to listen to her now. He was too involved with his own feelings. But sometimes, it was nice to fantasize about what it would be like to be close to him again. She shook her head impatiently and got up to go outside and check on the foghorn. The inspector's report had included a checklist of things for her to do, and deep-cleaning the foghorn was one of them. She wanted to see what needed to be done.

As she walked toward the shed housing the foghorn, she saw a car race up the path and stop and wondered who could be coming over at this hour. She gasped when she saw Carlotta step out of the car and stalk sternly toward her.

"You know where he is, don't you?" Carlotta said in a high, shrill voice, shaking her fist at Loralei. "I've been looking everywhere and checking with everyone, and he's gone. He's nowhere. What have you done with him, Loralei? What have you done with Jake? Where is he? I know, you know."

Loralei felt the hair on her arms prickle. She'd never seen Carlotta in such a state. Her face was red and perspiring, and the pupils of her eyes were wide, dark, and menacing. She looked to Loralei like a feral wolverine roving the woods and hunting for prey.

Loralei took a step back. "I don't know what you're talking about," Loralei said, looking for a way to escape. "How could I do anything to Jake? He's much bigger than I am."

"You know what I'm talking about. Jake told me you were sweet on him and that you went crazy when he broke things off with you. You were just looking for someone to blame for your own negligence. You spread all these lies about him, didn't you? You said he put out the beacon, and people believed you. What'd you do with him?" Carlotta asked.

"I think you'd better leave, Carlotta, before things go any further. This isn't your business," Loralei said firmly.

"You're damn right, it's my business. Jake is mine. If you did something to him, you'll pay. I'll see to it. You're crazy, Loralei. Crazy as your crazy old father was," Carlotta shouted.

"Get out," Loralei yelled. She felt her cheeks get warm and her body heat up. "Nobody talks about my father like that."

Her father had not been crazy, as Carlotta put it, but some people in town, put off by his aloof air of authority, his deep, often strict, religious faith, and their family's ancestral ties to the French aristocracy, had spread rumors to that effect in the past. He had been a wonderful, loving father when he was home, although slightly distant and extremely firm with his children, and Loralei had loved him desperately. It upset her to have to deal with people, obviously including Carlotta, who spread rumors like that.

"Is that right? Well, I do. Get used to it," Carlotta said.

"I said, get out," Loralei repeated, making a fist and lunging toward Carlotta.

Carlotta appeared taken aback for a moment. "If you did anything to Jake, I'll find out, and I'll come after you. You can bet on it. Oh, and by the way," Carlotta said, turning and heading for her car, "I'm telling Devon about you and Jake. Just so you know."

Carlotta flipped her long, black hair back and plunged into the car, slamming the door behind her before hurtling through the gravel down the path away from the lighthouse. Loralei watched her go and put her hand to her rapidly beating heart. She couldn't believe Carlotta had acted that way. She gulped in a deep breath and tried to settle her nerves. She'd had more than enough excitement for one day. She watched Carlotta's car disappear down the path through the woods before walking slowly back to the lighthouse and closing the door behind her.

CHAPTER 10

Loralei startled awake and stared into the inky blackness of the bedroom surrounding her. She'd heard something, something that terrified her, but she wasn't sure what it was. Since Jake's death and Carlotta's ensuing confrontation with her, she'd been so on edge that anything out of the ordinary rattled her nerves. She relived the horror of seeing Jake's death in her dreams and slept fitfully, waking up on and off during the nights in a cold sweat. It was a horrible thing she had witnessed, and she didn't know if she would ever get over it. She still cared for Jake and knowing she would never see him again hurt her heart. She had eventually forgiven Andre for killing him, out of the belief that what he had done was necessary to protect her and the town and the lighthouse, but she couldn't get the picture of Jake's death out of her mind. Seeing him strangled had been traumatic for her, and the feelings of guilt she had about not being able to stop the murder and then helping to cover it up tormented her. She had revisited Jake's grave in the fruit cellar that afternoon to say goodbye to him and try to get some relief from the guilt and loss she was feeling. Instead, she became more guilt-stricken and filled with dread. What if Jake's body was discovered by someone, and she and Andre were found out? What would happen to them? Loralei shook her head to clear it and tried to get her bearings. And then she heard the noise again. It was again a low moaning sound or maybe a wail. *Something must be wrong.*

"Andre," she whispered.

He was sleeping next to her, warm under the covers from their lovemaking earlier in the night.

"Andre," she said again, more loudly. "I hear something. Please wake up," she said.

"What? What is it?" Andre said, turning over.

"Something's outside the lighthouse. I hear it," Loralei said.

He sat up, and she tried to make out his form in the dark as he stood and padded to the window. He drew the curtains, and the pale light of the moon cast a low glow on the side of his face. She jumped out of bed and walked over to stand near him. Being close to him made her feel safe, and she was too frightened to stay in bed alone. He opened the window, and she heard the sound again. She gasped as she realized what it was.

"Wolves," she said.

"What?" he asked.

"Wolves," she said again, more decisively. "The wolves are back. They come out this way sometimes after the rains when the moon is full. I don't know why. I haven't heard them in a long time. But that's what it is, the howling of the wolves. They won't come near the lighthouse. They will just prowl the woods and make their mournful sound."

Loralei moved closer to Andre, and he turned and took her in his arms.

"Dio Mio," he said, drawing her close to him and hugging her tightly. "Wolves? How do you live out here in the wilderness by yourself, dealing with these dangers? You are the bravest woman I have ever known."

"I'm not, Andre. I'm frightened. Please hold me. I'm

frightened of the world tonight," she said. When Loralei felt Andre's arms encircle her, she leaned into him and put her head on his shoulder. "I need you so much," she murmured, feeling her body warm as he pulled her close.

She smelled the fresh scent of pine in the light breeze blowing in through the window and heard the soft sound of crickets filling the woods with song. The translucent half-moon dappled the bedroom with a pale light, filtered down through the fluttering leaves of the paper birch trees outside the window. She felt her fear begin to wane as she let the ambiance of the forest and the nearness of Andre lull her into a welcome peace.

"You saved me from Jake," she said quietly to Andre as she leaned into his embrace. "You saved everyone from Jake. And you're here with me now, after Devon has left me alone again. I have no words to describe what it means to me to have you here, to save me from the loneliness and the heartache and the fear I feel when I'm here by myself. There is so much to be responsible for at the lighthouse, and having you here, to help me and protect me and love my cares away, makes my life worth living."

She melted into him when she felt Andre embrace her more deeply and trembled when she felt him press his lips hard against hers. She moaned softly as she surrendered to the fierce need that emanated from him and gave herself up to the pleasure of being desired.

"You are so young and lovely and delicate. You deserve to be protected and loved and cared for like the precious jewel you are," Andre said. "Come. Let me show you how precious you are."

Andre led her back to the bed and laid her gently down on it before covering her body with his and nuzzling her cheeks with ardent kisses. Loralei sighed with pleasure at his expert touch. She felt the cool breeze that ruffled in through the curtains at the open window brush against her skin and cool her increasingly fevered body. She no longer heard the wolves howling in the woods or felt the agony and grief of her losses and fears. There was only the glorious oblivion of being suspended in time with her lover.

"You are bellissima," Andre murmured, drawing her to him and taking her as his own. "Cara mia, Lori."

Loralei gasped and quivered as she gave herself up to him. The cares of the world went away, and for a glorious fragment in time, there was only Andre and her and the way they felt about each other.

She snuggled next to him as he held her afterward, savoring the feeling of being safe and protected and loved.

"Andre," she said after a while, wondering if he had fallen asleep.

"Hmm?"

"Where are you from, originally?" She rested her head on his arm as she waited for him to answer.

"Italy. Florence. My parents brought me to the United States when I was a child," he said.

Loralei paused for a moment. "Do you miss Italy?"

She waited in the silence for his answer.

"Sometimes. Why do you ask?" he asked.

"I wondered if it was hard being so far away from where you were born. I've always lived in my home here at the lighthouse, and I can't imagine ever leaving. We're different in that way. I find it exciting that you've seen so much of the world and that you travel and work where you can. It's such a different life than my own," she said.

"Yes, it is. We are different in that way, but we both love our country. We have that in common," Andre said.

"Yes," Loralei agreed. She heard the mournful, distant howl of a wolf and snuggled in closer to Andre. "Where are your parents now?" When Andre didn't answer at first, she added, "If you don't mind my asking."

"Dead," he said.

"I'm sorry," she said, caressing his arm. "I know what that's like. It's very painful to lose your parents."

"Yes. We, unfortunately, have that in common as well," Andre said.

Loralei sighed as Andre drew her closer to the warm safety of his embrace. She had never before felt so accepted and loved. She closed her eyes and let the warmth and strength of his embrace lull her to sleep.

***

Andre took his plate of bacon and eggs to the breakfast table after kissing Loralei on the neck and listening to her lighthearted giggle. The terror of the wolves from the night before seemed far in the distant past. He was more than pleased with himself. The night had gone extremely well for him with Loralei, and he had never felt better in his life. He smiled as he remembered their lovemaking and allowed himself the fantasy of being her loving husband while she was the happy wife. It was a life he had seen others live as he looked in from afar, as though through a window, at a life he could never have. He had too many responsibilities, and he had killed too many people to live such a life. But now, after he'd gotten rid of Jake and confirmed that Loralei's husband was gone, he enjoyed pretending that he was living such a life in reality. Even as he did so, he couldn't help but be reminded of his true reason for living in the lighthouse. He needed to use the lighthouse radio to surreptitiously transmit the information he had received in Detroit to his spy network in Canada. And he needed to find a way to continue with his mission to secure information about the Soo Locks, perhaps by going there soon. He also needed to maintain his new facade as a lighthouse tender by repairing the electrical wiring for the beacon and restoring the Fresnel lens it used.

"I'm letting Misha sleep in," Loralei said as she brought her plate to the table and sat down across from him. "He was up late reading his picture books, and I want him to have his rest."

"Of course," Andre replied, smiling and thinking again about how lucky Misha was to have Loralei as his mother.

She obviously cared deeply for him, and Andre swallowed as he felt a deep yearning for something that he felt he had never had, the unconditional love of a mother. He remembered playing with his younger sister, Isabella, on the beach in Tuscany as children, long before the war had ever been imagined. It was long before he had thought of being an Italian deep-cover agent and long before he had seen and done the unspeakable things during his training as a spy that had changed him indefinitely and put him forever, he knew, on the outside of society looking in. He had yearned for his mother's love then, he remembered. But it wasn't to be. Now, he could see himself with Loralei on the beach in Tuscany, laughing and playing with the children when the war was over and after the baby was born. Perhaps he could find a way to put his past behind him. He and Loralei could forge a new life together, a life without killing and grief and the grim specter of death. They could be happy.

"Misha is lucky to have you," Andre said, gazing across the table at her.

He marveled at how her blonde tresses glimmered and glowed in the rays of the morning sun streaming in through the window. She looked to him like an ethereal angel shimmering in a halo of translucence, more beautiful, even than his *Mother and Child* painting by Mary Cassatt.

Loralei nodded and smiled back. "I'm lucky to have him."

They ate in silence for a moment, and Andre savored the perfectly crisped bacon and expertly seasoned scrambled eggs she had made for him.

"I was looking at your seascapes again," he said quietly. "They display the signature, 'Loralei Clairmont.' Is that your name before marriage?"

"Yes. That is the name I paint under."

"I see," Andre replied, realizing at that moment that she

was related to Maurice Clairmont in France and that Edmund was the brother Maurice had talked about visiting in Michigan. He looked away quickly and made a plan before looking back at her. "I hope you do not mind, but I have made arrangements with an old friend of mine to have them appraised. I am hoping you might consider allowing the Detroit Institute of the Arts to display a few of your paintings. My friend who works there would like to look at them."

"What?" Loralei asked.

Andre saw Loralei's bewildered expression and grinned. "It would be an honor to me if you would allow me to send your paintings to my friend. I can assure you he would take the utmost care of them."

Loralei shook her head. "I don't see how I could send my paintings anywhere, even if I wanted to. I only paint because I need to, because I love to, not because I want to show my art to someone."

"We could send them by freighter to Detroit," Andre said, rubbing his chin with his fingers. "It could be done, and I think it should be done. The art world needs to see these paintings. It would be a crime to keep them hidden away."

"Do you really think they're that good?" Loralei asked. She looked at him with seeming disbelief.

"They are magnifico."

Loralei smiled. "We'll see."

Andre smiled back and bit into another piece of bacon.

***

Devon flicked a queen onto the poker table next to the jack of the same suit he'd already turned up. He smiled to himself, being careful not to let the others at the table see the reaction on his face. With the cards on the table and the cards in his hand, he had a straight flush. He was pretty sure he was going to win the pot hands down, and he could use the extra money to hit the taverns in Detroit when they pulled into port in a few days.

"Hey, Tex, it's your bid," he said to the new hire sitting next to him, who had introduced Devon's crew to the new version of poker they were playing.

"Right, Captain," Tex said, throwing some chips in the pot.

Tex was one of the few crewmen still loyal to Devon, who called him Captain, despite Lanny's new claim to the title. The others, it seemed to Devon, hedged around the way they addressed him, usually calling him sir or old man, and saving the Captain title for Lanny, even though they professed their continued loyalty to Devon. The bidding went around the table and came back to Devon.

"All in," Devon said, shoving his chips into the middle.

"I fold," Tex said, throwing his cards down. "Dag nab it, if you're not going to beat me at my own game again."

The others folded as well, and Devon grinned as he scooped in the chips just as the five-minute warning call for lights out sounded.

"Okay, mates, that's it for tonight. I'll let you win it back tomorrow," Devon said, gathering up his chips.

He waved at the men before heading back to his cabin with a bottle of rum Tex had smuggled to him under the table in exchange for the empty one Devon had finished during the game. Tex said it was a free country, and a man ought to be able to have a drink if he wanted to. Devon had to agree.

He closed the door to his cabin and sighed at the heaviness of the silence that enveloped him. He was used to it by now. He'd been holed up in his room for three days, even though he knew he could roam around the freighter if he wanted to. He didn't want to. Being relieved of command had shocked him, and he felt himself walking around in a daze. He didn't want others to see how much the demotion had affected him, and he kept to himself for the most part, except when there was a poker game. He made an exception for that.

He threw his chips in a cubbyhole, uncorked the bottle of rum, and plopped down on his berth to drink himself into a stupor. It was the only thing that soothed his shattered ego and numbed his restless nerves. Loralei had told him he needed to feel his feelings and cry over losing his father in the shipwreck two years ago, but he scoffed with impatience at the idea. He'd lost many friends and family over the years to the ever-clutching grip of the lakes, and he prided himself on the fact that he was strong enough to overcome the deaths without a tear, at least not in front of others. Crying was for sissies, he thought to himself, taking a long draught of rum and reveling in the soothing feel of the sweet liquid trickling down his throat and warming his body. And he wasn't a sissy.

He thought of Loralei and wondered how she was doing with Misha and the pregnancy. A strange feeling of wistfulness came over him as he realized he didn't know much about his wife anymore. The love they had shared when they were first married struck him as a faded, faraway memory. They had been so distant from each other for so long. But with the war and his responsibilities, he hadn't felt much like working on his marriage. He wondered, briefly, now that he had more time to think if that was a mistake. He shook his head and took another swig of rum. He breathed a sigh of relief and laid back on the pillow, closing his eyes as he felt the numbness kick in.

Devon jolted awake at the first deafening blast of the fire siren and blinked his eyes open, trying to find his bearings in the smothering darkness of his cabin. The bottle in his hand dropped to the floor as he swung his legs quickly over the side of his berth and jumped up to hover unsteadily in the middle of the floor.

The siren sounded again, and Devon felt the blood drain from his face as he realized what it was.

"Fire!"

He heard the yells outside his door and thuds of footsteps in the passageway.

"All hands on deck!"

Fire on a freighter was one of the worst calamities a crew could face, especially in the middle of the lake. If it wasn't halted immediately, it could overtake a freighter and engulf the crew in a caged inferno. Devon felt the surface of his door for heat and, feeling nothing, yanked it open and stepped out into the passageway. He smelled the faint, noxious odor of burning oil and saw wisps of smoke drifting near the ladder to the engine room.

"Fire! All hands on deck!"

Devon heard the emergency call again. He wanted to help, but he didn't know where to turn. He knew he was still on duty to help with emergencies, but he wasn't sure what to do or where to go. He shook his head to clear the haziness of his thoughts, but he couldn't seem to do so. He stepped back as other crewmen tore past him down the passageway.

He covered his ears tightly upon hearing the incessant blasts of the siren. Each blast seemed to split his head open with a continuous cacophony of sound. Finally, he gave up, returned to his cabin, and collapsed on his bunk. He listened in agony to the repeated, muffled blasts of the siren until suddenly, the blasts stopped, replaced by an eerie silence. He took his hands away from his ears and lay in his bunk, holding his throbbing head and hoping the fire had been extinguished without incident. A short time later, Devon heard a knock on the cabin door and called out his permission to enter. He was surprised to see Lanny step into his cabin.

"Tex got burned," he said, looking at Devon and grimacing. "He's in the infirmary. He was trying to put out an oil fire in the engine room, and his clothes caught on fire. It's pretty bad. Thought you'd want to know. By the way, where were you?"

Devon felt a flash of anger at the tone of Lanny's voice. "Can't be everywhere at the same time," he answered gruffly, trying to cover his feelings of inadequacy. "I'm demoted, remember? I'm stuck in my cabin. The freighter's only big enough for one captain at a time."

"Get off your pity party," Lanny said loudly. "We needed you helping as much as anybody else. The *Manitoulin* could have gone down if we hadn't put the fire out, and you weren't anywhere to be found. You need to reevaluate your priorities if you want to stay on this boat."

"Go lecture somebody else, and leave me alone," Devon spat back. He had had it up to here with Lanny. Everything Lanny said grated on his nerves.

"We'll see," Lanny said, turning and leaving, slamming the door behind him.

Devon looked at the ceiling, trying to gauge what had just happened. He was relieved the fire was out but upset that Tex had been hurt. He had wanted to help put out the fire, but he hadn't felt like he was in any shape to do it. For a moment, he thought about Tex, burned and laying in the infirmary, and he wondered if Lanny was right about his needing to change his priorities. He didn't want to lose the *Manitoulin* to a disaster any more than he had wanted to lose command of it. *It wasn't his fault. It was just the way things were.* But then, as he thought about Loralei and Misha waiting for him at home, he wondered how close he had come to losing everything, including his own life and the lives of his crew, when he hadn't been there to help or take charge. It had worked out this time, except, unfortunately, for Tex, but maybe that was just luck. *Next time things would be different. Next time, he would be sober and take charge of things again in his rightful post as captain.* But he wasn't convinced, as he drifted off into what promised to be a troubled sleep, that would be the case.

CHAPTER 11

Loralei took the breakfast dishes to the sink and gazed out the kitchen window at the calm, low-rolling waves of Lake Superior rippling and shimmering in the morning light and breaking here and there into tiny whitecaps. A lazy sailboat, far out on the lake, caught the breeze and tacked and skimmed over the water.

She was relieved that she and Andre had enjoyed another quiet yet amorous night. He was a wonderful, generous lover, and she found herself developing an extreme affection for him. The wolves of a few weeks ago had gone and not returned and left Andre and her to share their passion in peace. But that would end for a while. Devon was returning from his voyage in the late afternoon, and she had asked Andre to move into the scullery quarters until Devon left again in a few days. She had locked the door leading down to the fruit cellar, as well, in anticipation of Devon's return. An unappealing odor had developed in the cellar that overwhelmed its usual mustiness, and she didn't want him to ask any questions. She tried not to worry about it and contented herself with the fact that Devon seldom went down in the fruit cellar, anyway.

She winced when she went in to make the bed and realized

Andre was gone from her bedroom. He had moved his things out of the Pointer House in town and into the lighthouse almost a month ago when he had accepted the job as a lighthouse tender and had stayed with her in her bed ever since.

But there was nothing else she could do. She was planning to explain Andre to Devon by telling him that, after the beacon had been sabotaged, the lighthouse inspector had insisted that she hire a live-in lighthouse tender to protect the lighthouse. It was true, after all. She hoped Devon would take it at that and believe her. She hoped her grandfather believed her, as well. She had seen him looking at her and Andre a few times when they were together and had felt uncomfortable with the look on his face. But her life was her own, not Devon's and not Edmund's. She would live it within the bounds of her duties to her family and the lighthouse, but in the way she wanted to. And she didn't want to live a life of indefinite celibacy, whether society considered it proper or not.

It was such a beautiful morning that Loralei decided it would be a good day to bring a picnic out to the meadow near the bluff. She could paint while Andre and Misha fished off the rocks below. She walked toward the scullery quarters to find Andre and ask if he'd like to do that when she heard a knock on the lighthouse door and went to answer it.

"Mrs. Petrova. Won't you come in? It's so nice to see you," she said when she saw Misha's teacher standing at the door.

"Hello, dear," Mrs. Petrova said.

Mrs. Petrova's smiling face and comforting personality always made Loralei feel happy.

"I've come for Misha's sign language lesson, and I brought some gingerbread, fresh from the oven," she said, handing Loralei a basket covered with a red-checked dishtowel. "I remember all of you liked it the last time I brought it over — Edmund especially. Is he here, by any chance?" she asked, looking around.

Loralei took the basket from Mrs. Petrova and turned

away so she wouldn't see her grin. She'd seen the way Mrs. Petrova looked at her grandfather when he was around and had determined long ago that she was sweet on him. Loralei decided that romance could blossom at any age.

"No, but I'm expecting him this afternoon. He's coming over to drive the Jeep into town to pick Devon up when his freighter comes in. Devon's staying for a few days while they load the ship with iron ore before they sail to Detroit again," Loralei said.

"So soon?" Mrs. Petrova asked.

"Yes, unfortunately," she replied. Loralei placed the basket on the counter and lifted the towel covering the gingerbread, enjoying the pleasant, gingered aroma that wafted through the kitchen. "At least we can see him in person for a while. Some wives go to the Soo Locks to wave to their husbands from shore as they pass by. I can't do that because I have to take care of the lighthouse, and it's an afternoon's ride through the woods to the locks from here, anyway. I'd like to make the trip sometime, but since I can't, it will be nice to have Devon home, if only for a few nights," she said.

"I'm glad for you. It must be hard to have him gone so much," Mrs. Petrova said.

"It is, but Misha and I manage. Misha's in his bedroom right now. I'll let him know you're here. Misha. Mrs. Petrova is here," she called.

Loralei placed the gingerbread, which she was pleased to find was still warm, on a plate and pulled a knife out of the drawer to slice it.

"People in town are still talking about Jake Calico putting out the beacon and disappearing like he did. They're wondering where he'll turn up next. I hope you're safe here, dear," Mrs. Petrova said.

"Yes, I am. I have the new lighthouse tender and Grandpapa, and we're all on the lookout for Jake now, especially since the shipwreck. I'll never forgive Jake for sabotaging the beacon like that and putting the lives of Dan and the other fishermen in danger. They could have died, and I could have been held responsible," Loralei said, forcing the knife down to cut a thick slice of bread.

"You're right, of course," Mrs. Petrova said, patting her on the arm.

Loralei sighed, feeling soothed by her comforting touch.

"It seems everyone in town feels the same way," Mrs. Petrova added.

Loralei noticed a quiver in her voice and put the knife down to listen to her more closely.

"I've heard talk that some of the men in town want to go after him themselves and not wait for the lawmen to act," Mrs. Petrova continued.

Loralei nipped her lip and looked up at Mrs. Petrova in the pause that followed. She seemed to think for a while before looking over at Loralei.

"Jake did a terrible thing. I agree. But we must always turn the other cheek, dear. It is the only thing that saves us from each other," she said.

Before Loralei could respond, Misha ran into the kitchen and bounded into Mrs. Petrova's open arms.

***

Devon slammed his beer mug down on a table in The Blue Lake Tavern, spilling beer and froth in a wide, swelling puddle, and stared at Carlotta in disbelief. She had followed him into the tavern where he'd gone after the *Manitoulin* docked and fluttered her eyelashes enticingly. He couldn't resist her dark-eyed charms. He'd asked her to join him at the table, and she had been flirting with him outrageously, in a way he found irresistible until she suddenly became serious and dropped a bomb on him.

"What do you mean, Loralei and Jake?" Devon asked, feeling a wave of heat course through his body.

Something about the way Carlotta said it set him on edge.

"Nothing really," Carlotta responded, seemingly taken aback at his forceful response to her statement.

Devon watched her lower her eyes in obvious pain. She looked back up at him after a moment and hesitated before she leaned toward him.

"I didn't want to be the one to tell you this, Devon, but I've heard that Jake was visiting Loralei while you were gone on your voyage in the spring. It's well known around town. And now that he's disappeared, well...." Carlotta paused for a moment. "I have to wonder if Loralei knows where he is," she said.

Devon stared at Carlotta and felt his head begin to throb. He couldn't believe what Carlotta had just said.

Loralei taking up with Jake Calico? It was impossible. She was his wife, devoted to caring for their family and the lighthouse, and Jake was a pirate bent on destroying everything dear to him and everyone in the town. It didn't make sense.

"You're mistaken, Carlotta," he said.

"I don't think so," she said.

Devon decided he'd heard enough. He was no longer interested in the charms Carlotta had to offer or her obvious interest in him, at least for the moment. He threw some bills down on the table and stood to leave.

"I'll thank you to keep your suspicions to yourself from now on," he said firmly, grabbing his duffel bag and turning to leave.

He saw Finn and Marie looking at him from behind the counter at the bar.

"Devon, I—" Carlotta said.

"Captain Lancaster to you, Carlotta," he said.

Devon swung his duffel over his shoulder and stormed out of the tavern without a backward glance.

***

Andre set Loralei's easel down on a grassy knoll near the lake overlook they had walked to with Misha after Mrs. Petrova left. Loralei had suggested they all have a picnic lunch by the lake, and Andre had jumped at the chance. He had spent much of the last few weeks repairing the electrical wiring on the beacon and making sure the Fresnel lens was polished to a smooth, shiny finish and rotating properly. He also helped Loralei with chores around the lighthouse and was amazed at how much there was to do to keep the lighthouse running smoothly. He was ready for a break.

"There's a freighter on the horizon. I think it must be Devon's," Loralei said.

He turned to see Loralei pointing into the distance.

"Grandpapa came by to take the Jeep into town while you were repairing the hole in the rescue boat. He said he'd be back with Devon as soon as his freighter docked," she said.

Andre nodded and took the picnic basket from her. He set it next to the easel and turned to smile at her.

"I will remove myself from your presence when he arrives and work around the lighthouse," he said.

He didn't want to be a problem for Loralei with her husband.

"I suppose that would be best. Misha, come sit down. And you, too, Andre. I've made bacon and tomato sandwiches," Loralei said, motioning to them as she pulled a blanket out of the basket and spread it out on the grass.

As they sat down to lunch, two plump, white and silver seagulls strutted over to peck at the basket, and Loralei dropped her sandwich and waved them away. Misha giggled and jumped up to run after them when they squawked and flew away through the meadow. Loralei smiled and signed to him when he ran past, saying not to go too far and to come back soon to finish his lunch. She watched him running through the meadow for a moment before turning back to Andre.

"I used to come here with my father. The seagulls did the

same thing the last time I came here with him, and they stole the bread from my father's sandwich. They must remember me," she said, laughing lightly.

Andre watched her eyes sparkle with amusement and then dim.

"They make me remember him. I miss him," she said, lowering her eyes and turning to look out over the lake.

She appeared to be lost in thought, and he waited in silence for a moment until she turned back around.

"I am sure you do. I am sorry you lost your father," he said.

He felt a wave of emotion as he watched Loralei's delicate features dissolve into an expression of grief. He couldn't stand to see such a beautiful woman in such obvious emotional pain. He had seen Loralei's expressions of pleasure and delight, and the contrast to the pain in her eyes was almost too much for him to bear. *There must be something*, he thought, *something that could relieve her pain and bring back the brightness to her eyes.*

"Perhaps you could make a painting of your father. Perhaps you could bring him back to you through your artistry," he said, touching Loralei's arm.

She turned and looked at him before nodding almost imperceptibly.

"Perhaps I will. I hadn't thought of that. Maybe I could capture him as the captain of his freighter before the shipwreck, with his crew and Devon's father as first mate. I could paint them and bring them back in some way," she said.

"Yes," Andre said, pulling Loralei to him and brushing his lips against her hair.

It was silky and smelled of lavender, and he tensed with desire as he felt her soft body yield to his. He gently tucked a soft lock of hair behind her ear and leaned in to press his lips against hers, thrilling when she met his lips with an ardent response. He pulled her to him and embraced her more tightly.

"No, not now. Misha is here. Later," she said.

He sighed and pulled back.

"You are right, of course. Later," he said, gazing into her eyes.

She nodded and looked away. Loralei waved at Misha, who was still running after the seagulls, to come back, and when he did, they finished their sandwiches and lemonade and ate the chocolate chip cookies Loralei had made.

"Shall we go fishing, Misha?" Andre asked, picking up a fishing pole. "We can fish and leave your mother to paint her pictures. Is that all right?" he asked, turning to Loralei.

"Yes, please do. I have some ideas now of what I want to paint. Go have fun," she said.

Andre handed Misha a pole and headed for the rocks where they usually fished. He wanted to spend some time with Misha and give Loralei time to herself to express herself through her painting. Sometimes he wondered at himself why he could have such deep, protective feelings for both Misha and Loralei. It reminded him of the protective feeling he had toward his sister, Isabella, in Italy. He smiled, thinking of his beautiful sister with her extraordinary musical gifts, playing in renowned musical venues all around Italy. He wanted to keep them all safe. He hoped nothing involving the war or his duty to his country would change that as it had in the past, with people like Jacques Boudrais at the Chateau de Chambord, who he had had to kill even though they had been his friends. He gave a backward wave to Loralei and smiled at Misha, who waved at Loralei and skipped through the meadow next to him.

***

Loralei gathered her paints together as the afternoon sun waned lower in the sky. Devon would be back at the lighthouse soon after Edmund picked him up when the freighter docked in town, and she looked around nervously for Andre and Misha. It was time they all headed back. She wanted to be home when Devon arrived. When she didn't see them, she went back to her painting. It had been a productive session for her, and she was pleased with the picture she had made of her father and Devon's father in their uniforms on their freighter at sea. The painting had come so easily for her once she started, and she found herself unable to stop.

She had mixed a pale grey with a creamy white to change the clear blue sky in front of her into what she remembered the sky had been like on the day of the storm in which her and Devon's fathers had perished. She added deep greys to her rendering of the puffy clouds that dolloped the sky before her to give them depth and make them look like storm clouds. She imagined her father on his freighter on the day of the storm, gazing at the sky with Devon's father beside him, and brushed away tears before adding more color to the painting. It was still hard for her to accept that they were gone. She used wide, sweeping brush strokes to further define the turbulent, indigo-blue waves and smaller brush strokes to add definition to the freighter she imagined sailing through the choppy waves.

The breeze on the lake picked up as she added the last details, and she sat back and looked at it, feeling satisfied and purged of her emotions at the same time. It was the first time she could remember that she had completed a painting in one sitting. As she put her brushes in the basket, she was relieved to see Andre and Misha walking toward her through the meadow.

"I don't see any fish," Loralei said lightheartedly as they drew near, feeling like teasing Andre.

"I do not believe they were hungry today. Perhaps some other time," Andre said, grinning at her.

Misha ran up next to her and handed her a Petosky stone. He signed to her that he had found it and wanted her to have it. She took it from him and patted his head. Petosky stones were fossilized stones that were treasured finds in the area, especially, Loralei knew, by Misha. She felt honored to receive one from him as a gift.

"Thank you, dear. Shall we head back? Papa could be home by now," she signed.

Misha jumped up and down, and Loralei laughed, picking up her things. She paused as Andre stopped her suddenly and took the painting from her.

"You painted this just now?" he asked, in seeming disbelief.

"Yes, do you like it? I mixed some new shades, and I hope I captured the light properly," she said.

Loralei watched as he slowly perused the painting with an expression of seeming incredulity.

"It is extraordinary. You are very gifted," he said.

Loralei felt her cheeks grow warm and realized she must be blushing. Andre's praise thrilled her.

"Thank you," she managed, trying not to show how touched she was by his obvious admiration.

She wasn't sure she was ready to believe her paintings were that good, especially since Devon had never paid any attention to them at all. They gathered up the picnic items and headed home to the lighthouse. Loralei felt happy and safe with Andre walking next to her through the meadow. It had been a wonderful day, and she would remember their time together for a long time to come.

When they reached the yard of the lighthouse, Misha saw the Jeep and ran toward the lighthouse door. Loralei realized he knew Devon was home and hurried to follow him. She wanted to see Devon, too. As they approached the door, it opened, and Loralei gasped with fear when she saw Devon step out into the yard.

***

"Devon. Is everything all right? I've been looking forward to seeing you," Loralei said as she walked nearer to the lighthouse.

"Is that right?" Devon said.

Loralei felt a sharp pain in her chest. She put her hand to her heart and felt it pounding in rhythm with the growing pain in her side. She sucked in a tortured breath when she saw the glowering look on Devon's face and wondered, for a moment, if he had found Jake's body in the fruit cellar.

"Yes. I've missed you," she choked out, watching Misha run up to hug him.

She sucked in another breath, trying to gain control of her quivering heart. Was it possible that Devon knew? Had he found Jake's body, despite the fact that Andre had covered the grave in the cellar with new shelving? She shivered as she realized the new carpentry might draw attention to the grave rather than away from it. But it was too late to worry about that now. Loralei shook her head. She had no idea how she would deal with Devon and his volatile emotions, especially if he had found Jake's body.

"Go see Grandpapa," Devon said, setting Misha down after hugging him and pointing him toward the kitchen.

Misha hesitated for a moment before looking at Devon's face and doing as he was told. Loralei was torn between treasuring the tender moment she had witnessed between Misha and his father and fearing what would happen to Misha and to her if Devon became more enraged. When Devon turned back toward her, Loralei clenched her hands and tried to control her shaking. She had never seen him look so angry.

"Where have you been? I've been home for a while now, and there was no one here to greet me. And who the hell is this?" he asked.

Loralei followed Devon's gaze to Andre, who was walking up next to her. She tried to choke out an answer, but her throat felt tight. Her tongue felt thick and dry. She looked over at Andre in desperation and was relieved to see that he didn't appear to be intimidated by Devon.

"I am Andre, the new lighthouse tender. At your service, sir," Andre said.

"At my service? Really? Loralei, what's going on?" Devon asked.

Loralei felt the shaking that had begun in her legs move up through her body. What if he knew about her and Andre? She didn't know how she would handle another jealous rage from him as she'd had to do in the past.

"Nothing, Devon, really. I took Misha for a picnic lunch, and Andre came along to make sure we were safe, given that Jake could still be around. That's all," she said. She turned to look at Andre. "Thank you, Andre. You may retire to the scullery quarters for the day if you'd like. I will have dinner ready around seven," she said.

Loralei tried to sound proud and dismissive to allay Devon's obvious suspicions about her and Andre's relationship.

"Yes, of course. Excuse me, sir," Andre said.

Andre moved to walk past Devon into the lighthouse.

"Just a minute," Devon said, holding up his hand and moving toward Andre in what Loralei thought of as a menacing manner. "Where'd you come from? Loralei, do you even know who he is?" he asked.

"Yes. He came in on Captain Blake's freighter a month ago with excellent recommendations, and I hired him at Finn and Marie's tavern. I needed someone to tend to the beacon and the lighthouse, and he's doing a wonderful job. Now, can we come in, please?" Loralei asked.

Loralei huffed and stomped forward, hoping to bluff her way past Devon with pretended indignation to cover her fear. She didn't know why he was so suspicious, but she didn't want to argue with him at the moment.

"I don't think so. Get your things, and go," Devon said to Andre. "Edmund told me he's been staying here, Loralei, and I don't like it," he said.

Loralei looked desperately at Andre and tried to think of something to say to save the situation.

"No, Devon, I need him," she said.

"What?" Devon asked.

Loralei shook her head in fear at the look in his eyes. She realized she had said the wrong thing."

"I don't mean...I mean...," she stammered.

Devon turned back to Andre, who stood, holding the easel and picnic basket in his hands, as he appeared to be waiting to see whose directions he should listen to.

"I said, get out," he said to Andre.

"No, Devon," Loralei said.

She struggled to regain her composure. She realized she didn't have the luxury to fall apart. If she lost Andre, she would be overwhelmed with the responsibilities at the lighthouse, and she didn't want that to happen. She didn't think she could handle everything by herself while she was pregnant. And she would no longer have Andre as her lover. She couldn't fathom that not after all she and Andre had shared. She couldn't stand to lose him, not now. Loralei straightened, threw her shoulders back, and faced Devon when he turned back to her.

"No," she said again, more loudly. We need him here, Misha and Grandpapa and I. Andre protects us and the lighthouse from Jake Calico when you're gone, and I won't have you dismissing him, especially when you're leaving again in a few days. Besides, the lighthouse inspector insisted on it," she said.

"The lighthouse inspector?" Devon asked.

Devon looked at her in seeming disbelief.

"The lighthouse inspector told me to hire someone to protect the beacon after Jake tried to sabotage it, and we can't go against his authority. Andre's here, and he's staying," Loralei said.

She clenched her fingers into fists against her sides as she waited to see how Devon would react to her words. She felt her stomach churn and unclenched a fist to place the palm of her hand on her abdomen. For a second, she thought she felt the baby kick. She ignored it as she saw Devon's cheeks turn a fiery red. A blue vein popped out on his forehead. Despite her trepidation, Loralei forced herself to meet his glare with a level gaze.

"I can't do this by myself anymore, Devon, not while I'm pregnant and not while Jake's around. We need Andre here," she said.

Devon looked from her to Andre and back again. She could see him gauging the situation and determining whether he should listen to her or not. When he lowered his hand after a moment and stepped away from Andre, Loralei breathed a sigh of relief as she realized he was going to listen to reason. She felt her stomach ease, and the baby stopped kicking.

"Thank you, Devon. You won't be sorry. I'm glad you're home," she said, walking toward him.

She waited as Andre nodded and walked past Devon into the lighthouse before following him toward the door. She held out her arms toward Devon as she neared him but lowered them when she saw his expression as he stepped toward her.

"We'll talk later. I have some things I want to talk to you about," he said in a low voice.

"Of course," she answered, feeling her heart drop. She supposed it was too much to hope Devon's visit would be a peaceful one and that the tension from their altercation would fade. "Perhaps we can talk tomorrow after things have settled down," she said, trying not to let her voice quiver as she spoke.

She wondered what Devon wanted to discuss, but she didn't want to talk to him when he was in such a frenzied state. She shivered as she stepped past him through the door into the lighthouse and walked into the kitchen to start dinner. As she pulled a cast iron skillet out of the cupboard, she decided she would come out later to make sure the door to the fruit cellar was still locked. She didn't know what Devon wanted to talk about, but she hoped it didn't have anything to do with Jake.

CHAPTER 12

Loralei busied herself with making shepherd's pie for dinner and tried not to think about the tension building in the lighthouse since Devon's return. She was happy that Misha, seemingly unaware that anything was wrong, was playing checkers with Devon in the living area. As Loralei continued browning meat in the cast iron skillet and reached for the spice rack, she realized Misha was pulling on her skirt.

"Mama, I get cherries?" Misha signed to her.

Loralei, startled by Misha's question, turned away from the stove to pat him on the head. "No, thank you, dear," she signed. "It's too dark in the fruit cellar for you."

"I'll go with him," Devon said, standing and walking into the kitchen.

Loralei tensed at Devon's words. "No. I locked the door."

"What'd you do that for? Come on, Misha, we'll get the cherries." Devon took Misha by the hand and looked up to address Loralei. "I'll take the key off the hook by the door."

"Devon, no," she said.

"Will you relax?" he said.

"Shouldn't you two finish your game of checkers?" Loralei

asked.

"We'll finish it later. What's the matter with you?" Devon asked.

Loralei moved sideways as Devon brushed past her with Misha and walked through the kitchen toward the lighthouse door.

"I think the key is missing," she said desperately.

"It's right here," he said.

Devon scoffed and pulled the key off the hook by the door, and walked out of the lighthouse with Misha. She put her hand to her mouth and shook as she realized there was nothing more she could do. She walked to the door of the lighthouse and watched, terrified, as Devon led Misha to the fruit cellar and lifted the door to go underground. He pulled back for a moment after opening the door and appeared to direct Misha to wait for him before descending into the cellar. Loralei felt a cold drop of sweat run down the back of her neck. Even though Andre had built new shelves over Jake's grave and had taken care to disguise the area around it, she was afraid that Devon would discover her secret. What would happen to her if he did? After a few minutes, Devon reappeared with a jar of cherries, took Misha's hand, and yelled something to her that she couldn't hear. She squinted to see the look on his face, but she couldn't tell what it was. She felt her heart beat faster and her body shake violently as she waited for him to draw closer.

"The rats got in the cellar again," he said when he reached her. "I can smell them. One must have died down there. Have your new man, Andre, get rid of them while I'm gone," he said.

Loralei relaxed and put her hand to her heart as she realized she hadn't been found out. She tried not to let Devon see what she supposed was her obvious agitation.

"Yes, of course, Devon. Whatever you say," she said, swallowing and turning away.

They all went back into the lighthouse together. Loralei

took one last look over her shoulder at the fruit cellar before taking the key from Devon and closing the door behind them.

***

Andre turned on the beacon at sunset and waited to make sure it rotated properly and flashed its bright light out over the darkening twilight of the lake. Lights blinked in the distance near the channel, and sailors navigated the waters in the deepening stillness of the night. After seeing Devon earlier, Andre knew he was going to have to keep his distance if he was going to survive in his job at the lighthouse. He had seen jealousy many times before and recognized it in Devon's dangerous demeanor. Andre didn't want to risk a confrontation with Devon if he didn't have to, given that Devon was Loralei's husband, and he didn't want to upset her. He had eaten his dinner in his room and had done various odd jobs outside the lighthouse before heading up the staircase to tend the beacon. He made a note in the logbook of the time, knowing that Loralei would check it later, and headed back down the stairwell. As he neared the bottom, he heard Devon and Edmund talking in the living area and paused to listen.

"They're building the new lock at the Soo. I saw them on my way through this time. It's going to be bigger to allow the larger freighters to sail through. They're really moving on it."

Andre heard Edmond say, "The MacArthur Lock at the Soo Locks?"

"Yes," Devon said.

"I read about that in the Portstown Gazette. It should be finished in the summer of next year. It's being built to allow more and larger freighters to go through the locks to bolster the shipping operation for the war effort," Edmund said.

"That's fine with me. Anything to speed up the wait to get into the locks gets my vote. The construction could be one of the reasons for the increased troop presence there and for the hydrogen balloons guarding the airspace around the locks," Devon said.

Andre slowed his breathing and became as quiet as possible as he listened to their conversation. He didn't want to risk being discovered eavesdropping. The information he had overheard was vital to his spy mission investigating the Great Lakes shipping operation, and he made a note to travel to the Soo Locks as soon as possible. He needed to find out what was going on there and to perhaps make sketches of the locks and the new MacArthur lock, in particular. He thought for a moment and wondered if he could persuade Loralei to go with him. Having her as a traveling companion could keep his presence at the Soo Locks from appearing suspicious and allow him more access to secured areas. And Loralei had access to the Jeep, which would solve his need for transportation.

He stood on the stairs for a while until he heard Loralei call to the men to come back to the table for cherry cobbler before descending the stairs to make his presence known. He walked quietly through the kitchen, nodding to Loralei, and went to spend the rest of the night in his room in the scullery quarters.

***

After she tucked Misha in for the night and waited for the men to leave the table and go into the other room, Loralei slipped out the door and strolled to the lake. A purple dusk descended, leaving only the hint of gold peeking over a pale pink horizon above the rippling, azure-blue waves. A great blue heron stood far down the beach, gazing with her at the twilight sky. The night was warm, and a light breeze rustled the silver-green leaves of the white ash trees behind her. Two sand-and-white piping plovers darted in and out of the low-rolling waves that washed to shore, and she made a note to record the sighting of the small shorebirds for the environmentalist group she tracked them for.

She looked out over the water and remembered the thrill of seeing Jake canoeing to shore toward her on a similar, beautiful evening. But he wasn't there. He would never be there again. How she wished the night he died had never happened.

But it did, and she missed him. She missed her connection with him and the way he had made her feel like she was a part of the world, a desirable woman and not just a dutiful worker. Even though she had broken things off, she hadn't gotten over their affair. Now, Andre made her feel desirable, and maybe she was beginning to love him, but it wasn't the same as it had been with Jake and Devon before that. She missed the way things were with Devon before the merciless fury of the historic storm had stolen their fathers from them and twisted and wrenched their love away in its vicious aftermath. Now, standing alone on the beach, she felt connected only to the lake and the wilderness. The loneliness punched her in the stomach and sucked her breath away, and she leaned over and struggled for air. *Did I feel the baby?* She took a deep breath and placed her hand on her girth to feel the restless fluttering of the new life inside her, feeling suddenly overwhelmed with love and hope. Would a new baby assuage the loneliness and end the desperation she felt in her relationship with Devon? She didn't know. It wasn't right to hope the baby would change things with her husband. Things needed to change between them because of each other, not because of the baby. But was that possible? She hoped for a happy family and a solid future for her child, but if the baby was Jake's, that hope could be dashed.

She patted her stomach and thought about the baby. *I will do what I can to give you a happy life and a happy home. You will be loved. You will be cherished. You will be a child of the light.* The night darkened as the sun disappeared, and Loralei turned and walked back to the lighthouse.

***

Devon poured another snifter of brandy from the bottle on the wood-hewn table in front of him. Edmund had finished his brandy earlier, pleaded exhaustion, and leaned on his cane to walk to the scullery quarters, where Devon knew he was going to spend the night. Devon had talked to Loralei earlier in the evening about needing Edmund to drive him into town in the morning to board his freighter. Edmund had said at the time that he would be happy to stay over and drive Devon to town in the Jeep.

He wasn't looking forward to sailing again on the *Manitoulin* as a crewman and not as the captain, but there wasn't anything he could do about it for now. Lanny was still in charge, and once the iron ore was loaded, they were heading back to Detroit. Devon bristled at the thought of having to endure Lanny's self-righteous attitude for another trip. He took a long sip of brandy to assuage his nerves and looked around for Loralei. When he didn't see her, he picked up his brandy and walked to the bedroom. She was there, dressing for bed.

"We need to talk," he said, aware that he was slurring his words but enjoying the familiar numbness he felt as the brandy warmed him.

"I thought we were going to wait until morning," she said.

"I want to talk now," Devon said, slamming his brandy down on the dresser. "I want to know about you and Jake Calico."

"What?" Loralei asked.

Loralei's cheeks flushed as she turned to look at him. He wasn't convinced the blameless look she gave him was real.

"You and Jake Calico. Carlotta Pomodoro told me there was something going on between you two. What is it, Loralei? Do I even know you anymore? Are you carrying on behind my back?" Devon asked.

Devon was surprised to feel his body shaking. The possibility that Loralei could be seeing someone infuriated him. His mother, long ago, had had beaus who brought her candy and flowers when his father was gone at sea, and it had upset him to no end. He hadn't known how to reconcile keeping such secrets from his father. He had retreated into himself as a child, trying to distance himself emotionally from his father and his mother to protect himself. When his mother ran off with one of her suitors several years ago while his father was sailing the lakes, Devon had been devastated, and he wasn't going to stand for the possibility of such a thing from his own wife.

"Of course not. Why would you say something like that?" Loralei asked.

Devon scoffed and shook his head. "Don't lie to me," he said.

"I'm not. I don't have anything going on with Jake," she said.

He looked at her for a moment, feeling the weight of his suspicions overwhelm his attempt at remaining calm. He thought Loralei was telling the truth, but something about the way she said it bothered him.

"I won't stand for it. Do you hear me? You're my wife, not some trollop from the bar," he said.

"Oh, really? And what about Carlotta? It seems to me you prefer a trollop from the bar to your wife," Loralei said.

Devon felt his face warm with the anger that coursed through him when he saw Loralei put her hands on her hips and stick out her chin. She had never talked to him like that before. He didn't know what could have gotten into her.

"I won't have you talking to me like that. I'm your husband, and I deserve respect," he said.

"So do I, and you're not giving it to me. I need more from you than you're willing to give, and I'm not going to listen to you talk to me about what Carlotta says when you don't know anything about my feelings. Nor do you care," she said.

Devon huffed in frustration. He wanted to yell at her, but for some reason, he held his tongue. He didn't understand how their marriage could have ended up this way, and for a moment, he was sorry it had.

"I care," he said, turning away. "If I didn't care, I wouldn't be so angry."

He sat down slowly on the bed and waited for Loralei to

say something. The events on the *Manitoulin* that had relieved him of his command and the arguments he was having today with Loralei had left him feeling outnumbered and defeated. And he was always on edge thinking about how close to home the front of the war could be getting, given the situation at the Soo Locks. He didn't know how his life or his marriage could have gotten so out of hand.

He leaned over and put his head in his hands. There was a long silence.

"Do you really care, Devon? After all this time? I care, too. I've been waiting for you to come back to me. I want our marriage to work," she said.

Loralei's soft words sifted through the pounding in his head. He rubbed his temples and turned to look at her. She was standing by the window in the glow of the moonlight. She looked to him like an ethereal angel, with her white nightdress reflecting the silver light and her silky hair in a halo of gold around her face. He had forgotten how truly lovely she was.

"Come to me. Please, I need you," he said.

"I need you, too," she said, walking toward him. "We'll get through this somehow. Time will heal the grief we both feel for the loss of our fathers in the shipwreck, and time will bring an end to the war. We will have our life together again. We have Misha and the baby coming. We can be a family," she said.

Devon breathed a sigh of relief when she reached him and touched him gently on the shoulder. He pulled her down onto the bed next to him and held her tightly, smelling the lavender scent of her hair and touching the silky smoothness of her hair. He wanted her, he realized. He wanted her so badly. But something between them wasn't right. He could sense it.

"You could be right," he said. "Time could heal our grief. But I will never forget my father. I will never get over losing him to the anger of the lake. The lake took him from me when I needed him the most. I needed him to be my father and Misha's grandfather. I needed him to be part of our family and part of my life. He was the only person I could talk to, besides Edmund, about the freighter and my command. I wanted so much to make him proud of me and to be the best ship captain there was. But I screwed up, Loralei. I made the biggest mistake of my life by telling my father I thought he should sail in the weeks before the storm that killed him. I'm no match for the lake. I should be because I'm the captain of the *Manitoulin*, but I'm not. And now he's gone," Devon said.

"It wasn't your fault," Loralei said.

He pulled Loralei to him and held her, burying his face in her hair.

"It just wasn't," she said. "You have to quit blaming yourself for something that was beyond your control."

He felt her tighten her arms around him.

"I want it to be the way it used to be between us, before everything that happened, before we lost each other to our grief," she said, caressing his neck.

"I want that, too," Devon said, pulling back to look at her.

He looked deep into Loralei's eyes, searching for something, but he didn't know what. For some reason, he felt as though she was a stranger to him. She seemed so different from the happy young girl he had married years ago. It had been so long since he'd had a meaningful conversation with her, and he realized that he hardly knew her anymore.

"I want that someday. Not now," he said, looking away and feeling lost and alone.

He was suddenly sorry that he had been so angry with Loralei for so long and so distant. He didn't even know who she was anymore. He released her, and as she slid over to her side of the bed, he leaned over and turned out the dimmed nightlight on the nightstand. He was exhausted from the arguments and the worries of the day, and he felt his body collapse onto the softness of the bed. He didn't even feel as though he had the strength to dress for bed.

"Don't go. I miss you so much when you're gone," she said.

"I know. I have to go. You know that. My country needs me," he said.

"I know that. And I'm proud of you. But I need you, too. And the fear that the lake will take you away from me the way it took my father away from me is more than I can bear. I can't stand to think of that happening to you. I worry about you every day you are gone. I'm afraid another deadly storm will take you away from me," Loralei said.

He heard her words, which sounded desperate and faltering to him, and tried to keep his eyes open as he felt a wave of defeat and exhaustion wash over him.

"Let us be together tonight, you and me, the way we used to be. I need you so much," she said.

Devon heard Loralei whisper softly to him in the quiet of the night before he turned over on his side and drifted off to sleep.

***

Devon lugged his duffel and the large, flat, brown-wrapped package Edmund had given him to take to Detroit when he dropped him off at his freighter that morning to his cabin, threw everything in a corner, and plopped down on his bunk. It had been a long few days, and he was relieved, although irritated, with the fact that Lanny remained the acting captain to be back on the *Manitoulin* and heading out to sea again. Devon had observed the breathtaking hues of the sunrise over Lake Superior as he walked up the gangplank to board the freighter. The scene's beauty had made him long to be out on the water, sailing the open seas with the wind at his back and the vastness of the majestic great lake stretching out before him. But first things first, he thought, reaching for the bottle of rum he had stashed in a hidden compartment in a cubbyhole. He needed to relax after the long weekend he had spent at home. His shore leave this time had been full of turbulence and conflict and arguing with Loralei, and the jealousy he felt over thinking she was seeing other men was unbearable. Despite the fact that she had said she cared about him and wanted their marriage to work, he didn't feel she was being truthful with him. It bothered him to think she could be deceiving him, even though he hadn't felt close to her in a long time.

Devon pulled the bottle away from his lips and turned to look at the package Edmund had handed him before he boarded the ship. Edmund had said that his brother, Maurice Clairmont, had sent him a letter asking him to talk to Loralei about sending one of her paintings to the Detroit Institute of the Arts. Edmund's brother, Maurice, who was a famous curator in France, had said that he received a letter from a curator at the Detroit Institute of the Arts who had been vacationing in Portstown and had seen Loralei's paintings on display there. The curator did not identify himself but wrote that he had seen seascapes, which Loralei had painted under the name of Loralei Clairmont, on display at the Methodist Church in Portstown. He wondered if she was any relation to Maurice and had been effusive about the genius of Loralei's work. Maurice was excited to think that Loralei could be so talented and wanted him to convince her to send a painting to the institute for inspection. Edmund asked Devon to take the painting with him on the freighter and deliver it to the art institute in Detroit.

Devon hadn't wanted to do it at first. It seemed silly to him that something Loralei did as a hobby could engender so much fuss, and he thought she should be spending her time tending to her family and her duties at the lighthouse instead. But he had relented at Edmund's insistence. He determined that if Loralei's grandfather and family in France thought it was so important, he would deliver the painting to the art institute. He didn't want to risk alienating them by refusing. Devon looked at the package containing the painting and wondered if he should open it. He wanted to see what Loralei had painted. Before he could climb out of his bunk, he heard a knock on the door.

"We're leaving port, Captain."

Devon heard a crewman call to him through the closed door.

"Aye," he responded from his bunk, standing to walk over to the package.

He picked it up gingerly and laid it on his berth, grabbing a letter opener to slice an opening in the brown paper wrapping. He ripped the paper off the front of the painting and set it upright against the wall. He stood back, stunned, and gasped at what he saw.

"Father," he murmured, looking at the painting of a freighter sailing the lake with its captain and crew.

The painting mesmerized him with its motion and light and its realistic rendering of a ship at sea. But most of all, it struck him because of the faces of the sailors. The sailor in the front of the ship was obviously Devon's father, dressed in his first mate's uniform and gazing out over the rippling blue water of the lake with an expression of concern. And the sailor to the port side of him was obviously Loralei's father, dressed in his captain's uniform and pointing toward storm clouds on the horizon, appearing to issue commands.

He stood gazing at the painting. He felt a surge of emotion as he realized that Loralei had captured both of their fathers in what he supposed was her idea of the way they looked when they first saw the storm on the horizon, the storm that had shipwrecked their freighter two years ago and sent them to their deaths. He realized she had painted what she thought of as their fathers' last moments of being alive. He paused for a moment, perusing the painting, before raising his hands to his face and impatiently wiping tears from his eyes. He felt suddenly overwhelmed with grief and began to sob in spite of himself. He had never cried before over his father's death. Something about the painting touched the wound in his soul.

"Captain, you're wanted on the bridge," Devon heard a crewman say through the door. He shook his head and tried to regain his composure.

"Be right there," he said.

He grabbed the painting and slid it under his bunk. He wiped the tears from his face and reached into a cubbyhole to pull out a lemon drop, which he quickly unwrapped and popped in his mouth to disguise his breath. He smoothed the wrinkles from his jacket, opened the door, and stepped into the passageway to make his way to the upper deck of the *Manitoulin*. He wanted to find out what Lanny wanted this time.

CHAPTER 13

Loralei drove the Jeep down the gravel road through the forest, trying to keep the steering wheel straight while bumping over ruts and rocks in her way. She tried to concentrate on driving, but her mind wandered to Devon and their last night together before he had left to sail the *Manitoulin* to Detroit. She brushed away tears as she thought again of the distance between them and of his continued physical rejection of her. She loved him so much, and she wanted to show him. But Devon wouldn't let her. She wondered if he ever would again.

She turned the wheel to avoid a fallen branch blocking part of the road. She splashed through a puddle, fresh from the rain the night before, that hadn't yet evaporated in the early-afternoon sun and felt the cold drops of water from the puddle mix with the hot teardrops on her cheeks and cool her face. As she steered around the branch and neared the spot where she had told Andre to meet her, she heard his familiar voice call to her from the woods.

"Lori, I am over here. Stop on the side of the road, and I shall walk over," he said.

She breathed a sigh of relief that he was there. They had

set up a rendezvous point two nights before when Andre had left the lighthouse and told Edmund that he was going into Portstown for a few days.

"Andre, my love, I'm so glad you are here," she said when Andre reached the Jeep.

When he climbed in and grinned at her, she caught her breath, realizing again what an attractive man he was.

"I was afraid for you. Were you caught in the storm last night?" she asked.

"No. I found a cave near the lake, not far from the river that runs through the woods," he answered. "I slept there, protected from the storm until I could rise to meet you near the circle of white birch trees here, as we agreed." Andre paused for a moment. "I trust you had no problem with Edmund about leaving?" he asked.

"No. He suspects nothing," Loralei said.

She had told Edmund a few days before Andre left that she needed him to watch Misha and the lighthouse for her for a few nights while she went to the Sault Ste. Marie to get special replacement parts for the beacon they needed. They did need the parts, and her gas ration for the week would be larger if the trip was classified as a necessary business trip. Edmund had been reluctant to let her leave to travel through the woods by herself on what was at least an afternoon's drive, but she had eventually convinced him of the importance of the trip. He had agreed to let her go when she told him she would be careful and that she would stay at a nice hotel at the Soo.

"Good. Then, we are free to be together, mia cara," Andre said.

Loralei smiled at Andre and steered the Jeep back onto the gravel road to continue their journey toward the Sault Ste. Marie and the Soo Locks, as they had planned. Andre had told her that he had seen the Soo Locks when he had sailed to Portstown and thought they would make a wonderful background for one of her seascapes. And, he said, it would give them a reason to spend time alone together, away from the lighthouse. She had been thrilled at the prospect of a romantic rendezvous with Andre and also of painting a new seascape incorporating the locks. The painting she had made of her and Devon's fathers, at Andre's suggestion, was one of the best paintings she had ever done, and she was inclined to listen to his advice.

"I'm afraid it may rain before we get to the Soo," she said. "I listened to the weather report at the lighthouse before I left, and the rainstorms may continue. I know of another cave beneath a waterfall that we could camp in tonight if we need to."

"Wherever we are, as long as I am with you, is benissimo," Andre said.

Loralei smiled and glanced over at Andre. He smiled back at her, and she shivered at the prospect of being with him that night. But she saw something in his eyes that frightened her, and she wondered if he had other things on his mind besides her. He seemed determined about something, and Loralei felt a sudden distance between them.

She concentrated on keeping the Jeep on the road as she drove through the dripping forest. The road was shadowed by a canopy of trees that let in occasional filters of light, and the air underneath the canopy was cool and damp. They travelled for a few hours before the rain began again. It started as a light downpour before the wind picked up, and the raindrops splattered the windshield and slapped against their faces.

"We must find shelter," Loralei said, turning the Jeep off the road and heading down a dirt path toward the lake. "The cave behind the waterfall on the river is not far from here. We can spend the night there."

"Yes. Let us hurry for cover," Andre said.

Loralei raced the Jeep down the dirt path as fast as it would go until she reached the spot near the river rapids where the waterfall tumbled over the rocks. "This is it," she said, parking the Jeep in a dense copse of trees. "The Jeep will be dry enough here. Grab your things, and I'll show you the way to the cave," Loralei said, pulling a basket and a plastic bag out of the back of the Jeep and running down to the riverbank through the downpour.

Andre pulled a canvas bag out of the Jeep and followed her. She ran until she reached the rocks in the river near the cave entrance and knelt to climb over them to a dry space on the side of the waterfall that led to the entrance to the cave. She looked back for Andre when she reached the cave entrance and saw him kneeling and slipping over the rocks on his way to join her.

"I fear that I have become an animal in the wilderness," Andre said when he reached her, shaking the rain from his hair as he climbed up and stood beside her. "I shall be after spending another night in the forest with you."

She saw him grin at her.

"There are more than enough wolves in the forest already," Loralei said, laughing and noticing how the wet curls of Andre's thick, dark hair glistened as he shook his head. "You don't need to be another one." She felt her body tingle. "Come. We must set up a place to eat and sleep, and we need to build a fire to keep us warm tonight. We need to gather dry wood. Perhaps there is wood that is not too wet under the thicker brush in the woods. I have brought matches with me."

"I will help you find some wood," he said.

She set about her task, and before long, she had an armful of dry branches, which she took back to the cave with her. She built a fire, and Andre returned with more wood to add to it. Loralei prepared the cave for the night and opened the basket of food as Andre tended the fire. She set about preparing a simple dinner of leftover chicken, which she placed near the fire to warm, along with a loaf of fresh, homemade bread she had brought. She added the blueberry cobbler she had made from the berries in the garden to the array, and called to Andre to sit down and eat with her. They talked and ate their dinner by the light of the fire. Twilight turned to darkness by the time they finished eating. Loralei stood and went to the front of the cave to look out at the river and the woods from behind the waterfall.

"There is a pond here that the water falls into. I have been here before. The underground springs that feed the river with water are warm, and they mix with the turbulence of the water from the falls to create a wonderful sensation as you swim. I swam in the pond once as a child. I felt like a water nymph," she said.

She turned to see Andre gazing at her.

"Let us swim together in the pond," he said. His eyes were glinting in the glow of the fire. "I would like to see you as a water nymph," he said, unbuttoning his shirt. "I would like that very much," he continued, moving toward her and unfastening her dress. "The night is dark. No one will see us. Come to the water with me, Lori."

Loralei gazed back at Andre and nodded.

She dropped her dress to the floor of the cave before following Andre behind the waterfall and out into the quiet of the warm night. As they slipped into the pond together, Loralei felt the silkiness of the warm water against her skin and the coarseness of Andre's warm body next to hers and sighed. The soft singing of crickets warbled with the rustling of the leaves in the trees. She felt herself move as one with Andre in the water. He kissed her and caressed her until she felt free and wild and consumed with an urgent desire greater than anything she had ever felt before. She arched her back and gave herself up to Andre when he lifted her from the water and pulled her to him. The waterfall sprayed them and glistened with the light of a thousand shimmering stars from the night sky above the river. Loralei clutched Andre and moaned as she felt herself become one with him, and their spirits soar into the vastness of the wilderness. She held him and kissed him until she felt her spirit return to her, and she took his hand

and ran with him back to the cave.

They dried themselves in front of the fire and dressed again before huddling together on the bed of pine needles and leaves that Loralei had made to cover the damp floor of the cave. As the fire crackled and warmed her, the spray of the waterfall flickered with the orange colors of the flames. The patter of the rain that had begun again outside mingled with the rushing sound of the water falling in front of them.

"I wish we could stay together like this forever," Loralei said, reveling in the warmth of the fire and the nearness of Andre.

The desire she felt for him seemed endless, and its intensity took her breath away.

"I have never known a man like you," she said.

"I have never known a woman like you," Andre said. "You are the most intriguing woman I have ever met."

Loralei smiled and nuzzled next to him.

"I think my hair is almost dry," Loralei said after a while, running her fingers through the damp strands.

"Let me see," Andre said, touching her hair as he gazed deeply into her eyes.

Loralei felt his fingers caress her temple and trembled as she closed her eyes.

"Yes, it does feel drier," he said.

Andre's lips found hers, and she moaned with pleasure at his touch.

"You fill me with so much love. I don't know what I would do without you," she said.

"You are the light of my life," Andre said, pulling her to him and laying her back on the soft bed of pine needles, which smelled fragrant and fresh to her. "You do not ever have to be without me. I will take you with me wherever I go."

He kissed her more deeply, and she let her mind relax. She didn't want to think about what Andre said. She could never leave the lighthouse forever, to go with him wherever he went, but, for the moment, she didn't care about that. She was here with him now, and that was all that mattered to her.

"Yes, Andre. Take me with you. Let us go again to where only you and I can take each other in the pathways of our minds. Be one with me," she said.

"Yes, Lori. We will be one," Andre answered.

Loralei sighed and laid back, and let Andre take her where she wanted to go.

***

Devon strolled along the deck of the *Manitoulin,* looking out over the railing at the low-rolling waves of Lake Huron. Lanny had summoned him to the bridge once again, as he had many times over the last few weeks as they sailed to Detroit to deliver the iron ore. Even though Lanny was the acting captain and supposedly in charge of the freighter, he seemed to have more questions for him than he thought necessary. He had begun to wonder if Lanny knew what he was doing and if he could handle the command of the *Manitoulin* without him. Devon stepped into the pilot house on the bridge to find Lanny looking out the window and giving orders to the wheelsman.

"You wanted to see me?" he asked.

Lanny turned to look at him. "Yes. Could you come out on the deck with me? I have something I need to discuss with you in private."

Devon was surprised that Lanny didn't address him as Captain, as he had continued to do even after the change in command. He wondered what was going on as he followed him back out onto the deck and over to the railing. A light breeze blew some whitecaps onto the waves, and they tumbled over each other as they gently washed against the sides of the freighter.

"I have some news that I don't think you're going to want to hear," Lanny said.

Devon didn't know what more it could be. So many things had happened over the last few weeks on the freighter to make him realize he was no longer in charge and only a crewman that he wasn't sure he wanted to hear what Lanny had to say. The crew had started to treat him like one of them and seemed to be transferring their loyalty to Lanny, which was intolerable to Devon. But he didn't know what to do about it. He had spent a lot of time drinking in his cabin to assuage his feelings of inferiority.

"What is it?" he asked, bracing himself.

"I'm afraid I've been asked to permanently relieve you of your command of the *Manitoulin*. The trip back from Detroit, after we reach the city and load the coal for the return trip, will be your last trip on the *Manitoulin*. I'm sorry, Devon. The orders from the shipping corporation are clear. I'll show them to you if you want. There's nothing I can do," Lanny said.

Devon stared at him. He felt his eyes begin to lose focus as a stunned feeling of anger raced through his body.

"Relieved of command?" Devon shouted. "I've been the captain of the *Manitoulin* for years and a lot longer than you have. Who's taking over? You? God help us all."

"I'm sorry you feel that way. Maybe we can talk another time when you've calmed down. I have things to do," Lanny said, turning and walking back toward the pilothouse.

"Yeah, I'll bet you do," Devon shouted after him. "Go ahead and try it, Lanny. Try being in charge of the *Manitoulin* by yourself. But when you get into trouble, and you will call me. I'm still the captain of the *Manitoulin*, whether you believe it or not, and the lives of this crew are on my mind every day. Call me. Call me when you need your captain back."

He shook his head in disgust and headed back to his cabin. He didn't take this kind of treatment from anybody, least of all Lanny. Devon stomped into his cabin and slammed the door behind him. He knew Lanny would need his advice again sometime. He grabbed the bottle of rum out of the cubbyhole and threw himself on his bunk to drink himself into another stupor.

He paused for a moment and pulled Loralei's painting out

from under the bed to look at it again.

"Father," he said softly, taking a long swig of rum as he perused the hazy brushstrokes of the painting Loralei had made of his father and her father on their freighter in the gathering storm. It seemed to him that it was the kind of storm raging around him emotionally all the time. "Father, tell me what to do," he said aloud.

***

Loralei stepped out of the Jeep in front of the guard tower and chain link fence at the entrance to the Soo Locks and sighed with relief that they had finally arrived. She was struck by the new realities of the war as she looked at the fencing and the guard tower shadowing the sparkling blue water of the channel that led to the locks. She remembered coming here as a child, before the locks were under such tight security, to wave to her father when he sailed through on his freighter. He had looked down at her over the side of the freighter that appeared to her to be a great wall and waved back.

The locks and channel looked completely different now. The park she had once come to with Misha and Devon was different now, too. The playground was still there near the St. Mary's River, but it was fortified by the menacing fencing and the isolated guard tower near the woods at the entrance to the park.

She felt a momentary pang of loss as she remembered how happy she and Devon had been when they had come here with Misha when he was a baby. It seemed so long ago. She gasped as she looked beyond the playground and across the channel at what she supposed was the new MacArthur Lock under construction. It looked like a vast open canyon, and she was amazed at the scope of the project.

"Identification, please."

Loralei turned to see a young man in a soldier's uniform shouldering a gun.

"Yes, of course," she replied, grabbing her purse off the seat of the Jeep and rummaging through it.

The soldier took the papers she held out and glanced at them before looking up.

"These appear to be in order, but I'm sorry, ma'am, civilians are not allowed in the park at this time by orders of the U.S. Coast Guard."

"The coast guard? But why ever not? I only want to do some painting and have a picnic. And I was hoping to wave to my husband. He's on his freighter, and it's been ever so long since I've seen him." Loralei tried to sound naive about the war situation and distressed about Devon, hoping she could convince the young soldier to let her through the gates.

"I'm sure my husband, Captain Lancaster, wouldn't have wanted me to have come all this way for nothing," she said.

"Captain Devon Lancaster of the *Manitoulin*?" the guard asked.

"Why, yes," she said.

"I shipped out with him on my first job on a freighter out of high school. I didn't know he was your husband. Are you the Lady of the Lighthouse in Portstown, then? I've followed that lighthouse beacon through the channel there, myself."

"Yes, I'm the lighthouse keeper. My grandfather, Captain Clairmont, is watching the lighthouse while I'm on holiday," she said.

"Captain Edmund Clairmont?" the guard asked, eyes widening. "He's a legend on the Great Lakes. His crew saved the crew of a sister ship that wrecked on Lake Superior in the great storm of 1913."

Loralei nodded. The soldier smiled at her and handed her back her papers.

"I suppose an exception could be made in this case. Who's that?" he asked, tipping his chin.

Loralei followed the guard's gaze to where Andre was

pouring a paper cup of water from a thermos under the shade of a nearby tree.

"He's the lighthouse tender in Portstown for Captain Lancaster and me. I can vouch for him," she said.

Loralei saw the soldier hesitate for a moment. She smiled her most charming smile and ran her fingers through her hair. She really wanted to add a painting of the locks to her collection of seascapes.

The guard smiled back and nodded. "All right. I'll make arrangements to let you set things up in the park, but please, only for a few hours. I change shifts at the end of the afternoon. Nice to meet you, Mrs. Lancaster," he said.

"You, too, I'm sure," Loralei said.

She climbed back into the Jeep and waited for the soldier to open the gate. She waited for Andre to return and climb back into the Jeep before driving through and waving as they passed the soldier. The soldier waved back as Loralei drove past him and the guard tower toward the park by the bank of the river.

CHAPTER 14

Andre helped Loralei gather things from the Jeep and walked with her through the park to an open space on the grass near the water. He gazed at the construction raging in the distance of what was obviously the new MacArthur Lock and felt a thrill of satisfaction that he had made it past the guard. This was what he had come to the United States for, to find the Soo Locks, the hub of the Great Lakes shipping operation. It was spread out in front of him in a glorious panorama.

He planned to gather information about the new lock, which he didn't think his country knew about, draw a map of its location, and make sketches to relay to his spy network as soon as possible, to apprise his side of the amount of firepower it would take to destroy both the new lock and the other locks. He had also secured a camera at a shop at the Sault Ste. Marie — while Loralei had purchased replacement parts for the beacon in another store — to take pictures, especially of the new lock. The completion and integration of the new lock could change the course of the war forever if more and larger ships, bound for Detroit and its steel-making factories, could sail through the Soo more quickly with the precious iron ore needed for making weapons to send to Europe. They could face a massive arsenal of resistance from the Allies, and Andre was determined to prevent that from happening.

He spread a blanket out on the grass and set up Loralei's easel and canvases next to it. He positioned the easel in a way that would make it easy for her to capture the lock under construction on canvas. He also made sure she would have a clear view to paint the operating lock, traversed by freighters on the river in front of them.

He looked up as sunlight turned to shadow over the grass. A hydrogen barrage balloon was floating over the park, the same type of balloon he had seen when he sailed through the locks on his way to Portstown months ago. He had heard about their air-defense capabilities at the tavern in Portstown. Another one hovered in the distance and more behind that. He decided to photograph the balloons flying thousands of feet overhead, their tentacled cables piercing the airspace below. Any aircraft entering the area would be destroyed by the cables. He would photograph the security of the area, as well, to present the option that the locks could be breached by foot and sabotaged from the ground instead. He could then escape through Canada with the photographs and other vital information he was able to uncover.

They had picked up sandwiches from a local restaurant, and Andre was glad they were finally ready to eat. All the running around and the trip from the day before had made him hungry. He ate with relish as he watched a freighter glide through the channel in front of them. He thought to himself what a grand ship it was, similar to the one he had sailed to Portstown on. He was amazed at the technology that made it possible for a freighter of that size to be lowered from one lake to another.

"Would you like another sandwich?" Loralei asked.

Andre shook his head at Loralei's question and sat back. He pulled a pen and notepad from his pocket. "I thought I might make some sketches of my own while we are here if that would be agreeable to you," he said.

"Of course. I've brought my sketch pad and charcoal. You're welcome to use those if you'd like," she said. She reached into a portfolio folder, pulled out the items, and handed them to Andre.

"E perfetto. I also sketch with charcoal," Andre said.

He sketched for a while as Loralei painted next to him and relaxed in the beauty and quiet of the afternoon. The sun dappled the grass under a tree nearby and sparkled on the water of the channel. A light breeze blew off the lake, and seagulls soared through the tranquil blue sky.

She paused for a moment and turned to him. "Do you still have family in Italy, where you grew up before you came here years ago?"

He looked at her for a moment. He wasn't sure how to answer. Thinking of Italy made him wistful. He longed for his country and the people there. "Yes, I do. I have a beautiful younger sister, Isabella. She plays the piano like an angel and sings like a nightingale. She lives in a villa near Florence with my parents, who are curators at an art museum there. My mother is a painter, and my father is a sculptor. It was a wonderful life." He set his charcoal down and looked away.

"I thought you said your parents were dead," Loralei said.

He looked back quickly. "What? Oh no, mia cara. Sometimes I only say that to those I do not know well because it is so painful being away from them that I do not want to talk about them," he said.

She nodded slowly. "I understand. Why did you come here?" she asked.

He paused to think of an answer, hoping she didn't realize she'd caught him in a lie. It didn't seem so. "I came here to see an old friend, and I never left," he said evasively. "Shall we continue with our drawings? You have begun with an exceptional hue for the underpainting." He began to sketch again.

"Thank you," she replied, dabbing her paintbrush into a color on her palette.

He breathed deeply of the clean, lake water fresh air as he watched her sweep elegant brush strokes across the canvas in front of her and was awed by how graceful she was. She was a natural painter, a casual genius, and he was enthralled. He grinned when he saw her catch him looking at her. The sunlight highlighted the golden tresses of her hair.

"What is it?" she asked, pausing in her movements for a moment and blushing in a shy way that Andre found enticing.

"You are very beautiful and very talented," he said.

She blushed more deeply, and he leaned toward her.

"Come away with me, Lori. We could go to Italy together and live there. We could be happy and put the war behind us. It will end someday," he said.

Andre waited in silence, surprised at himself that he had poured out his emotions to a woman he barely knew — although, after the passionate nights they had shared, he felt as though he had known her all his life. Her artistic genius was unparalleled, as was his admiration for her. She was the feminine light in the impressionist paintings he so enjoyed perusing. She was the luminous woman in the masterpieces he sought to acquire. She was the radiant angel he had been searching for all his life.

"Come with me to Italy, amore mio," he said.

He waited for her to answer, but she looked away out over the channel in silence.

"I can't, Andre. There's so much you don't know about me. And I can't leave my post or my family, especially during this time of war. It just isn't possible. Let's just enjoy our time together as we have it now," she said.

"Lori," he said.

"Please, Andre. Leave it at that," she said.

"But what do I not know?" Andre asked, setting the sketch pad on the grass next to him and turning to her. "After all we have been through together? What is it you are not telling me?" he asked.

"Andre, I...," she said.

He touched her arm and leaned nearer.

"What is it?"

He waited as she paused for a moment before answering.

"The baby could be Jake's. It might not be Devon's and my child. Do you still want me to come away with you?" Loralei asked.

Andre gazed deeply into her eyes. "That is of no concern to me. Come away with me, Lori. La mia bella signora della luce. We can be a family."

Loralei looked down.

"I'll think about it," she said. "Now, shall we finish our pictures?"

"Si," Andre replied.

He smiled as he watched her blush and return to her painting.

"If you do not mind, I believe I will take some photographs now. We can use them later to create more detailed pictures," Andre said, standing to retrieve his camera from the nearby bag.

"Of course," Loralei said.

He stood and walked toward the channel. The view was open and clear, and he snapped several photographs of the MacArthur Lock. He also took pictures of the hydrogen barrage balloons, the operating locks, and the St. Mary's canal.

Andre walked nearer to the guard tower near the woods as he concentrated on taking pictures. He wanted to show the security around the area, as well. As he neared the woods, he noticed that he could no longer see Loralei over the grassy knoll between them and decided he had gone far enough. He began to head back.

"You didn't tell me you were going to take photographs."

Andre heard a stern voice behind him.

"Photographs are not allowed in this area. I'm afraid I'll have to confiscate the camera."

Andre turned to see the young soldier from the guard tower walking toward him. He grimaced as he realized he should have been more discreet.

"You'll have to leave now. I'll return the camera without the film to Mrs. Lancaster when you drive out," the guard said.

Andre smiled at the guard.

"I should have thought of that. Mrs. Lancaster wanted the pictures to remember the day. I am sure you can understand," Andre said.

"It's not allowed. And, could I see your identification?" the guard asked.

"Of course," Andre said, smiling again as he lifted the camera strap he had around his neck over his head and began to hand the camera to the guard. "I have identification in my pocket. Allow me to get it for you," Andre said.

As the guard moved to take the camera from Andre, Andre lifted it sideways and caught the guard under the chin with a strong left hook. He smashed the camera onto the guard's head and heard a satisfying thump before lassoing the strap around his neck and pushing him to the ground. Andre knelt on the guard's back and twisted the strap until he no longer heard him gasping for breath before checking to make sure he was dead and dragging him into the nearby woods.

Andre tightened his hold on the camera and glanced around quickly before walking out of the woods to return to Loralei. It occurred to Andre as he walked by the guard tower that their visit could have been logged, and he glanced around before slipping into the tower to look around. He found a logbook open on a wooden counter with Loralei's name at the top of the inside page. He ripped the page out and crumpled it into his pocket before running out of the guardhouse and back to Loralei. He slowed as he approached her.

"It is time to go," he said as he neared her. "Let me help you pack up," he said.

***

Loralei packed up her things and carried them to the Jeep in the parking lot at the Soo Locks. She placed everything in the back seat and waited for Andre to follow with her easel and paints. He had seemed extremely pleased with himself and happy earlier in the afternoon, but when he returned from taking photographs, he seemed agitated and upset. She didn't know what had changed, but she was ready to leave. It had been a long afternoon, albeit a productive one. She was happy that Andre had taken pictures for her to make more paintings of the locks later and was surprised that he didn't seem to feel the same way. Was he hiding something? She grabbed the picnic blanket off the seat and went to shake out the crumbs in the woods as she waved at Andre, who was calling to her from the park, but she couldn't hear what he was saying. The woods were dark and filled with mosquitoes, so she hurried to shake out the blanket and return. She shook her head when she saw a pair of boots in the bushes because they seemed so out of place in the area. Loralei looked more closely and screamed.

"Andre," Loralei called, turning and running back toward the Jeep.

"Andre. It's the guard. He's on the ground in the woods."

Loralei waited as Andre ran toward her and ran with him back into the woods to show him what she had seen when he reached her. She put her hand to her mouth as she looked at the sprawled body of the guard in the dark of the woods.

"I think he's dead," she said to Andre.

Loralei felt her body shake as she watched Andre lean over and peer through the bushes. She grabbed his arm to steady herself.

"Yes, I think you are right. We must leave immediately," he said, pulling her to him.

"Leave? We have to tell someone. What could have happened?" Loralei asked, trying to control her trembling as she realized what she was seeing.

"We cannot, Lori. There could be saboteurs in the woods. We are in danger standing here even now. We must go. We must go back to the lighthouse now. Leave this for the war department and the coast guard. In this time of war, it is their responsibility. There is nothing you or I can do. Come quickly. We are in danger," Andre said.

Loralei sighed with dismay as she realized he was right and turned to leave with him. She took one last look at the crumpled body of the young guard in the woods before swallowing her fear and sadness and running with Andre back to the Jeep. She realized, when she climbed in the Jeep and saw Andre's tense face, that they had to get away from the Soo Locks and back to the lighthouse as soon as possible. And she didn't know how they were going to do that.

***

Devon signaled to the bartender to send him another beer. He was drinking at a table in his favorite tavern in Detroit, waiting for the *Manitoulin* to shed her red shipment of iron ore and load up with coal. He'd been in the tavern since early evening after dropping Loralei's painting off at the reception desk at the Detroit Institute of the Arts. Devon shuddered as he thought of the black-painted windows of the factories by the river he had passed and the somber atmosphere of the city. The war seemed to be taking its toll everywhere. There were rumors in Detroit, too, of possible bombing raids, even though the logistics of such an operation, given what he had read in the newspapers, were sketchy at best. The windows were blacked out to keep the light from showing through at night and alerting possible bombers to the factory locations.

He shook his head. The front of the war seemed much closer to home than before, and it weighed on his mind. He was more concerned about Loralei and his family than he had ever been. They could be in real, immediate danger, and it bothered him that he wasn't there to keep them safe.

He had been approached by several women he'd known from past trips to Detroit, but he didn't feel like talking. For some reason, Loralei had become uppermost in his mind, and he didn't want to dally with other women at the moment. He wondered if she still loved him. It had seemed that way when he had been home the last time, but for some nagging reason, he wasn't sure.

Devon took a long draught of the beer the waitress set in front of him and looked around the dimly lit tavern. A few sailors from the *Manitoulin* were carousing at another table, but he didn't feel like joining them. He felt like drowning himself in drink instead. He looked up and saw Lanny walk in.

"Okay, mates, it's time to sail. The *Manitoulin* is loaded and ready to go. Let's get going. I want to pull out of port tonight. Some long-term weather forecasts don't look good, and I want to get back to Portstown ahead of schedule. The corporation is on my back to keep things moving, too. Let's go," Lanny said.

Devon scowled and drained his beer mug. He didn't like Lanny telling him what to do, and he didn't like not being the captain anymore. He wanted his command back. He wasn't looking forward to the return trip to Portstown with Lanny in charge, and he didn't know how he was going to keep his temper. Somehow he was going to have to make it work. He walked to the door and stood a few feet away from Lanny. They waited for the others to join him, and they all walked out of the tavern and headed back to the *Manitoulin* together. There was safety in numbers, Devon thought, looking around at the deserted streets. He hoped the war would end soon, although he didn't have any assurances of that. And he hoped that he would somehow get his command back and make it safely home to Loralei.

***

"Drive faster. The only way to leave the park is to drive through the gate in the chain-link fence," Loralei said.

"I know that," Andre said.

Andre pressed his foot down hard on the accelerator and steered the Jeep out of the parking lot and toward the guard tower.

"We have to leave before the shift changes. The guard told me someone would be taking over for him. If the new guard sees us, we won't be able to leave," Loralei said.

She tried to see if anyone was near the guard tower. The gate was down and blocking the exit to the road home.

"The gate is down. We can't leave," Loralei said loudly. She felt the Jeep bolt forward and grabbed the side of the door to steady herself. "What are you doing?"

"We are going to leave," Andre said.

He pressed his foot down harder on the accelerator as he raced the Jeep toward the gate.

"No, Andre. We can't run through the gate," she said.

"Watch me," Andre said.

"No. You can't," she said. She grabbed the door more tightly and gasped when she saw something in the distance. "There's the new guard. I see him. He's by the fence, running out of the woods toward us with a gun. He must have found the body of the other guard. We have to stay and help. He sees you. You have to stop," she yelled.

"I am not stopping. Hold on, Lori," Andre yelled back.

Loralei grabbed the door of the Jeep with one hand and the windshield with the other as they raced closer and closer to the gate. She gasped again when she heard popping sounds and realized the new guard was shooting at them.

"He's going to kill us," she screamed.

The Jeep hit the gate hard. The gate made a loud cracking sound and splintered into jagged pieces around them as they crashed through.

"Go faster," Loralei shouted, ducking below the door and

trying not to listen to the sound of bullets whizzing by the Jeep. "He saw us," she said, shaking with fear that they would be caught by the authorities at some future date.

"He does not know who we are. Keep your head down," Andre said.

Andre screeched the Jeep down the road. She stayed in a crouch until all she could hear was the sound of the Jeep's motor and Andre calling to her.

"We did it, Lori. We are out of sight of the guard. You can sit up now. We are in the woods. I am driving back to the lighthouse," Andre said.

She sat up slowly. "Are we really safe?" she asked.

"Yes. Do not worry. The guard tower was so isolated that no one was around. No one else saw us. I know that. I checked," he said.

"We should have stayed," Loralei said, feeling helpless to change what might have been a terrible mistake.

She didn't understand what had happened. But she loved Andre and wanted to do what he thought was best. She felt her body tremble, and suddenly, she grabbed her stomach and doubled over.

"What is it?" Andre asked.

Loralei heard the concern in his voice. "The baby's kicking," she said, groaning.

"You need to rest. I shall find a place for us to go," he said.

Andre slowed the Jeep, and they drove for a while through the woods until he turned the Jeep off the road and drove down a dirt path through the woods to a bluff overlooking the lake. He said he wanted to make sure no one who might have followed them could find them.

He came around and helped her out, and Loralei followed him down to the beach. She removed her shoes and breathed a sigh of relief when she stepped onto the cool sand and scrunched its grittiness between her toes. The lake soothed her, as it always did, with its exquisite beauty and quiet shore. She gazed out at the sun setting in hues of red and orange on the horizon and thought of the view from the lighthouse. No matter where she was on the lake, it filled her with awe. She walked with Andre down the beach and listened to the soft, lapping of the waves. A bird glided in the breeze nearby and landed on the sand near them.

"Look, Andre," Loralei said. "This is one of the birds I put bands on to keep track of its migration. It's a piping plover. There are many of them on the shores of Lake Superior. I'm so glad to see its location when it's not at the lighthouse. I will record it when we return home," Loralei said.

Andre nodded and took her hand.

"Your many talents amaze me," he said.

They walked together down the beach, making footprints in the sand until they reached a small peninsula dotted with grey driftwood. Andre sat down on a large piece of driftwood and helped Loralei sit beside him. He put his arm around her and let her rest her weary head on his shoulder as she gazed out over the lake. A sense of wistfulness washed over her as she watched a seagull soar into the clouds and swoop back down over the water. It was free to live its life of leisure. It didn't know war or loneliness or fear. It was an unfettered spirit in the vast majesty of the wilderness.

"Do you ever think about God, Andre?" she asked.

"God? I suppose. Why do you ask?" he asked.

"No reason. I do. I think about God a lot lately. I wonder what he would think about the war and all the killing. But mostly, I wonder what he would think about what happened to Jake. I wonder what he would think about what you did and about what I did. Do you wonder about that?"

Loralei waited through the silence that followed her question for Andre to answer. She tilted her head and saw him looking out over the lake.

"No, I do not wonder about that. I stopped wondering about what God thought of those kinds of things a long time ago," he said quietly.

She thought Andre sounded distracted and distant when he answered her. She wondered what it was about him and his past that made him seem so detached and far away from everyone in the world but her.

"I think about Italy," he said, after a moment. "I think of returning home someday to the country I love. It is so beautiful, Lori. The hills are low and rolling and stretch out for miles in blankets of green and gold. The ancient villas of the countryside are more splendid than you could ever imagine. I will own one someday and fill it with exquisite antiques and magnificent paintings and, perhaps, a family and the beautiful woman that I love," he said quietly, caressing her arm.

Loralei took a quiet breath. Andre's words were so lovely. She could picture Italy and feel his deep love for the country he grew up in. And she realized, at that moment, how much he cared for her, although she wasn't sure how to respond. She cared for him, but the country he loved was on the other side of the war and far away, and the country she loved was here. She didn't know how they could ever overcome their differences to be together. She tried not to think of the future and to concentrate, instead, on the present and her feelings for him at this moment.

"I'm so glad you're here for me now," she murmured, nuzzling his shoulder.

"I will always be here for you," he replied, smoothing her hair with his hand.

Loralei realized as she gazed out over the lake that Andre was becoming more than a lover to her. He was becoming a part of her soul. He was there for her when Devon was not, and she loved him for that. But she still felt, deep within herself, a strong tie to Devon, and she wasn't sure how her relationship with Andre was going to fit in with that. She watched the sunset with him until all that was left was a bluish twilight.

"I believe we can go home. Anyone who followed us would not know where we are now," he said.

"You're right," she said.

"Are you feeling better?" he asked.

"Yes. I'm glad we could rest a while," she said, smiling.

"Come. We must head back to the lighthouse now. We can make it before it becomes too late at night if we leave now," he said, standing and helping her up.

"Yes, Andre," she said.

She saw something in his eyes, but she wasn't sure what it was. It was a faraway look, as though he had left her for another time and place. It was as if he were someone else, someone other than who she knew him to be. But then the look was gone, and he smiled at her again.

"Let us go," he said.

"Yes. It is time for us to go home to the lighthouse," Loralei said.

She stood and took Andre's hand, and they walked together down the beach toward the Jeep on the hill.

CHAPTER 15

Andre slid his feet toward the side of the bed after hearing the soft, slow breaths that told him Loralei was asleep. It had been difficult for Loralei to recover from the unfortunate incident with the guard at the Soo Locks a few days ago, and she had been terrified to return home through the woods in the Jeep at night. But they had no other options, and he had promised to keep her safe. As he had driven the Jeep back to the lighthouse, he had assured her that there was nothing more they could do and had talked her through her fear and sadness over the guard's death. He was relieved that she had eventually agreed that they had done the right thing by leaving and had turned to him again for solace.

Andre had waited patiently after their lovemaking, in the moonlit shadows of the quiet night, to further execute his plan. He needed to radio the information he had discovered about the new MacArthur lock to his spy network and discuss plans for leaving the country through Canada soon. He wanted to personally hand over the sketches and paintings he and Loralei had made and the photographs he had taken while they were at the Soo Locks to his spy network as soon as possible. He knew that delivering the information and pictures was vital to the successful completion of his mission.

He had used the radio under cover of night several weeks before without incident. He had radioed his spy network the secret information about the new minesweeping technology he had discovered in the valise given to him by his unfortunate messenger in Detroit. He hoped to perform a similar operation tonight and contact his spy network clandestinely. His network had approached him during his last transmission about the possibility of smuggling parts of a bomb to him to assemble and place on a freighter heading to the Soo Locks. Bombing a freighter sailing through the Soo Locks could destroy the locks in the same way a bombing raid could, but with fewer logistical complications. It was important. He knew that he should find out more about that possibility. Andre thought if he could get a package on a freighter, which he had done, surreptitiously, by anonymously writing to Maurice Clairmont about Loralei's painting and having Edmund send it via Devon to the Detroit Institute of the Arts at Maurice's request, he could get a bomb on a freighter. Andre knew his spy network was waiting for his answer and for his transmission.

Andre carefully rolled to the side and silently pushed the covers away as he slipped out of bed. He breathed in slightly when he felt the cold floor on his bare feet as he moved toward the door, finding his way across the room by the light of the alabaster moon shining softly through the window.

"Where are you going? Stay with me. It was so lovely being together."

He paused at hearing Loralei's quiet, languorous voice.

"Yes, amore mio. It was lovely indeed," he said.

"I don't want to be without you for a moment, my darling," she said. "My arms feel so empty without you, and the bed seems so cold. You fill up my life when you're with me. Your touch makes me whole. I've never felt this way before about anyone.

Stay, please. We can love each other all night."

Andre paused, thinking of another way he could complete his mission. *Perhaps, tomorrow.* Perhaps while she was otherwise occupied, he could find time to use the radio. The transmission could wait until morning, he decided, giving in to the desire that overtook him at Loralei's invitation. He turned and walked back to bed. He climbed in and buried himself in the pleasurable warmth of her arms, leaving the cares of the world for another time.

***

"Are you sure you know what you're doing, Loralei?" Loralei heard Edmund say. She looked up from changing the bed in her bedroom to see him looking at her from the doorway, his white eyebrows furrowed over his grey eyes. He had come over to the lighthouse this morning to take Misha fishing.

"I don't know what you mean," she said.

"You know what I mean," he said.

She looked at him for a moment before looking away and nipping her lip as she contemplated her answer. She didn't want to talk about her relationship with Andre with Edmund because she didn't want to talk about something so intimate with her grandfather. But, after seeing the look in Edmund's eyes, she knew she didn't have a choice if she wanted to maintain an honest relationship with him. She'd never lied to him.

"Andre is important to me," she said.

"It's more than that, isn't it? I see the way you look at him. You love him, don't you?" Edmund said gruffly.

She sighed with exasperation. "No, of course not. Can we not talk about this?"

"We need to talk about this. I know how lonely you are, but keep your eyes open. People aren't always what they seem. I know you give them the benefit of the doubt, but that might not be a good idea in this situation," he said.

"What situation are you talking about?" she asked.

"You're a married woman," he said.

"I'm well aware of that. I love Devon. I would never do anything to jeopardize our relationship or our family," she said.

Loralei tried not to raise her voice, but Edmund's words made her feel defensive. She could hear herself sounding shrill.

"I think you already have," he said quietly. "I talked to Blake. He told me he never hired Andre in Detroit to be a cook on his freighter. He just showed up one night and sailed to Portstown with them. No one knows where he came from or who he is. If you want to keep your family safe, and I know you do, I think you need to take another look at who you let into your bedroom. That's all I'm going to say," he said, before turning and leaving the room.

Loralei felt her cheeks warm and flush as she looked after him. Who was Edmund to tell her what to do? He didn't know what it was like to be her, to wait night after night for a man like Devon, who was seldom home and distant when he was. He didn't know what it was like to reach out to a husband over and over again through a wall of misery that he wouldn't allow you to breach. He could never understand what it was like to so desperately need someone like Andre to help heal the pain of a broken marriage and make life bearable for a while. She wished her mother was still alive. She needed another woman to talk to about Devon and Andre, not Edmund. How could her grandfather ever understand what it was like to be a woman with a broken heart?

She ripped the sheets off the bed and tossed the pillows against the wall. She threw herself down on the naked bed and buried her face in her hands. She wanted Devon back, but not the way he was now. She needed a real marriage and a real life with a real husband who loved her and cared for her, not someone who showed up once in a while to fight with her and then leave again. *How could she make a marriage work if she was the only one working on it?*

Edmund was talking to someone in the kitchen. She shook her head impatiently and brushed the tears away. She didn't have the time or the strength to deal with her emotions right then. Loralei stood up and walked to the kitchen to see who Edmund was talking to. She avoided his gaze and greeted Mrs. Petrova, who she saw standing near the doorway.

"Mrs. Petrova. How nice to see you," she said.

"You too, dear. And you, Mishka," Mrs. Petrova said, patting Misha on the head as she walked by him and Edmund into the kitchen to put some books on the table. "Shall we have our lesson now? I have a new word for you," Mrs. Petrova said.

Misha nodded and walked over to her. Mrs. Petrova closed one of her hands and bent her arm sideways in front of her. She held out the thumb of her other hand while making a fist and raised and lowered that hand in front of her other hand two times.

"This is the sign for 'danger.' If you ever need help or if you know a storm is coming, you can use this sign to tell other people there is danger. Okay?" Mrs. Petrova signed.

Mrs. Petrova knew that Misha was afraid of storms. He didn't like the flashes of light from the lightning, and he seemed to be aware of the vibrations in the air from the cracks and rumbles of the ensuing thunder. He usually ran to hide under his bed. Misha nodded and made the sign himself.

"That's very good. You learn these signs very quickly for a boy your age," she signed. Mrs. Petrova smiled and turned to talk to Loralei and Edmund. "I've found a school for Mishka." There is a teacher at the school on the peninsula who teaches deaf children and hearing children together in her class. She is very good and very well known in the area. I think you might want to consider sending Mishka to her class. He is a very intelligent boy, and I think it would be helpful for him to have more ways to communicate than I alone can teach him. I think he would be a good writer," she said.

Mrs. Petrova stopped talking and looked at Loralei as though waiting for her to say something.

"The school across the bay? That's very far away. I don't know how we would get there, but I suppose we could think about it if you think it's important," Loralei said.

"I do, dear. The school begins again soon in the fall, and Mishka is old enough to attend the kindergarten occasionally. And maybe next year, he could attend the kindergarten full-time. I showed the teacher some of the writing he has done under my tutelage, and she agrees that he is exceptionally gifted, especially for his age," Mrs. Petrova said.

"Maybe. What do you think, Grandpapa?" Loralei asked.

She turned to look at Edmund, forgiving him for his earlier comments as she concentrated on this new idea.

"I think it's a good idea. We could cross the bay in the rescue boat. That would cut down the distance to the school considerably. I would be happy to come over in the mornings and row Misha to school in the boat," he said.

"What do you think, Misha? Would you like to go to school?" Loralei signed to him.

Misha nodded.

She looked back at Mrs. Petrova. "We'll do it," she said.

"It's settled then," Mrs. Petrova said, smiling at them all. "This will be a wonderful opportunity for Mishka. Edmund, I think it's wonderful that you will take him to school," she said.

Loralei thought Mrs. Petrova seemed to make a special point to smile at Edmund.

"Yes. Well. We'll see to it," he said.

"I'm so glad. He will benefit greatly from the school. I've always said I thought he was lucky to have such a nice grandfather. I've always said that. He really is, you know. You're to be commended," Mrs. Petrova said, patting her hair into place as she gazed at Edmund.

Loralei watched Edmund smile slightly at Mrs. Petrova

before turning away and heading into the living area.

"He's a very charming man," Mrs. Petrova said.

"He is, isn't he?" Loralei said, smiling at the tender look on Mrs. Petrova's face as she watched Edmund walk away.

***

Andre tapped out the message on the telegraph in Morse Code to his undercover contact on a ship in the Canadian waters. He had waited until Loralei told him she was leaving the lighthouse to check on the foghorn, and on the lock on the fruit cellar, before walking to the communications room and using the radio to send his transmission. He alerted his network that he was available for a covert bombing operation involving freighters sailing through the Soo Locks and was awaiting further instructions. He continued to tap, concentrating as he sent his message again for verification.

"What are you doing?"

Andre heard. He flinched and turned to see Mrs. Petrova standing in the doorway. He paused in his tapping on the telegraph to give her what he hoped was a winning smile.

"Mrs. Petrova," he said, raising his hands to his ears and removing his headphones. "I did not hear you come in. I was listening to some music. Will you join me?"

She looked at him warily and stepped back slowly. "I don't think so." She looked behind her at the door and then back at him with what Andre thought of as an unwavering gaze. "I know what you're doing, young man. You won't get away with this."

He grinned at her. "I am sure I do not know what you are referring to, dear lady. Will you not join me in a dance?" He took a step toward her and watched her take another step back toward the stairwell. "Another time, perhaps?" he asked, grinning again.

"No. This is my country. This is my home. I will not allow you to endanger it," she said.

"That is very noble. You should be very proud of how devoted you are to your country. In the same way, I am devoted to mine," Andre said, taking another step toward her.

"God Bless America," Mrs. Petrova said.

"Dio benedica, l'Italia," Andre said.

***

Loralei pulled open the door of the lighthouse, stepped into the kitchen, and screamed. She had just returned from performing scheduled maintenance on the foghorn and checking the fruit cellar to make sure Jake's grave remained undisturbed and walked in to see a terrible scene. "Mrs. Petrova!"

She ran through the kitchen toward the stairwell. She had seen a crumpled figure lying on the floor when she stepped through the door into the lighthouse. The familiar print on the dress the figure was wearing made Loralei shriek in horror. "Mrs. Petrova. What's happened? Are you okay?"

Loralei sucked in short, shallow breaths as she neared the bottom of the stairwell, trying to comprehend what she was seeing. She groaned and dropped to her knees when she reached the stairwell and felt the baby kick her hard in the stomach.

"No." She turned the figure on the floor at the bottom of the stairwell over to see the fixed, unfocused eyes of Mrs. Petrova staring back at her. Loralei screamed again when she saw the position of Mrs. Petrova's neck. It left no doubt in her mind that Mrs. Petrova was dead. "What could have happened?" she asked, cradling Mrs. Petrova's lifeless body in her arms.

She rocked back and forth, gritting her teeth against the pain in her stomach while holding Mrs. Petrova, unable to accept that she could no longer respond. "We have to get you to a hospital. We have to get you some help," she said, hearing herself sob.

She was barely aware that Andre had come into the lighthouse and was kneeling beside her.

"It is too late for that, Lori. I can tell by the position of her body. What a dreadful accident," Andre said.

Loralei leaned into Andre and wept uncontrollably as

he put his arm around her. "I don't know how this could have happened. I thought she had left."

"Perhaps she returned for something and went looking to find you," Andre said.

"Maybe. I saw some books on the kitchen table," she said. Loralei stiffened. "Where's Misha? I don't want him to see this."

"I believe he is still fishing with Edmund. I will take care of Mrs. Petrova. I will put her in a bedroom, so Misha does not see her, and we will alert the authorities," he said.

Loralei moaned when she felt the baby kick again and put her head on Andre's chest. "Not another death. How could this have happened? What a terrible thing."

"Yes, it is very sad. But Mrs. Petrova was old and not so steady on her feet. These things sometimes happen. It is a high staircase," he said.

"You're right, of course," Loralei said, stifling her sobs as she garnered strength from the comfort she felt from Andre's words.

"Here. Let me take her," Andre said, taking Mrs. Petrova's body from Loralei's embrace. "I believe this is too upsetting for you. You must try to relax and take care of yourself and the baby. I will move Mrs. Petrova to the scullery quarters so she will not be seen."

"Yes, thank you. I don't know what I'd do without you," she said. She felt so relieved to have Andre there to take charge and comfort her in such a horrible situation.

Andre cradled Mrs. Petrova's body in his arms and picked her up to take her through the kitchen to the scullery quarters. "I will take the Jeep into town and alert the authorities. I do not want you to have to go through that," he said as they parted ways in the kitchen.

"Thank you. You're right. I don't feel up to it," Loralei said, massaging the tightness in her stomach and trying to relax.

She was relieved that Andre was taking care of everything

for her. She realized she didn't know anymore how she would live without him. He always seemed to be there for her when things were at their worst, and he made her life so much easier.

"Do not worry, cara mia. I have everything under control. I will take care of everything," he said.

Loralei nodded with relief and took a deep breath as she felt the pain in her stomach begin to lessen. She looked after Andre to take one last glance at Mrs. Petrova before lowering her eyes and preparing to grieve.

***

Andre drove the Jeep into Portstown and parked in front of the sheriff's office on Main Street. He wasn't sure what he was going to say to the sheriff, but Andre knew he would think of something. He was confident his way with words and his ability to tell believable lies would see him through.

Andre pulled open the door to the sheriff's office and stepped inside. The office smelled musty to him, like an unopened closet of old clothes. The black bars of jail cells lined the wall to his left. Andre saw the sheriff, who was sitting behind a desk to his right, look up when he walked in.

"Sheriff, there has been a terrible tragedy," Andre said, thinking it would be best to tell the sheriff right away and dispense with any greetings. "Mrs. Petrova, a citizen of Portstown, fell down the stairs at the lighthouse and died. I have come to alert you to the tragedy. It is such a terrible thing and too much for Mrs. Lancaster, the lighthouse keeper, to bear. She asked me to drive in and talk to you in her stead. I am Andre Soren, the lighthouse tender," Andre said, extending his hand.

Andre saw the sheriff look back at him and sit back in his chair. When the sheriff didn't shake his hand, Andre pulled it back to himself and waited for the sheriff to say something.

"Mrs. Petrova fell? How did that happen?" the sheriff asked.

Andre thought the sheriff was looking at him suspiciously,

and he hurried to give a plausible answer,

"It is not possible for me to say," Andre said, choosing his words carefully. "I was not there. Mrs. Lancaster found Mrs. Petrova's body at the bottom of the stairwell when she returned from working outside the lighthouse. I found Mrs. Lancaster with her when I returned later."

"Where were you?" the sheriff asked.

Andre was beginning to feel uncomfortable. The conversation was not going as he had anticipated. "I was outside doing work as well. I had no way of knowing that Mrs. Petrova was in distress."

"Distress?" the sheriff asked, looking at Andre closely. "That's a strange word to use to describe it. You're the sailor that came in on the Intrepid a few months ago that Mrs. Lancaster hired, aren't you? I've heard about you. Where are you from originally?" the sheriff asked, standing and walking toward him.

Andre was not happy with the way things were going. "I am from Detroit. I have lived there a long time," he said, thinking quickly of something to say. "I have been working at various jobs since the war started because of the layoffs in Detroit, and I am happy to help out at the lighthouse in my current position. I am sure you understand."

"Yeah, sure, I understand," the sheriff said, scowling as he walked closer to him.

"I shall return to the lighthouse now after having alerted you to this terrible tragedy," Andre said, taking a step back and turning to go.

"Yeah, good idea. I'll meet you out there," the sheriff said.

Andre walked quickly to the door.

"Don't go anywhere," the sheriff added.

"I would not think of it," Andre said, pulling open the door and stepping out into the street.

He walked as quickly as he could to the Jeep and climbed in. He started the vehicle, pushed his foot down hard on the accelerator, and raced out of town. He wanted to get back to the lighthouse as soon as possible. The meeting with the sheriff had not gone well, and he realized now what a precarious situation he was in. It seemed his presence in Portstown was not as covert as he had hoped. The sheriff was well aware of his whereabouts and, possibly, it seemed, of his comings and goings about town. And the sheriff knew Andre worked at the lighthouse and had come in on a freighter from Detroit two months ago. The sheriff did not appear, to Andre, to have much trust in him, and when Andre told him about Mrs. Petrova's death, he hadn't been sure the sheriff was going to let him leave. He'd seemed inordinately suspicious. Andre knew that strangers were suspect in this time of war, especially in small towns around the Soo Locks, and he realized his presence had not gone unnoticed. Getting away with murder in this town, it seemed to him, might be more difficult than he had imagined.

He turned off the road and screeched up the gravel path to the lighthouse. He wasn't sure what he was going to do when the sheriff came out to the lighthouse to investigate Mrs. Petrova's death, but he knew he was going to have to make plans to leave Portstown as soon as possible, maybe even sooner than he had planned. He didn't know if the sheriff or the townspeople, for that matter, would allow him to stay around for much longer.

CHAPTER 16

Andre pulled the Jeep into the small shed near the lighthouse and jumped out to run to the lighthouse and find Loralei. He found her in the kitchen talking with Edmund and Misha. Edmund gave him a long, contemplative stare.

"Andre, I'm so glad you're back. Did you talk to the authorities?" Loralei asked.

"Yes, the sheriff will come out soon," he said.

Loralei nodded. "Misha, it's time for bed. Go and put your pajamas on, and I'll come in later to read you a story. Okay?" she signed to him.

Misha nodded as he got up from his chair and left the room.

Andre looked at Edmund, who had continued to stare at him throughout the conversation.

"Where were you while Mrs. Petrova was in the lighthouse? I should have thought you would have stayed here with her while she finished grading the papers and done some work," Edmund said, frowning.

"Yes, that had been my plan, sir. But instead, I went to the beach and made further repairs to the rescue boat. It was very unnerving to return and find Loralei dealing with such a dreadful situation," Andre said.

He held Edmund's gaze without wavering. He had already told a similar story about working outside the lighthouse to the sheriff in town, although he wasn't sure it had been accepted as the truth. Andre was relieved to see Edmund nod and look away. It seemed to him that his explanation had satisfied Edmund, at least for the moment. Loralei made coffee, and they sat at the table to wait for the sheriff.

"Did the sheriff say what time he was coming out?" she asked after a while.

Before he could answer, Loralei jumped at what sounded like a car crunching through the gravel path outside the lighthouse.

"He's here," she said.

Her face turned bright red, and she appeared to be perspiring. Andre wondered how she would handle the interrogation that was almost certain to take place when the sheriff came in. He wondered how he would handle it, too. But he calmed himself with the fact that he had been in perilous situations many times before and had always been able to talk his way out of them. He stood back to appraise the unfolding situation as Loralei went to answer the knock on the lighthouse door.

***

"Sheriff, won't you come in?" Loralei asked when she opened the door.

"Mrs. Lancaster," he said, nodding and walking past her into the kitchen. "I understand there's been an accident."

"Yes, a terrible tragedy," Loralei answered, trying to control the tremor in her voice. "Mrs. Petrova fell down the stairs. I found her when I came back from doing my outdoor chores. It's unbelievable."

"Yes, it is. That's how I would describe it, too. Unbelievable," the sheriff said, giving Loralei what she thought of as a penetrating stare.

She was taken aback by the sheriff's tone of voice. She didn't know what to say in return to such an obvious statement of distrust. The sheriff walked past her further into the kitchen. She looked behind him to see a man in a suit and two men in work clothes rolling a stretcher through the door.

"This is the coroner. He'll need to see the body," the sheriff said.

"Of course," Loralei said, heading toward the scullery quarters.

"First, show me where you found her," the sheriff said. "Maybe one of you gentlemen could show the coroner the body," he said, looking at Edmund.

Edmund stood at the sheriff's request and walked over to lead the men to the scullery quarters. Loralei shivered as she watched them walk past, rolling the stretcher. She turned and walked to the stairwell with the sheriff following behind her.

"Here," she said, feeling a catch in her throat. "She was lying here at the bottom of the stairs. I didn't see her face until I turned her over. That's when I knew she was...dead," she said, sobbing in spite of herself.

"I'm sure it was very upsetting. Where was your lighthouse tender at the time?" the sheriff asked.

"I'm not sure. I assume he was outside somewhere. He came in later after I found her and helped me carry her into the scullery quarters so my son wouldn't see what had happened," she said.

"That was very chivalrous of him. Unfortunately, he disturbed a crime scene by moving the body. That's not considered lawful behavior. We're going to need to talk about this further," the sheriff said.

"Of course," Loralei said.

"How far up does this go?" he asked, climbing the stairs.

"Sixty-five feet to the top, up seventy-two steps. She must

have fallen down the staircase or over the railing. I don't know," she said.

He climbed the stairs and came back down. "Yes, well, it's certainly high enough to kill someone. I'll have some other people come out to do a more thorough investigation. I'm going to leave it at this for now because I can see how hard this is on you. But make no mistake, Mrs. Lancaster, we take this kind of tragedy seriously in this town."

"Of course," she said again.

"One other thing. Jake Calico disappeared around here about two months ago after an investigation showed he sabotaged the lighthouse beacon. We've been looking for him ever since to bring him to justice. Any idea what happened to him?"

Loralei paused and looked away. "No, I'm sorry. I have no idea," she answered.

"Yeah, I didn't think so," the sheriff said, shaking his head.

Loralei heard him scoff as he walked past her toward the kitchen. She felt her heart skip a beat as she wondered if it was possible a further investigation could uncover Jake's body in the fruit cellar. She shook her head to put such a disturbing thought out of her mind and made a note to herself to get rid of the unseemly smell that had developed in the cellar. As she followed him into the kitchen, she saw the two men in work clothes roll a stretcher into the kitchen that carried a long, black, zippered body bag, following the coroner. Loralei cringed, knowing that it was Mrs. Petrova on the stretcher. The sheriff walked over to them.

"Looks like the cause of death is a broken neck, likely the result of the fall. I understand from Edmund here that's what happened. The woman fell down the lighthouse stairwell," the coroner said, addressing the sheriff.

"Apparently," the sheriff said.

The coroner turned to address the rest of them. "I'm sorry, everyone. I'm sure this is very hard on you. It's very sad. We'll be going now."

He walked through the kitchen with the men rolling the stretcher behind him, and they left through the lighthouse door. Loralei swallowed hard. She knew Mrs. Petrova was dead, but hearing it from the coroner seemed so final and dreadful. She looked over to see the sheriff looking at her with his penetrating black eyes.

"Call me anytime, Mrs. Lancaster, if you want to talk. You can reach me at the department in town," he said.

Loralei was uneasy with the shrewd look he gave her when he talked to her.

He turned to Andre and scowled. "We'll talk again soon," he said.

He turned and walked out, giving Andre a short, backward glance. Loralei walked over and closed the door behind him. She leaned forward and covered her face with her hands. She stood there for a moment, struggling to regain control of her scattered emotions before lowering her hands and looking at Andre and Edmund.

"We are not to talk of this again," she said firmly, standing up straight and walking through the kitchen. "We will remember Mrs. Petrova for the wonderful way she lived and not for the terrible way she died."

She lowered her eyes and walked past Andre and her silent grandfather. She headed into the other room to read Misha his bedtime story.

Later in the evening, Loralei walked back into the kitchen and heard the door close behind Edmund as he left. She was glad she was alone in the kitchen with Andre because she wanted to talk to him about Mrs. Petrova's death and about what the sheriff had said.

"What a dreadful day. I didn't think it would ever end," she said, sitting next to Andre at the kitchen table.

"It was a long day," Andre said, looking over at her.

She paused for a moment before deciding to talk to Andre about the sheriff.

"I thought the sheriff seemed unusually suspicious of Mrs. Petrova's death. He made me feel very guilty, as though it was my fault she fell down the stairwell. I wonder why he was like that," she said.

"He did seem suspicious. I felt the same way, but you cannot let it bother you. You must recover from the death in your own way and not think about the sheriff. It was an unfortunate occurrence, but time will help you deal with it," Andre said, touching her arm.

"I hope so," she said, glad that Andre was there for her once again at such a traumatic time. "I was also afraid that the sheriff might search the lighthouse for clues about Jake. He asked me about Jake's death. Did he ask you about it?"

"No. Not yet, anyway. Do not worry about such things. Jake is buried in the fruit cellar under the shelves. I do not think you need to worry about his body being discovered. It is well hidden," Andre said.

"I hope so. If his body was ever discovered, my life at the lighthouse would most certainly come to an end," she said.

"He will not be discovered," Andre said firmly. He stood and took her hand. "Come to bed, Lori. You need your sleep, as do I." He gently pulled her from her chair to stand.

"Yes, you're right. We need to put this day behind us," she said.

And for the first time, as she let Andre put his arm around her and walk with her toward the bedroom, Loralei felt as though Andre was a trusted friend and not just her lover.

***

Loralei stepped through the door into the narthex of the old Methodist Church in town. She was relieved to be out of the sprinkling rain of the cold fall morning. The church smelled musty and damp, like old logs of pine left to rot in the woods by the lake. What had happened, she wondered, to the light, airy church brightened with sun-streamed colors from the stained glass windows in the sanctuary she remembered from her youth? She had visited the church a few times with Misha on Sundays in the past, and she had been there to see her seascapes displayed in the alcove off the narthex a few years ago, but that was all. She looked around at the townspeople silently gathered in the sanctuary and hoped she was on time for Mrs. Petrova's funeral. The last few days had been difficult for her, dealing with the authorities and her own personal grief over Mrs. Petrova's tragic accident at the lighthouse. She needed the formal ceremony of the funeral to help her deal with her grief. She also hoped gathering with others to pay tribute to Mrs. Petrova would help her find a way to talk to Misha about why they wouldn't be seeing her anymore.

She took Misha's hand and turned to look back at Edmund, leaning on his cane and following her through the door into the church. He looked so old and sad to her, not at all like the stalwart, stoic figure she knew him to be. Mrs. Petrova's death seemed to weigh heavily on his mind. Loralei was relieved that Andre had insisted on tending the lighthouse for them while they attended the funeral. He had been adamant that they allow him to do that for them so they could pay their last tributes to their friend in peace. She felt so blessed to have him there for her.

Loralei saw Annie Paxton, her friend from high school, walking over to talk to her.

"Loralei, I'm so glad you could make it. I'm sure Mrs. Petrova would have been glad to know you are here. It's such a terrible tragedy. God will see us through this. I know Mrs. Petrova would have said that if she were still with us," Annie said.

"Thank you. I wanted to be here. My lighthouse tender is watching the lighthouse for me," Loralei said.

"How nice. And is this Misha? Aren't you getting big?" Annie said.

Misha didn't say anything. Loralei knew it was because he hadn't heard Annie, but Loralei didn't want to sign to him at the moment. She had spotted Carlotta sitting in a side pew with her lustrous, black hair done up in what Loralei thought was a rather overabundant amount of curls for a funeral, and she was trying to think of a way to walk in without Carlotta seeing her. It didn't seem the appropriate time to risk another confrontation with her about Jake. Loralei looked back at Edmund. She was relieved to see that he was talking to Finn and Marie, who had apparently just come in. Loralei gasped when she saw the sheriff walk in behind them. She hoped he wasn't there to ask questions. Misha released her hand and ran over to hug Marie. Maybe, Loralei thought, she and her family could all sit together in the back, and Carlotta and the sheriff would leave them alone.

"Come sit with us," Marie said, walking toward Loralei with Misha in tow. "What a terrible thing for you to have to deal with. Mrs. Petrova was a wonderful person, and we'll all miss her. I'm sure you and Misha will miss her the most, though. I know what a good sign language teacher she was for him," she said.

"Yes. She was like a grandmother to Misha, although, of course, she wasn't the same as Mother would have been if she was still alive. I still can't believe she's gone," Loralei said.

Marie hugged Loralei and took her by the arm. Loralei let her lead her into the church as she kept an eye out for what Carlotta was doing and looked around for the sheriff. She didn't see him. They found an open pew where they could all sit together and scooted in. Marie touched Loralei's arm when they sat down together and whispered to her.

"I saw you looking at Carlotta. You won't have to worry about her and Devon anymore. I heard she's marrying Captain Blake at the end of the month, and they're moving out east. Captain Blake's going to sail freighters on the ocean instead of here on the lakes. Carlotta won't be around to bother you much longer," Marie said.

Loralei breathed a sigh of relief. "Thanks for telling me."

Loralei settled back to listen to the soothing music of the organ that had begun playing a traditional hymn. She saw Marie leaning toward her out of the corner of her eye.

"How is Andre working out? Some of the people in town that I've talked to seem a little concerned that he's staying at the lighthouse. No one really knows who he is or where he's from. Dan Paxton said he could come out and help with the lighthouse maintenance if you need it," she said.

Loralei wasn't sure what Marie meant about Andre, but she was quick to defend him. "Andre's wonderful. He's doing a great job, and I don't know what I'd do without him. There's nothing to worry about," Loralei said.

"Okay. Just thought I'd ask," Marie said.

Loralei wasn't sure Marie was convinced that everything was all right.

"By the way, Finn and I were talking. If you need help after the baby's born, I could stay with you at the lighthouse for a while. We'll get some other help for Finn at the tavern, and I'll come stay with you. I miss the lighthouse, and I'm sure you could use an extra hand."

"I really could. Thanks, Marie," Loralei said.

Loralei breathed another sigh of relief, thankful her sister was apparently looking out for her. They got through the funeral in the church in peace, and Loralei was glad she had come into town for it. As they stood out on the lawn drinking lemonade and eating cookies afterward with the surprisingly large crowd that had gathered, Loralei exchanged pleasantries with many of the townspeople she hadn't seen since the fundraising dance for the war effort. She kept her distance from Carlotta and from the sheriff, who she noticed seemed to be talking to a lot of people.

Loralei felt a drop of rain on her cheek and looked up at the sky. It was starting to sprinkle again. She saw low-lying grey clouds in the distance moving slowly across the pale-grey sky, and she wasn't sure she liked the look of them. She'd seen clouds like that before, before the Armistice Day storm on the Great Lakes two years ago and before other storms in the past, usually in November. Deadly gales that sometimes lasted for days didn't usually come this early in the fall, but it wasn't unheard of. Loralei took one last look over her shoulder at the sheriff and hurried to retrieve Misha and find her grandfather. She wanted to get back to the lighthouse as soon as possible and listen to a weather report.

***

The weather forecast called for rain. Devon had heard it while he was on the bridge of the *Manitoulin* on their return trip to Portstown after leaving Detroit more than a week ago. He had been talking to Lanny about the paperwork involved in officially transferring command from him to Lanny when the transmission for the weather report came through. Storms were in the area, and the coast guard had issued a high seas warning for the following morning. He hoped they could make it to the channel entering the Soo Locks before the storms rolled in and wait out the storms there, but he wasn't sure they would make it. If they did make it, he thought they should stay on the St. Mary's River and not sail through into Lake Superior. Lake Superior could oftentimes be extremely rough sailing in bad weather. Devon grimaced as he remembered that he didn't have much say in that type of decision anymore.

Devon had read the radio transmission from Loralei a few days ago, informing him and Lanny of Mrs. Petrova's untimely death at the lighthouse. He wanted to return to Portstown as soon as possible to find out exactly what had happened and to be there for Loralei, but he didn't want to risk the safety of the *Manitoulin* to do so. It upset him that Lanny didn't seem to feel the same way about the safety of the *Manitoulin* as he did. Devon knew Lanny wanted to sail ahead through the forecasted bad weather to keep on schedule and impress the shipping corporation with his expertise as a captain by arriving, on time or sooner, in Portstown. He had tried to convince Lanny to reconsider his position and to anchor in the St. Mary's River at the Soo Locks instead of sailing through into Lake Superior. The weather reports and his gut told him they were in for a legendary squall, but it did not appear that Lanny agreed with him. Devon was beside himself with frustration.

He stood on deck, looking across the grey waves of Lake Huron at the sky above the horizon. It seemed a strange color to him, one he hadn't seen often. He tried to remember when the last time was that he'd seen a sky like that. And then it came to him. Armistice Day. The sky had been that color before the Armistice Day storm on the Great Lakes in November two years ago that had shipwrecked his and Loralei's fathers' freighter on Lake Superior and taken their lives. He thought of Loralei's painting of that day. It was the painting of their fathers on their freighter right before the deadly storm that had sent them to their deaths. It was the painting he had delivered to the Detroit Institute of the Arts when the *Manitoulin* was in port in Detroit several days ago. It was the painting with the sky of the same pale grey color he was looking at right now. Devon turned and headed to the pilot house to find Lanny. It was time they had another talk.

CHAPTER 17

Andre walked to the communications room off the kitchen after making sure the door to the lighthouse was securely locked. He didn't want anyone walking in on him again while he radioed his spy network. He had determined, after meeting with the sheriff about the death of Mrs. Petrova, that it was imperative that he leave Portstown as soon as possible. His mission, as it had been initially laid out, of gathering information on the Great Lakes shipping operation — and the Soo Locks, in particular — was complete. He wanted to deliver the information, sketches, and paintings to his spy network as soon as possible. He didn't want to stay any longer to act as an intermediary to smuggle bombs on freighters or attempt to sabotage the Soo Locks himself. He feared for his freedom and perhaps even his life. It appeared to him, from what the sheriff had said, that he was suspected by the townspeople of having something to do with the disappearance of Jake Calico, who the townspeople had wanted to bring to justice themselves for sabotaging the lighthouse beacon. For the first time, Andre began to think of himself in the way the townspeople could be thinking of him. He was a stranger, an interloper, who was upsetting the socially set ways of the town, and they didn't like it. They didn't like him. He needed to escape Portstown and return to his own country of Italy as soon as possible. He was not even going to return to France first. He needed to return to the safety and security of his motherland.

He sat down in front of the telegraph and put on the headphones. He twisted the dial on the transmitter until he reached the pre-set frequency he used to communicate with his contact. He hoped his contact on a ship in the Canadian waters would pick up his signal even though his transmission was not being sent at a predetermined time, as it usually was. It was imperative that he send his message and set up a rendezvous point with the ship to leave the country. Andre sat up straight when he received the signal to transmit. His contact had picked up his signal.

Andre tapped out the secret code message in French, "Tu es en cheval?" along with his location, signaling to his contact that he was ready for pick up. He held his breath, waiting for the return transmission. His life could depend on the response. He thought of Loralei, his lovely Loralei, and of Misha, and of Loralei's unborn child. He wanted to bring them with him. He didn't want to leave Loralei here by herself, without a husband to take care of her, in this vast, lonely wilderness of isolation and danger. He wanted to bring her with him and raise a family with her in Italy. He tried to think of how that was possible.

The return transmission tapped and crackled in his ear.

"Oui. Three days. Portstown pier at midnight. Red flag on the mast. Leave no one behind," it said.

Andre sat stunned for a moment, feeling a shiver of dread. He had been expecting the transmission, but still, the contact's sign-off shook him to the core. He knew what it meant. His mission was concluded. Before he left the country, he was to kill anyone who had any knowledge of his actions and could alert the authorities. That included Loralei, who had gone to the Soo Locks with him. Andre shook his head. His spy training told him that he wasn't to feel anything. He was only to carry out his orders and fulfill his mission. But he did feel something. He loved Loralei.

Andre tapped his affirmation and signed off. He took his headphones off and sat for a moment, contemplating his next move. He took a deep breath and decided on a course of action. He was going to bring Loralei with him, along with Misha. It could be difficult to convince Loralei to leave, but it was the only option. He would make it work.

Andre stood and headed for the stairwell. They would have to make it to the ship between midnight and dawn in three days when it docked in Portstown. The ship would leave by dawn if he didn't show up to avoid detection by the coast guard. And he needed to make plans to assure that he was able to escape the townspeople and the sheriff without incident. At some point, he knew he would have to get in touch with the Statler Hotel in Detroit to have his trunk and personal items sent to his address in Italy, where he had decided to return instead of France. But he would do that later. Loralei and Misha and Edmund would be in town, at least the rest of the morning, for Mrs. Petrova's funeral. He would work around the lighthouse and act as though nothing had changed when they returned.

Andre suspected, from the way that Edmund had acted during the sheriff's investigation, that Edmund was beginning to question his background and integrity. Edmund could have suspicions that he had something to do with Mrs. Petrova's death and maybe even Jake's disappearance. Andre realized he was going to have to be on his guard around the lighthouse, and around Edmund, in particular.

Andre climbed the staircase to the top of the lighthouse to check on the beacon. He needed to make sure the beacon was in working order, especially to ensure that his contact and escape ship would make it into Portstown safely for the rendezvous.

As he stepped from the top step into the lantern room,

he was struck by the greyness of the light in the fall morning. He walked over to the window and looked out across the lake. Wisps of feathery, silver clouds floated in the distance above the rippling waves of the lake. It was an odd color for the sky, he thought, its pale grey, almost pearly luminescence reflected in the pale grey color of the lake. But he was used to how quickly the weather changed in Portstown, and he wasn't too concerned.

He turned his attention to the lighthouse beacon and went about checking the electrical wiring and polishing the Fresnel lens and brass workings. It was important to Loralei, he knew, that he keep the beacon in pristine condition to bring the sailors home safely. Andre smiled as he thought of Loralei and their future together in Italy. He knew she would come with him. It was the only way. Andre concentrated on completing his meticulous work, checking the beacon for proper rotation to ensure that the flashes it emitted were properly timed and uniform in the way that Loralei wanted them to be. He smiled as he went about his work, thinking of Loralei and how happy she would be when he told her that he had taken care of everything and that they could be together at last. He wanted to please his lovely lady of the light.

***

Loralei sat on a wooden bench in the familiar, makeshift chapel in the woods in front of a handmade cross nailed to a wood-slatted backdrop. She had gone to the chapel with Misha after Mrs. Petrova's funeral to seek solace by being in a place that reminded her of her father. Loralei remembered asking her father, when they were praying by themselves at the small log-sided chapel with its wood-shingled roof that her father had built for their family long ago, how he was so sure that there was a god, even though she had been frightened as a child to question his stalwart faith. He had looked up from his prayer for a moment, gazed at her intently with his deep, hazel-brown eyes that warmed when he talked to her alone, and said, "Anyone who has ever looked north over the vast, wild beauty of Lake Superior, washed in the rich, tranquil rays of the rising or setting sun, knows there is a god."

She thought of that now as she remembered her father's sometimes poetic voice when he talked to her. She remembered his stoic, commanding ways and his fierce, protective love for their family. Loralei felt a momentary pang of guilt when she thought about how her father would have reacted to her keeping Jake's death a secret. He wouldn't have approved, just as he wouldn't have approved of the way she found solace in the arms of men other than her husband. But she had come to terms with that. What she hadn't yet come to terms with was being an unwilling accomplice to Jake's murder and her father's almost certain disapproval of that. It bothered her to think she could have let him down. She had always wanted him to be proud of her. Her father had loved her, Loralei knew, in the same fierce, protective way he loved his family and his country. And she had loved him back. She still loved him and always would, no matter that he was no longer physically present. She held him in her heart.

"Mama, you cry," Misha signed.

She brushed the tears from her cheeks and hugged him. He was sitting next to her and raising his fingers toward her face.

"Is there 'danger'?" he signed.

"No. I'm okay, dear," she said.

"I will always save you, Mama. I don't want you to cry," he signed.

She held Misha close and thought of her family and how they had always lived by the moods of the sun, by its rising and setting, by its dawning and gloaming, and by its presence by day and disappearance by night. In the same way, the beacon lived by the moods of the sun. It shone in the evening when the sun went down and rested in the morning when the sun rose again. She was proud to be the lady of the light, tending the beacon as a mother tends her child, keeping the beacon alive and secure. And she was proud of the beacon, the lady of the night, holding out her brilliant, nocturnal arms to her sons, the sailors, who watched for her bright light to bring them safely home.

Loralei looked down at Misha. "Did you know I used to come here with my father?" she asked.

"Your father who went to heaven and isn't coming back?" Misha signed.

"Yes," Loralei said, nodding.

"Where Mrs. Petrova is?" Misha signed.

She nodded again. Loralei watched as Misha appeared to contemplate her answer for a while. He looked to her like he was deep in thought.

"Come with me. I will show you where my father is buried," she said.

Loralei took Misha's hand and led him deeper into the woods down a gnarled path to the family graveyard that was in an open meadow under a copse of trees. She paused in front of her father's gravestone. She remembered coming here on Armistice Day to remember him after ringing the lighthouse bell. She had received special permission from the town to ring the lighthouse bell twenty-four times on that day, to honor her father and Devon's father and the twenty-two other members of the crew who had perished with them when their freighter went down in the Great Lakes storm on Armistice Day two years before. Many of those onboard the freighter had left friends and family behind in Portstown. The ringing of the bell had provided some solace to her, and she hoped, to the town as well. But her grief still felt raw and unassuaged as she stood in front of her father's gravestone today.

"Here. This is where my father is buried. I come here to talk to him sometimes," Loralei signed after touching the gravestone.

"Can he hear you?" Misha asked with his hands.

"I think he can, and that's good enough for me," Loralei

signed.

Misha stood in front of the gravestone silently for a moment before reaching into his pocket and pulling out a Petosky stone. He walked over and placed it carefully on the grave.

"I will leave this here for him," he signed.

Loralei was enthralled. She couldn't believe Misha had done something so sentimental that meant so much to her.

"He would like that," she said, walking over and holding Misha close.

"Maybe he can give it to Mrs. Petrova if he sees her in heaven," he signed.

Loralei didn't know what to say. Her heart swelled in her chest as she looked at her lovely young son's hopeful, upturned face and trusting eyes.

"Maybe," she replied, signing.

They stood together in stillness until the wind picked up and rustled the leaves in the surrounding trees.

"We must go before the storm comes in. Perhaps we'll return another time," Loralei signed to Misha.

Misha nodded and turned with her to leave the meadow. She took Misha's hand and walked with him back through the rustling woods to the lighthouse.

***

Devon stood, fuming, on the upper deck outside the pilot house. He had just talked to Lanny again about the incoming storms and was not happy with the way their conversation was going. While Lanny had agreed with him about pushing the *Manitoulin* to reach the Soo Locks ahead of schedule to outrun the storms on Lake Huron, he had not agreed that anchoring in the channel at the Soo Locks was a good idea. Lanny wanted to press on into Lake Superior and get back to port in Portstown as soon as possible. He wanted to make points with the shipping corporation by sailing as far ahead of schedule as possible and bringing the shipment of coal to Portstown in record time. Devon vehemently disagreed.

He wanted to wait out the storm in the locks to avoid sailing on into Lake Superior in what the weather report forecasted to be extremely hazardous conditions. He had seen the way Lake Superior treated its sailors during blustery gales, and he didn't want any part of it. He was standing on deck to cool down before heading back into the pilot house to argue with Lanny some more

Devon saw the dark grey bank of thunderheads forming to the north even before the officer of the deck gave warning of its appearance on the horizon. He felt it suck the oxygen from the air, even from its distance, as it puffed out its bloated, menacing clouds. He stomped across the deck toward the pilothouse and threw open the door when he reached it.

"Lanny. It's a gale. The storms are coming in from Canada in the north down over Lake Huron. I can see them. We have to get to the Soo Locks now. There's no time to waste," he shouted as he stomped inside.

"It's Captain Thompson to you, Devon. We're going as fast as safely possible. You know that. We're not going to increase knots. We'll make up for lost time once we get into Lake Superior," Lanny said.

"No. That won't work. Lake Superior is the last place we want to be in this gale. You know as well as I do what the lake does to its sailors during a storm. We'll be at the bottom of the lake before we know what hit us," Devon said, feeling his face grow hot as the anger rushed through his body.

"I don't agree," Lanny said.

"Damnit, Lanny. I've been captain a lot longer than you have. Listen to me," Devon shouted.

"First mate, confine this man to his quarters," Lanny said, throwing his hands up in obvious frustration. "You're confined to your cabin until further notice," he said to Devon.

"What? You can't do that. You need me," Devon said.

"I think it best that you follow orders, Devon if you know what's good for you. That will be all," Lanny said.

He turned his back on Devon, and it was all Devon could do to keep from tackling him and wrestling him to the ground. Lanny didn't have a clue what he was doing, and the *Manitoulin* and its crew would suffer for it. Devon was sure of it. He looked at the crewmen standing between him and Lanny, gesturing him toward the door. Devon took a deep breath and tried to regain control of himself. Finally, feeling as though he had no other options, he turned around and left through the door with the crewmen following him. He walked across the deck, taking another look at the growing menace of the imminent storm, before descending the ladder to the lower deck and heading back to his cabin.

***

Loralei slipped her new, yellow gingham curtains onto a curtain rod and hung them in the window of the bedroom next to Misha's bedroom. She was decorating the small room as a nursery for the baby when he or she came. She smiled as she looked at the wooden crib her grandfather had set up for her near the wall and the rocking chair she had rocked in to nurse Misha that she had placed nearby. Just a few more weeks, or maybe a month, according to Doc Bailey, and she would have a new son or daughter to care for. Loralei smiled at the thought.

When she had returned to the lighthouse from the chapel, she had put Misha down for a nap and done some mending on Devon's work shirts in case he returned at some time and needed to wear them. Andre was outside near the woods, chopping wood for the stove that she was planning to use later to boil potatoes for dinner. Loralei was comforted by the routine, domestic nature of the afternoon, and she found herself relaxing and putting her cares away for another day. She was tired of feeling sad and remembered she had happy things to think about, too. She had stopped at the post office on the way home from the funeral and found a letter from the Detroit Institute of the Arts. The letter said that the curators at the institute were very impressed with her painting and wanted her permission to display it at the institute. Loralei was excited, although somewhat timorous, to think her art could generate such a response and so quickly. She had been waiting for the appropriate time to tell Andre and her grandfather about it.

As she adjusted the curtains on the rod, she glanced out the window at the gloomy sky. She saw the trees bending in the wind and decided to use the radio again to find a weather report. As she turned to go, she saw Edmund standing in the doorway of the bedroom. The look on his face sent a shiver of fear down her spine.

"What is it? What happened?" she asked.

"I found this in Andre's room in the scullery quarters," Edmund said.

Edmund handed her a small booklet with a leather cover.

Loralei took it from him.

"What is this?" she asked.

"A passport," he said.

Loralei opened it to find Andre's photo inside with an inscription written underneath it. Loralei read it out loud.

"'Tu es un cheval?' What does that mean?" she asked.

That means, "Are you a horse? In French," Edmund said.

She furrowed her eyebrows together. "'Are you a horse?' Why would anyone write something like that?" she asked.

"It's a code phrase," Edmund said.

Loralei had seldom seen him look so serious.

"It's a code phrase to cross the border into or out of French-speaking Canada. There's only one reason someone would have this. Andre's a spy," he said.

Loralei felt her spine go rigid. "A spy? The French are on our side, and so is Canada. How could Andre be a spy? Why couldn't he just speak in French without a code?" She thought about it for a moment before it dawned on her. She met Edmund's gaze. "That's right, Loralei. He wouldn't need a code unless he was a spy. He must be working for the other side. And I think he knows that I know."

"I don't believe you. It can't be true," Loralei said.

She felt herself beginning to shake. After all they'd shared and all they'd meant to each other, she couldn't accept that Andre could be the enemy.

"It's true. He's probably here as part of an operation to sabotage the Soo Locks. It's what we've all been told to look out for. It's what all the soldiers are stationed here for. They're protecting the Soo Locks. They're protecting our country from an attack. Do you understand what I'm saying? Andre's a threat to our national security. We have to save our country from him," Edmund said.

She shook her head. She couldn't believe that what Edmund was saying was true. "I don't believe you. Andre would never do something like this."

"Believe me. There's something else. I'm not sure you'll understand what this means to the security of our country, but I do. I found invoices from Davison's shipyard, a shipbuilding company, showing where minesweepers are going to be sent. They're specially equipped wooden boats that can sweep shallow water for mines and destroy them. If the Germans find out where these boats are, they'll know where we're sweeping for mines, and they'll know what beaches in Europe we want to land on. We could lose the war over this. It's that important."

Loralei gasped. She couldn't believe what Edmund was telling her. Andre couldn't possibly be a spy. She shook her head. "I don't believe it. Andre would never do something like this."

Edmund took the passport back from her and turned to go. "I'm going to walk into town and talk to the sheriff. I don't want to take the Jeep and have Andre wonder where it is. Keep the doors locked, and don't let him know that I know about him. It's very important that you listen to me, Loralei," he said, firmly.

Loralei watched Edmund through the kitchen window as

he walked down the gravel road outside the lighthouse. She was sure he was wrong. The phrase on the passport could have meant anything. She was positive it was just a silly saying. And as for the rest? How could invoices possibly be that important?

It was getting dark and hard to see. She impatiently brushed the mist from her eyes and started making dinner.

**

Andre stacked his last load of chopped wood in the woodshed next to the lighthouse. The air was thick and humid, and he wiped his brow to clear it of the sweat that dripped into his eyes. The evening had tiptoed in amongst the heavy clouds of the darkening afternoon, and he found himself struggling to see his way back to the lighthouse. Loralei had left a light on in the kitchen window, and he followed its dim glow to the door and stepped inside. He found Loralei standing at the stove and walked over to add some wood to the firebox.

"There is enough wood for a few months, cara mia (my beloved). I stacked it in the shed. The air is heavy outside. Perhaps the storm will arrive soon," Andre said.

Loralei looked up from her work and gazed at him intently.

"What is it? Did something happen?" he asked when he saw the look in her eyes.

"No, of course not. Why do you ask?" she asked.

Andre felt himself suddenly on alert. He didn't know what it was that made him uneasy. "I saw Edmund leave earlier. I thought he was staying for dinner," he said.

"He was, but something came up. He left and said he wouldn't be back tonight," she said.

"I see," Andre said.

He watched her warily for a moment before deciding his feelings had more to do with knowing that he had to leave the country soon than anything personal to do with him and Loralei. He knew she had had a long day and that the funeral had been difficult for her. He decided to give her some peace and leave her alone. He turned to go and wash up for dinner.

"Andre, wait," Loralei said.

"Yes? What is it?" he asked, turning back toward her.

"Do you love me?" she asked.

He paused and smiled slowly. "More than you can know, la mia bella signora della luce," he said.

She looked down.

"You would never hurt me?" she asked.

"Never. You are my love," Andre said.

Loralei looked back up at him, and he held her gaze, wondering what it was that he saw in her eyes.

"I'm glad," she said softly, as she looked away again.

Andre stood for a moment and watched her as she went back to her work. She was so beautiful and vulnerable. He hoped they might spend another romantic night together, sequestered in their cozy room of love against the turmoil of a raging storm. He smiled to himself as he turned and left the kitchen, leaving her behind.

***

Andre made sure Loralei was busy washing the dinner dishes before he picked up the telephone in the room off the kitchen and called the long distance operator. He asked to be put through to the number of the Statler Hotel in Detroit. Andre didn't want to use the phone, but he had no other options. He was planning to leave the country soon and needed to have his belongings shipped from his hotel room at the Statler Hotel in Detroit back to Italy, where he was planning to return.

"Statler Hotel. How may I assist you?"

He heard when the phone was answered on the other end.

"Yes, this is the city utilities regulations inspector," Andre said. "I have been asked to check the hotel for violations. It is imperative that I speak with the registration clerk about the absence of heat in several rooms. I have been informed that the hotel rooms are very cold."

"One moment, please," Andre heard on the phone. After a moment, the phone was answered again. "Hello. Is this the city's inspector? I have been informed that the rooms are cold. Is it also cold in the rooms up north?" he asked.

"Yes, very cold," Andre replied, using the code phrase of the spy network.

"One moment."

He heard. Shortly thereafter, the phone was answered again.

"Andre, is it you? Is it really you?"

He heard Angelina Rossi's shaky voice on the other end of the phone. He realized she must have been staying in his room while he was gone. Il Capo must have arranged everything related to Angelina's secret mission as well as his own.

"Yes, it is. I need my things returned to our home. I am leaving soon," he said evasively, in case someone was listening in on their conversation.

"You must leave now. I will take care of everything here. It is cold up north for people taking photographs with cameras and for those who recognize them," Angelina said.

He felt a stab of dread as he realized Angelina was telling him he had been seen and recognized buying the camera or taking pictures with it in the Sault Ste. Marie. He realized he needed to leave the country immediately for his own safety.

"Yes, of course. Be well," he said, feeling suddenly nostalgic about their trip together across the ocean from France but realizing he felt nothing more for Angelina than for that of a charming acquaintance.

He realized at that moment while talking to Angelina that he was in love with Loralei.

"I must go," Andre said quietly, knowing that he would probably never see Angelina again.

"Be well," Angelina said.

Andre heard the phone go silent and hung up. He stared

at it for a moment before standing to leave the room. He had things to do. He needed to leave the country through Canada immediately.

CHAPTER 18

Loralei finished washing the dinner dishes and stacked them next to the sink to dry. She would put them away in the morning. It had been a long day, and she was ready for bed. She had checked on Misha and found him sleeping soundly with Bear-bear tucked in next to him before heading to the lantern room. She had checked the beacon to make sure it cast its bright light across the dark, churning lake and flashed its signal into the leaden, fast-moving clouds of the blustery night before coming back down to the kitchen to finish the dishes. The storm was building, and rain poured down on and off and pummeled the windows, but for now, they were safe inside until such time as the storm worsened. She headed for the bedroom and slipped in the door, trying not to awaken Andre.

"Lori?"

Loralei paused as she neared the bed and heard Andre's quiet voice over the tapping of the rain on the windows.

"Yes, I'm sorry I woke you. You worked so hard today. You must need to rest," she said.

"I need you. I missed you. It was a long day," he said.

She sat on the bed next to him and caressed his arm. She let herself relax and enjoy the pleasure she felt at being with Andre. His presence over the past few months had lessened the loneliness and isolation she felt from living day to day at the lighthouse. And the loss she felt today that mirrored and rekindled the losses she had felt in the past was lessened by having him there.

"I missed you, too. I need you, too," she said, finding his lips with her own.

He pulled her to him and kissed her with even more passion than she had felt from him before. She moaned and leaned into him, giving herself up to the pleasure of the kiss.

"Stay with me always. Be my love forever," Andre murmured, raising the covers and pulling her under them with him.

"I will," she said. She wasn't sure she meant what she said. But she felt what she said, and that was enough for her, for now. "I will be your love forever," she said, softly melting into the warmth of his embrace.

Loralei sighed and closed her eyes, and let Andre take her away from it all.

***

Andre drove the Jeep away from the lighthouse the next day when the raging storm let up a bit in the early afternoon and made sure he was out of view before heading down the gravel road toward Edmund's cottage. He had seen the corner of the valise peeking out from the top of the weathered wood beam in the alcove of the scullery quarters where he had hidden it, thinking it would be safe. When he'd pulled it down and checked it, he found his passport upside down inside. He realized that Edmund must have somehow climbed up and found it, even with his bad leg, and rifled through his things while he was gone. Andre always kept track of details, and he could not think of any other reason for the passport to be disturbed. He could not let the discovery go unanswered. His life as a spy depended on it.

He slowed the Jeep as he neared the cottage. Edmund

was standing on the rocky bluff near his cottage, looking across the lake with a telescope, seemingly unaware that he was there. Andre parked behind a nearby tree before getting out and walking toward him. The wind howled over the bluff, and storm clouds gathered in the distance. He realized he had the advantage of not being seen or heard. He walked nearer to Edmund, glancing at the tumultuous waves crashing on the rocks below. It appeared to him that it was going to be easy to remove Edmund as a threat to his life as a spy. He pulled his arms back as he walked up behind him and prepared to push him over the bluff's edge.

Edmund suddenly turned and looked behind him as though something had alerted him to Andre's presence.

"You," Edmund yelled.

He pulled back and hit Andre in the side with the telescope. Andre grunted and doubled over. He was amazed that Edmund was strong enough to hit him that hard.

"This is my country, you damn spy. Everybody knows about you now. You're not going to be around much longer. I'll kill you before I let you get to me first, you bastard," Edmund yelled, swinging the telescope again.

Andre raised his arm to fend off the blow and reassessed his options. He had no idea that Edmund would put up such a fight. Andre dropped to the ground and rolled, holding his side where Edmund had hit him. He sucked in deep breaths of air and pulled himself to standing. Edmund ran toward him, raising the telescope again. Andre lowered his head and barreled toward him, ramming him in the stomach as Edmund brought the telescope down hard on his back. Andre groaned and heard Edmund scream as he stood to grab him. He saw Edmund drop the telescope and bend over to clutch his stomach as he spit out drops of blood.

"You're never going to have Loralei. She doesn't belong to you," Edmund said.

"She doesn't belong to anyone. She's a free spirit. She can

do what she wants," Andre said, rubbing his side.

"She'll never be with you. She loves her country too much," Edmund said, seeming to choke on his words and struggle to walk toward Andre.

"She'll be with me. She doesn't belong to you anymore," Andre said.

Andre grabbed the telescope and ran toward Edmund. He smashed it into his head and watched him drop to the ground. After a moment, he checked Edmund's breathing and determined he was dead. He grabbed him under his arms and pulled him to the edge of the bluff. He rolled him off the bluff and watched as his body hit the rocks below and rolled off into the surf.

"You put up a good fight, Captain," Andre said, as he watched him disappear into the lake.

***

Loralei stood in the lighthouse lantern room gazing across the lake at the sky. The rain had swept in on and off all day. It had pounded in sheets against the lighthouse windows and obscured the view. Now that the rain had paused, she could see more clouds forming in tall, dark-gray banks above the muted indigo blue line of the far horizon and knew that more rain would be coming soon. The evening was hazy in a dusky twilight. She wondered where Andre was. The passion they shared for each other bound her to him in a way she could not control, and she missed him when he was away. He had driven her body into a frenzy of need and desire that only abated when he touched her, and she longed for him. She longed for him to return and fill the void of her empty heart. If only, she thought, watching the seagulls peck and swoop at each other in the sky, Devon would come back to her and fill her heart again with love. But that was something he was no longer willing to do. Loralei sighed and turned her thoughts to Andre instead.

Andre had gone into town for replacement parts for the beacon earlier in the afternoon and never returned. He'd told her that the revolving mechanism that turned the Fresnel lens and made it appear to flash had failed and that he would repair it as soon as possible. Loralei thought Andre was very brave to go out in the storm. She watched the menacing clouds heading toward her over Lake Superior and hoped he would return soon. In a storm as serious as this one, she wanted the beacon to flash. The timing of the flashes indicated to sailors the location of the lighthouse and distinguished it from other lighthouses and warning lights in the area. Flashes from the light could be seen from miles away. But she was afraid that in a tumultuous gale, a still beacon with a static light could be mistaken for the wrong location and lead unsuspecting sailors in the wrong direction. And, she was afraid that if the beacon wasn't flashing, it would be more difficult for the sailors to see the light and follow it home through the storm. Loralei nipped her lip and wondered why Andre was taking so long to return.

She looked east and thought about Devon. She wondered if he was caught in the storms on Lake Huron or if he was farther north, heading toward the Soo Locks. The radio had spat static for the last hour, and she hadn't been able to raise a signal. There was no way to radio the coast guard or the *Manitoulin* and find out if Devon was caught in the storms or headed for home. The storms were coming down from Canada and had already battered Lake Huron to the south. If she couldn't guide the ships into the channel entrance properly because of the beacon's failure to flash in a storm, they could wreck on the rocks. The loss of life would be horrific, and the town could never withstand another tragedy like the one that took the lives of their sons, brothers, uncles, and fathers two years ago. She couldn't stand to lose Devon, either. It was her job to bring the ships home safely. She had to do something, but she didn't know what. She gritted her teeth and resolved to calm herself and wait for Andre to return and fix the mechanism. She hoped he would return soon.

***

Andre saw the storm clouds, too, as he drove the Jeep up the path to the lighthouse during a welcome break in the rain. The clouds looked even more menacing than they had the day before when he had radioed his ship and set up a rendezvous point, and he wanted to restore the beacon to its full operating capacity to bring the ships in safely. It was imperative that he leave the country, and soon. He wasn't sure yet what he was going to tell Loralei about Edmund's whereabouts if she asked him, but he would come up with something. He always did.

It was unfortunate that he was once again in the position of having to cover up a murder. He didn't want to be in this situation, but there was nothing he could do about it. Edmund had obviously discovered he was a spy, leaving him with no alternative but to protect himself. He hadn't wanted to kill him because he didn't want to hurt Loralei, but his country needed him, and he couldn't let Edmund turn him in. In his mind, he had no other choice.

He grabbed his bag and stepped out of the Jeep into the deepening dusk of the evening. The beacon on top of the lighthouse, though shining, was static and still, as he knew it would be without the rotation that caused it to flash. He had sabotaged the beacon earlier in the day to provide himself with a plausible reason to leave and a place to be. He had told Loralei that he needed to go into town to get parts to fix the beacon and had gone to see Edmund at his cottage before driving into town for the parts.

He walked quickly toward the warm glow of amber light from the window of the kitchen, where he hoped Loralei was making dinner. She'd mentioned beef stew that morning, and as he stepped through the door into the warmth of the kitchen, his mouth watered at the smell of simmering meat. He imagined he was coming home for dinner with Loralei and Misha like a regular married man. It was a world he had never known and one he hoped to soon enter. He had always been on the outside looking in at other men's happiness, though he had never before thought of contenting himself with one woman. He grinned, enjoying the fantasy of the moment and his hope for the future. He stepped through the lighthouse door into the kitchen. He saw Loralei turn to look at him from where she was washing dishes at the sink.

"Andre, I'm so glad you're back. I've been so worried. The storms are coming in again fast," she said. She wiped her hands on her apron and ran to him, kissing him on the cheek and completing his fantasy.

"I know. I saw the clouds on the way back. I will begin work on the beacon immediately," he said.

"Have you heard anything from Grandpapa? I'm so concerned about him. It isn't like him to stay away from the lighthouse during a storm. I wonder if his joints are acting up in the humidity," Loralei said.

Andre paused for a moment, considering his answer. "He will be here soon. Do not worry. He is a very capable man."

"Yes. You're right, of course," she said.

Andre smiled and touched her arm. "Do not worry, cara mia. I will take care of you."

She smiled back at him before turning to head up the stairs to the lantern room. He wasn't worried about Loralei believing him when he told a lie. He had learned, as Loralei's lover, that he could convince her to believe him when he told one. He was worried about the sheriff believing him, and Andre knew he wouldn't. Andre had determined that he would have to leave the country sooner than he had anticipated in order to avoid further confrontation with the sheriff and the townspeople over Edmund's death, and he was making plans even as he walked up the stairwell.

If Loralei was going to leave the country with him, she would have to believe that her grandfather would take over her duties at the lighthouse as the lighthouse keeper. She would never leave her post if she thought no one was there to keep the beacon going.

And Andre needed her to leave the country with him. He didn't want to kill her if he didn't have to. Something about her touched him deep in his soul in a way he had never been touched before. She was so lovely and strong and vulnerable. And she gave herself to him so freely in a way that made him feel he knew her deepest treasures.

Her lack of tears broke his heart. She was so much like him in the way that she accepted her situation and her life. It moved him, and he felt things for her he had never felt for another woman. It was as though she had broken through all his defenses and reached deep into his soul through a barricade he thought could never be breached. For the first time in his life, he didn't know if he could overcome his feelings for her to carry out his sacred duty to his country.

Andre stepped into the lantern room and walked over to look out the window at the lake, imagining the freedom beyond his view across the lake in Canada. Taking Loralei with him when he left the country was his only option.

***

Devon lay fuming on his bunk. Lanny had insisted on pressing on through the Soo Locks into Lake Superior in the storm to beat the scheduled time and please the shipping corporation despite his best efforts to dissuade him. Lanny's brashness reminded him of himself when he was young and new to command and thought he knew everything. He remembered when he had told his own father that he thought he knew better than him about sailing on the inland seas, even though his father had so much more experience at sailing freighters on the lakes. He would always regret the advice he thought had put his father in the path of the storm that led to his death. It reminded him of the helplessness he had felt when his father was trapped in the gale, and there was nothing he could do about it. Now he was beside himself with frustration at what he saw as the certain peril Lanny had placed the *Manitoulin* and its crew in. Devon had sailed in gales before and knew they were nothing to trifle with. He didn't know what else he could do. He had argued with Lanny to the best of his ability but to no avail, and he felt helpless and angry, confined to his cabin.

He wanted a drink, and he wanted one bad. He stood and reached for the bottle of rum, but something stopped him. He wasn't sure what it was. Maybe it was thinking about Tex having been burned in the fire on the last trip when he was drunk in his cabin and unable to assume command or help with the firefight. Maybe it was thinking about Loralei and Misha and the awaited new baby and wanting to be sober for them as their family grew. Maybe it was thinking about his father and how he would have wanted him to get on with his life and not bury himself in a bottle to numb his grief over his death. For whatever reason, Devon battled the storm of his addiction and turned away from the bottle.

The first giant wave hit with a force that knocked Devon off his feet and pummeled him into a corner. He fought for balance against the dizzying spin of the cabin, but he careened sideways into the door and banged his head on the door jam.

What the hell, he thought, grabbing for the doorknob to pull himself up. The cabin tipped over in the other direction, and Devon braced his foot against the floor to keep from sliding back toward his bunk.

"Lanny," he shouted, knowing it was to no avail.

He had to get to the bridge as soon as possible and find out what was going on. He needed to tell Lanny what to do. The freighter had obviously almost capsized. Devon yanked open the door and staggered into the passageway. The freighter was unsteady under his feet. He saw water pouring down the ladders from the hatch to the upper deck and filling the passageway. Crewmen were sloshing through the water, running desperately for the ladders.

"Batten down the hatches, men. Now," Devon yelled.

He couldn't believe Lanny hadn't already given those orders. It was a gross dereliction of duty and extremely negligent, given the strength of the storm. He sloshed toward the ladder, planning to make his way to the upper deck before the hatch was closed behind him. But another torrent of water washed down the ladder and threw him against the bulkhead. Devon grabbed for the handrail and tried to shake off the dizziness that overcame him after hitting his head on the railing. He careened back through the passageway as the freighter rolled again to the side.

"Damnit, Lanny, we're rolling. What are you doing?" Devon screamed in spite of himself, knowing Lanny couldn't hear him.

He gritted his teeth against the pain in his head and pulled himself along the handrail toward the ladder. When he reached it, he struggled to climb up through the hatch to the upper deck. He got to the top of the ladder and saw the dark lake churning like a whirlpool of inky blackness. The *Manitoulin* was struggling to remain afloat amid the crashing crests and swallowing valleys of a vortex of turbulent, black waves.

Devon fell to his knees and crawled desperately along the slippery deck toward the pilothouse. He needed to get to Lanny, and he needed to get to him now. He stood and ran before falling to the deck as the freighter tipped to the starboard side. He stood again, ran to the pilothouse, and threw open the door.

"Lanny, turn her on the diagonal. Run her forty degrees in the trough," Devon screamed.

His life and the lives of the crew depended on the quick action of the captain. And Lanny wasn't doing anything. Lanny turned from looking out the window of the pilothouse, his eyes wide and fearful. Devon looked at Lanny and then out the window, Lanny had turned from. He gasped.

A second giant wave towered over the bow of the *Manitoulin*. Devon only had time to shut the door behind him before it crashed into the freighter, shattering the windows of the pilot house and tossing the crew into a vertiginous, spinning deluge of cold water. The water closed over him, and he struggled to find a pocket of air in the torrential wave filling the pilothouse to catch his breath. The freighter leaned to the port side, and Devon pulled himself above the surface to suck in a breath. Lanny flailed nearby.

"She's all yours, Captain. The *Manitoulin* is yours. This is over my head. We need you back, Captain. For God's sake, Devon, save the *Manitoulin*," Lanny yelled.

Lanny went under again before surfacing and struggling for air. Devon started to swim toward him to rescue him, but Lanny shook his head at him.

"Leave me be. Save the *Manitoulin*," Lanny said again.

Devon rushed to assume command as the water lowered slightly in the pilothouse. He shouted orders to the crew to navigate the freighter through the storm.

"Turn into the swell," he yelled to the wheelsman, who had managed to regain his position.

He was going to fight the angry lake to the death for the *Manitoulin*. He battled to keep the freighter afloat and gain momentum against the growing furor of the angry waves. He shook his head in disbelief at the growing height of the cresting waves around them. He had heard legends of waves like this arising during the storms of Lake Superior, but he had never fully experienced the terror of them himself. Sailors who had sworn by their accounts of horrific waves washing over the hulls of ships and drowning sailors. Few had survived to tell their stories. Devon stiffened as he came to a sudden realization. The growing height and turbulence of the churning waves in a sea like this could only mean one thing. The three sisters.

A cold wave of terror rushed through his body. That's

what this was. The three sisters. The three legendary rogue waves of Lake Superior that arose one after the other in the trapped fishbowl between the rocky shores of the churning inland sea, each larger than the one before, to tower across the lake and take the lives of unsuspecting mariners in their wake.

He stared across the inky blackness of the turbulent lake. He had seen something, but he wasn't sure what it was. The *Manitoulin* was bucking and rolling underneath him, barreling through the crashing crests and swallowing valleys of the treacherous waves. He peered more closely into the stormy night and gasped in horror.

A monstrous wall of water loomed in the distance, obscuring the horizon and even the stars that were left in the sky. It appeared not to be moving, but Devon knew it was. It was coming for them. It was the third wave of the three sisters, and it was coming for them to suck them down with it into the cold, lethal depths of Lake Superior. Devon gazed in terror at the towering, mountainous wave of almost certain death and destruction, knowing there was nowhere for them to run.

CHAPTER 19

The rain was showering in the distance, far across the lake. Loralei could see it wisping down in misty spirals. It didn't look like rain from where she was looking out the window in the lighthouse, but she knew it was. She'd seen the rain disguise itself like that before in gales and whip in unexpectedly in a sudden torrent. It looked the same way now.

She was worried about Edmund. She hadn't seen him since he left to go into town last night, and Edmund considered it his duty to be at the lighthouse during storms. She made a sudden decision. She was going to run to Edmund's cottage with Misha to check on him before the storm crashed in again because she couldn't stand to worry about him anymore. She turned the stove off, took her cast iron skillet off the burner, and signed to Misha, who was reading at the table, to come with her. She estimated she had just enough time to get to the cottage and back. She bundled Misha into his Macintosh and put hers on, as well. For a moment, she contemplated telling Andre she was leaving, but she didn't want to bother him while he was fixing the beacon. She decided she could make it back before he knew she was gone.

Loralei pushed open the lighthouse door against the

gathering wind and pulled Misha with her toward the muddy path along the lake. Waves foamed and swelled in the false tides caused by the gale, and she shivered as she realized the storm was already on its way in. She tightened her grip on Misha's hand and hurried faster, pulling her raincoat around her. She hoped Edmund wasn't sick or that he hadn't tripped over his cane because of his sore joints and was lying unconscious on the ground somewhere. They were the only things she could think of that would keep him from the lighthouse during a storm.

But maybe not the only things. Maybe Edmund was, even now, making plans with the townspeople to come after Andre. There was no way for her to know for certain until she talked to him. Loralei hurried down the path, feeling a sudden prickle of goosebumps on her arms. Something was wrong. She was sure of it.

She tried to peer ahead along the bluff to get a glimpse of the cottage, but they were still too far away to see it. A gust of wind blew her sideways into Misha. She pushed back against the wind and glanced out at the lake. There was something on the rocks near the shore. She gasped as she realized that it appeared to be a small yellow raft crashing against the rocks. It was hard to tell from her vantage point if there was anyone in it, but she had to find out if there was and help them, if necessary. She kept Misha close to her as she left the path and inched down to the first slab of flat rock jutting out from the side of the bluff. The rock was moss-covered and slippery and far too treacherous to keep herself and Misha from slipping.

"Don't move until I come back for you. Unless the storm worsens. Then run back to the lighthouse. Do you understand?" Loralei said firmly, signing and tying Misha's hood snugly under his chin to protect him from the wind.

Misha nodded.

Loralei squeezed his hand, then turned and climbed carefully down the slippery, jutting rocks of the bluff, trying to keep her balance as the weight from her seventh-month pregnancy destabilized her.

"Ahoy," she shouted as she drew closer to the raft being tossed about in the waves. She squinted through the mist, trying to see if anyone was there. "Do you need help?" she called.

She picked her way over the rocks. As she neared the raft, she realized it wasn't a raft at all—it was a rubber raincoat. She stopped suddenly, unable to comprehend what she was seeing. It wasn't a raft floating in the water. It was a person.

Her heart pounded in her ears louder than the surf. She glanced up at Misha, praying he couldn't see much from the ledge. The person wasn't moving.

Still, she tried calling out again, hoping she was wrong. "I can help you," she called. "Grab my hand."

She balanced on the lowest rock, reached out her hand, and grabbed the hood of the raincoat. As she pulled it toward her, the waves turned the body over. Suddenly she heard a low, anguished moan and realized it was coming from her.

The body in the coat was Edmund. And yet it wasn't. Those pale, unseeing eyes, the slack, water-filled mouth. They couldn't belong to the warm, gruff man who'd comforted her when her mother died and held her when she grieved the loss of her father.

"Grandpapa. What has happened? Did you fall in? Can you answer me?" she asked. "Grandpapa. No!" she sobbed. "It isn't possible. No!"

Loralei struggled against the surf, trying to pull Edmund onto the rock. The lake wanted to suck him back into its dark, stormy shallows.

"Talk to me," Loralei pleaded. "Please. Please."

She cradled his head and tried to hold on. It was useless. He was already gone, but she couldn't make herself let him go. Loralei touched the face that was so dear to her and cried out in fear and desperation. Who would be left for her if her grandfather left her?

"You can't leave me, Grandpapa. You can't. Not like everyone else. I need you. I won't let the lake take you from me," she said.

She held onto him with all the strength she could muster, but the pounding of the waves was relentless, and she could feel herself losing her grip on the slick hood of the raincoat.

"No," she moaned as she felt the raincoat slip from her grasp. "You can't leave me. I won't let you. I love you," she cried.

With a heartless gust of wind and wave, the incoming storm ripped the yellow hood from her fingers. Loralei watched helplessly as Edmund's body floated away from her and back into the rolling, sloshing surf. She sat back on the rock and wept uncontrollably as she watched her grandfather float out to sea, buffeted by the churning water. Only after he'd disappeared into the surf did she wipe her tears and hug her arms around herself to stop the shivering.

"Fair winds and following seas, Grandpapa," Loralei whispered, murmuring the words she knew as a navy goodbye. "God be with you," she said.

She got to her feet, looking across the dark lake at the swirling black clouds racing toward her. All of the questions she had—had Edmund slipped and fallen? Had he been heading toward the lighthouse? Or had something worse happened?— would have to wait. She struggled quickly to regain her composure and climbed desperately back up the jutting rocks to the sharp, level slice of slate where she had left Misha.

"Come quickly," she said, grabbing Misha's hand, ignoring the real question in his frantic signing: What's wrong?

"We must hurry back to the lighthouse," she said. "The storm is getting worse."

As she turned and led them up the path, she realized that Edmund hadn't been wearing the galoshes he always wore when he walked in the rain.

***

Andre slipped quickly into the communications room and sat down in front of the telegraph to confirm his pick-up for tonight with his contact. He had decided, after talking with Angelina Rossi and thinking about the sheriff's suspicions of him, that it was too risky to remain in Portstown until the original date of pick-up and had rescheduled the rendezvous for tonight. Hearing what Edmund had to say before he pushed him off the bluff and watched him disappear into the crashing surf confirmed his fears that the townspeople suspected he was a spy and made him even more anxious to escape the country. When he'd looked out the window of the lantern room at the growing intensity of the storm, he'd decided he needed to radio his contact to make sure his ship was still going to be at the Portstown dock. He took a break from fixing the beacon and realized Loralei had left the lighthouse with Misha. He didn't know where she had gone or why, but he assumed she would be back soon.

He decided it was the perfect opportunity to use the radio. The storm would make tonight's pick-up dangerous, but Edmund's disappearance would not go unnoticed for long. And the townspeople were starting to suspect that he had something to do with Jake Calico's disappearance and Mrs. Petrova's death. He couldn't risk being around when the town discovered Edmund had disappeared.

Andre turned on the radio and put the headphones on. He adjusted the dial to the agreed-upon frequency and tapped out his message in Morse Code. He had to begin his escape through Canada, and he had decided to take Loralei with him. He loved her, and she loved him. His passion for her and hers for him knew no bounds, and he was never going to give that up. The news of the increasing threat of the conflict in the war drawing near to Portstown concerned him, too. The tightened security measures and increased surveillance made him wonder if some sort of an attack really was imminent. And, even if it wasn't to happen at this time, it could happen in the future. He didn't want to leave Loralei in danger.

It was his obligation to the safety and security of his country, as well, not to leave her behind. His orders were not to leave anyone behind, at least not alive, and the alternative, where Loralei was concerned, had become incomprehensible to him. Despite his training as a spy and a killer and despite his need to carry out his patriotic duty to his country, he couldn't overcome his passionate feelings for her. He loved her. He loved her more than any woman he had ever known, and he wanted her for himself.

He couldn't imagine crawling back into the tortured recesses of his mind to carry out his duty to his country and take her life. Not after the way she had given herself so freely to him by the river in the wilderness. Not after the way she gazed lovingly up at him with her trusting, clear blue eyes. Not after the way she made him feel like a whole person again and not the fractured, tormented murderer he had become. It was unfathomable. He couldn't live his life without her. The only answer was to take her with him. He planned to tell her they were leaving tonight with Misha. He wasn't going to take no for an answer.

Andre tapped out an urgent message on the telegraph requesting confirmation of the rendezvous for tonight. He was relieved that after an initial moment or two of static, his signal was picked up and responded to. The rendezvous was on.

***

Devon pushed with all his strength to shove open the door of the pilothouse and scream orders to the crew.

"All sailors below deck," he shouted through the door at the few remaining crewmen.

He needed them to get to the relative safety of their quarters while he tried to save the *Manitoulin* from almost certain destruction. He wasn't going to let the giant wave take them down with it if he could help it.

"Heave to," he shouted, turning back to the wheelsman who was desperately trying to retain control of the *Manitoulin*.

"Turn into the wave, damnit," Devon yelled.

He pointed off the starboard side at the wall of water in the distance. The wave was closer than before, pulling the black lake up into itself as it crawled stealthily toward them. It glistened like a mountainous black diamond polished to liquid perfection and slewing its facets to the sky. It was coming for them. Devon could feel it. It was coming for them to cut through the *Manitoulin* and take them down into the dark emerald and sapphire depths of the lake. Devon heard the muffled shouts of horror and dismay from the remaining crewmen, many of whom stood frozen, staring across the lake at the monstrous wall of water with open mouths.

He stepped out on deck. "We're going to ride this one out," he shouted, trying to make himself heard over the howling of the wind and the slashing of the rain. "We're not abandoning ship."

Devon knew there was no way anyone would survive in a lifeboat in the turbulent water. And he wanted to survive. He wanted them all to survive.

"Repeat, we are not abandoning ship," he yelled to make himself heard over the wind. "Get below. Batten down the hatches and secure yourself to your bunks."

Devon watched for a moment as the men ran to do as he ordered before turning and sloshing through the water on deck to run back into the pilothouse. He grabbed the wheel from the wheelsman, who was trying desperately to turn the *Manitoulin* into the wave, but seemed unable to do as he was ordered.

"Turn, turn," Devon yelled, turning the wheel with all his might, even though he knew it was too late.

He felt the freighter begin to sway and list.

"She's going over," he yelled.

The third giant wave smashed into the *Manitoulin* and rolled her upside down into the swirling vortex of the inland sea, plunging Devon and his crew into the deep, churning waters of Lake Superior. The cold water hit him with monstrous force. He closed his eyes and tried not to suck in water as he felt himself pulled under by the wave. But the frigid water pummeled him as he struggled to recover from the shock of the impact and find a way to surface and breathe. He felt as though he were floating in a silent netherworld of watery nothingness, and he wondered, for a moment, if his life was over.

Sharp pain stabbed through his head as the force of the wave smashed him into the side of the pilothouse. Devon closed his eyes as he began to lose consciousness. He knew he was going to die. He could think of no other outcome. He tried to open his eyes, but he couldn't shake the numbing pall that paralyzed him.

Through the enveloping blackness that sprang from the haze of his pain, Devon saw a light. In the light, Loralei was running down the Portstown beach toward him. It was day, and they were engaged to be married. She laughed, and he saw her wide smile and her happiness that he'd come to the lighthouse to see her. He wished he could see the face of that happy, young girl again, holding her arms out to him and drawing him close, her long, silky, blonde hair flowing behind her in the breeze from the lake and her smile as bright as the morning sun. He wished he could go back in time and be with his lovely Loralei again.

The pain stabbed through his head again, and darkness overtook him. *I'm coming home, Loralei,* he said. *Keep the light on for me. If there's a God in heaven, we're all coming home now, one way or another.*

As he spun with the freighter into the deep, dizzying vortex of the sea and felt himself lose consciousness, Devon didn't know whether the wave had won the battle for the *Manitoulin* or not.

***

Loralei gripped Misha's hand and ran, stumbling and crying, back up the path to the lighthouse, struggling to maintain her balance as gusts howled over the bluff and threatened to blow her sideways off the path. She bent low against the wind as she sucked in ragged breaths between deep sobs of terror. What could have happened to her grandfather? Loralei couldn't believe she would never see him again. Someone had to help her. Someone had to do something.

She had to tell Andre. He would know what to do. Loralei reached the lighthouse and pushed through the door into the kitchen, pulling Misha in beside her.

"Andre!" she called. He didn't answer. "Andre!"

She was bending over to take off Misha's Macintosh when she heard Andre call from the stairwell. "I will be right down. I have been working on the beacon."

Loralei breathed a sigh of relief that he was home and had answered. He would know what to do. He always knew what to do.

"Edmund came by and showed me what the problem was. He asked me where you'd gone, but I told him I didn't know," Andre called down.

Loralei stopped abruptly and stood up straight. She wasn't sure she had heard what he said. She paused for a moment, feeling her arms prickle with goosebumps. Was he the same man who held her close and murmured words of love during the long, lonely nights while Devon was gone? She told Misha to stand still and walked slowly over to the bottom of the stairwell.

"Grandpapa stopped by?" Loralei asked.

"Yes, he helped me with the beacon," Andre shouted.

"Just now?" she asked.

"A little while ago. He said to tell you he was spending the night at the cottage. I am almost done."

Loralei stood rigid, looking up at the stairwell. She glanced at Misha and then up at the stairwell again, feeling her eyes begin to sting. She heard Andre start down the stairs and felt a stab of fear as she tried to think of what to do. She had to protect Misha. And she also had to make sure Andre had repaired the beacon to bring Devon and the ships safely home through the storm. *What should she do?* Loralei gritted her teeth in anguish and refastened Misha's Macintosh. She crouched down beside him and put her face next to his, holding her hands out in front of him.

"Danger," she signed, mouthing the word to Misha. "Danger, Misha. Run to Grandpapa's cottage and stay there. Don't let anyone in. Do you understand?"

Misha's eyes widened as he looked at her. He shook his head.

"I save you," he signed.

"No," she signed back. "I will be okay. Danger. Run, Misha."

He leaned in to hug her, and she held him tightly for a moment, blinking the tears from her eyes as she felt him squeeze her hard. She released him after a moment and led him to the lighthouse door. She pushed it open against the blustery wind and guided him through it, biting her lip against the fear she felt at letting him go in the approaching storm. She had no other choice.

Misha turned around briefly and gave her a worried glance. "I save you," he signed again before running away into the night.

***

Devon coughed, choked, and opened his eyes, realizing he was entombed in a cubic sea of icy, black water. The pilothouse was filled with lake water, and he was wedged against the ceiling in a small pocket of remaining air. He could see Lanny and the wheelsman across from him, struggling to gulp oxygen from the air pocket in the same way he now was. He could hardly separate the water of the lake from the water in the pilothouse and realized the freighter must be rolling underneath the surface, sucked under by the clenching, arctic grip of the third wave of the three sisters.

Devon struggled to say something but found himself

struggling to breathe instead. He felt helpless to stop the Manitoulin from taking them with her to the bottom of the icy lake, entombing them all forever in a silent, watery coffin. He wondered if his father had felt the same way about his freighter and crew at the end of his life. He closed his eyes and prayed.

"Help us, O God," he said aloud.

He felt himself lose consciousness again. When he opened his eyes, he was on the floor, jammed into a corner of the pilothouse. The water had lowered, although it was still sloshing and churning him. The bitter taste of fishy bile stung his tongue, and he coughed and choked out water from his lungs. He groaned and stood to look through the shattered windows of the pilothouse out to sea. He saw the outline of the bow of the Manitoulin pulling out of the water in an upward diagonal glide and separating from the rest of the lake. Water poured out of the windows and off the deck, and drenched crewmen in the pilothouse struggled to stand and balance as the freighter began to level off and right itself. Devon realized that, in some impossible way, the Manitoulin was surfacing from the roll. She had survived, and somehow, so had they.

"Have we lost anyone?" he yelled, sloshing over to the wheel and peering through the shattered windows at the torrents of rain, knowing it was impossible to tell at this point but hoping for a positive response.

"Crewmen were below deck in the roll," Lanny shouted to him from the doorway of the pilothouse where he was struggling to stand. "I see men now running toward the bow. We need to regain control of the boat."

"Stations, everyone," Devon shouted to Lanny and the wheelsman and the few crewmen who had ventured on deck. "We're taking the Manitoulin back from the lake."

The freighter continued to separate from the dark, turbulent water as it leveled off. More crewmen came on deck and ran to their stations. For a moment, he dared to hope that the

Manitoulin and her crew had survived the awesome power of the wave.

"Captain. Come quick. There's a crack in the hull. You're needed on the forward deck," a crewman yelled through the door.

Devon released the wheel to the helmsman standing near him, and followed the crewman out on deck, bending against the wind and rain to run to the bow of the freighter.

"It's a three-inch crack, Captain," another crewman yelled over the wind when Devon arrived. "It runs across the deck and at least a dozen feet down both sides. We can't keep her afloat like this, Captain. The *Manitoulin* is splitting in half."

Devon took in the scene and clenched his jaw. It was bad. He'd never seen a freighter crack like this, and he knew they wouldn't survive the night if he didn't do something. The storm was still raging, and the Manitoulin was severely wounded. He paused for a moment to analyze the situation before deciding on a course of action.

"Okay, men, here's what we're going to do," he yelled. "Winch her up, men. We're going to winch the *Manitoulin* back together and make her whole. Run cables fore and aft on both sides and crank them tight. We're going to winch her back together and take her home."

The crew jumped to carry out Devon's orders. They stretched steel cables from the front to the back of the wounded freighter, secured them, and desperately cranked them as tight as possible to close the gap in the hull as the storm raged around them. Devon watched them work from his position in the pilothouse as he steered the *Manitoulin* through the storm. He hoped the winches would hold and prevent the freighter from splitting in half and sinking to the bottom of the lake with his crew on board. He and his crew and the *Manitoulin* had survived the wave. Now they had to survive its aftermath. He prayed they would.

Eventually, Devon saw that the winching of the crack was working. It was closing out the water and sealing up the freighter's hull. They were going to survive, and he was going to make his father proud that he was the captain of the *Manitoulin*. He was going to make it home to Loralei. They were all going to make it home to Portstown, he decided, one way or another.

CHAPTER 20

Loralei closed the door behind Misha and ran toward the stairwell.

"Don't come down," she called to Andre. "I'm on my way up. I want to see what you've done." She slipped off her raincoat and tossed it on a kitchen chair.

She hurried to the stairwell, glad she could no longer hear Andre's footsteps on the stairs. She didn't want him to come down and know she had sent Misha away. For a moment, she wondered if she should run away, too. The pounding of her heart and trembling of her body told her yes, but the aching in her soul told her no. She could never leave the lighthouse or the lives of her countrymen in the care of a man who'd killed her grandfather. And yet, she was putting herself in danger by staying. She couldn't act as though nothing had happened because Andre would want to know where Misha was. She couldn't pretend Misha was in his room and leave him at Edmund's cottage because Misha was too young to stay there alone overnight. She didn't know what to do. She didn't know what would happen if Andre found out she knew Edmund was dead.

"I'm sending Misha to his room to get ready for bed. Be right there," she called.

Loralei climbed the staircase, taking deep breaths to mitigate the trembling in her legs. She paused for a moment. Her head felt foggy, and her thoughts were muddled. She felt like she was floating in a drifting haze of shock.

How could it be possible that Andre had killed Edmund? There was no other explanation for the way he was acting, but it seemed unbelievable to her. Andre had shared her bed. He had been her lover. He had told her he would never hurt her.

Loralei wiped the perspiration from her brow and tried to concentrate. Edmund had shown her the passport. Was it possible that the words on it really were a code phrase? And he had mentioned shipyard invoices. Could they really contain information that could put her country in danger? Was Andre really a spy? It all came down to one thing and one thing only. Edmund was dead, and Andre had told her that he wasn't. There was no other way to look at it. He had murdered her dear grandfather.

She shook her head to clear it. She had to do something. What if Andre planned to kill her or even Misha? She struggled through a haze of denial to the realization that her grandfather had been right. Andre was a spy. Edmund had been trying to protect her by telling her and showing her the proof, but she hadn't wanted to believe it. And now he was dead, and she was left to deal with his killer.

She grabbed the railing to steady herself as a wave of nausea washed over her. She felt dizzy and struggled to remain standing on her trembling legs. Her world was in danger. She had to think of some way to stop Andre, not only to save herself and Misha but to save her country. Loralei squeezed her eyes shut.

After what seemed like forever, she opened them and knew what she was going to do. She'd tell Andre there was something wrong with the way the foghorn sounded and go with him to fix it. She had left the door to the fruit cellar open earlier to air it out in the afternoon when the rain had let up. When he walked past the fruit cellar, she could ask him to close the door, and when he bent over to do so, she could push him down the stairs, lock the door behind him, and have the authorities deal with him later. She would have to risk the possibility that the authorities could find Jake's body at the same time and know that she was an accomplice to his murder. But her country and saving it from harm were more important to her than her freedom or her life. She couldn't think of anything else to do.

"Is everything all right?" Andre called to her down the stairwell.

"Everything's fine," she said in what she hoped was a bright and happy manner. "I'm coming up now."

Loralei gritted her teeth. She took a tentative step up the stairs before coming to terms with her new plan and marching forward. She climbed to the top of the staircase and stepped into the lantern room.

***

"Let me show you what I have done," Andre said when he saw Loralei crossing the lantern room toward him. "I have repaired the mechanism that rotates the beacon. The flashes are every thirty seconds, as required."

He watched her for a reaction to his words. He thought she looked dazed for a moment and wondered if the stress of the last few days and of the storm had affected her health. The pregnancy made her tire more easily lately.

"Thank you," she said. "Andre?"

"Yes?" he replied.

"When you came to Portstown on Captain Blake's freighter this summer, was it after he hired you in Detroit?"

Andre looked up. "Yes. Why do you ask that now?" He gave her a sideways glance.

"No reason. I just wondered." Loralei looked away. "Is that where you lived?"

"Yes, I told you that, remember?" he answered.

"I remember. Do you know where Davison's shipyard is?" she asked.

Andre walked over to her. "Why do you want to know that?" He looked at her more closely. How did she know the name of the shipyard? She seemed nervous and uneasy, and he felt suddenly on edge.

Loralei stepped back. "I know someone that used to work there, that's all. I wondered if you knew where it was."

Andre paused for a moment before responding. "I did not work in a shipyard there, if that is what you are asking, and I did not captain a ship. But I assure you that I am capable of doing anything your grandfather can do around here. Now, are you done asking questions?" he asked, smiling.

She smiled back. "Yes. How silly of me. We have things to do. It's very important for the beacon to flash properly when the storm comes in again, so the sailors can see it. And it's important for the foghorn to work properly, as well. I think there's something wrong with it. Could you come with me to take a look at it? It should be louder."

"Yes, of course," Andre said.

"I will step outside the lantern room onto the gallery and watch the flashes of the beacon from there first," she said.

"Of course," he said.

Andre turned sideways to counter the gathering wind and followed her out onto the balcony that overlooked the turbulent lake. Menacing, dark banks of indigo clouds raced toward them across the night sky. The wind whipped Loralei's hair about her face, and when she raised her hand to tuck it behind her ear, she seemed dazed and disoriented, as though lost in thought. She grasped the iron railing of the balcony to hold herself steady in the wind and leaned against it to look up at the beacon. He stood next to her.

"Yes, it's perfect," she said after a few moments. "The

flashes are well-timed, and the mechanism appears to be fixed," she said, rubbing her temple. "Now, perhaps, we can go outside and check on the foghorn. The storm is almost here. You can wear Devon's raincoat since Grandpapa is wearing the yellow one."

Andre was silent for a moment. "How did you know that?" he asked, feeling suddenly wary.

"Know what?" she asked.

"How did you know Edmund was wearing a yellow raincoat?" he asked, watching her face for any sign of falsehood.

"I didn't. I just assumed. He has one, and it is raining," she stammered.

He sucked in a breath when he saw her look away quickly. He knew what deception looked like from his training as a spy. And it was obvious to him that she was lying. "Don't lie to me, Lori. You know, don't you? Somehow, you know that Edmund is dead."

He cringed when she looked back at him with accusatory eyes that misted over at his words.

"You killed him," she said.

"No," Andre said.

He tried to lie to her but stopped, stunned by the cold, unforgiving look in her eyes. He couldn't believe what he was seeing. *It wasn't possible that he had lost her.* He couldn't let this happen. He couldn't let this be the end of their relationship. He wanted her so much. But he could tell, by the way she looked at him, that she didn't believe him. And he could tell, by the cold tone of her voice, that she couldn't accept what she now knew about him.

"Lori, I did not want this to happen. I did not want any of this to happen," Andre said.

"You're a spy. You're a spy for the enemy," she said.

He tried to think of something to say that would soften the look in her eyes.

"I want us to be together, Lori. Please believe me. If it were not for the war, this would never have happened. None of this would have happened. Nothing would be as it is now. There would be only the two of us loving each other, with nothing in the world to separate us. Can you not put this part of our life behind us and think of the life we could share in the future?" he asked. "A life where I am not a spy. A life where you are not trapped in a lighthouse. A life where there is only you and me and our glorious love for each other, raising our children in peace. Please, Lori. Come with me."

He cringed again when he saw her steady, unchanging gaze. "Lori. Please. I am leaving the country tonight. I have radioed my ship for a rendezvous. I cannot leave you here now that you know about me. You can bring Misha. We will run away together, all of us. We can start over in my country. We can have a life in Italy."

Andre heard himself pleading with her and wondered at the intensity of the feelings he had for her. He had never felt this way about any other woman, and he knew that he would never feel this way again. He wanted Loralei more than anything else he had ever wanted in his life. She made him feel like a real person again. She made him feel like someone who could love and care about someone else instead of the emotional shell of the man he had become. He held out his arms to her.

"I can't leave," Loralei said, holding his gaze and ignoring his gesture. "I will never leave my post, and I could never leave my country."

He gritted his teeth and felt his face get hot. "You have to. We have no other options."

"I'm not leaving," she said, as he walked slowly toward her.

The anger he felt at the impossible situation surged through him, and he felt unable to control it.

Loralei looked behind her at the drop below. "I have nowhere to go."

"Italy," he said again. "You can come to Italy with me."

"Never. It will never happen."

Andre dropped his head. "Then you leave me no choice."

Loralei inched along the railing as he stepped toward her. He wrapped the end of the polishing cloth he had used on the beacon around one hand and stretched it taut with the other, holding it out in front of him. He had her trapped, and he could see, from the way she raised her chin and looked at him, that she knew it. And she would not give in to him. He could see it in her eyes as she backed away from him. How could he possibly twist the cloth around her lovely neck?

"Lori," he said softly, hesitating for a split second as he neared her.

Her beauty, at that moment, rivaled any he had ever seen in a Mother and Child painting or anywhere. She was breathtakingly beautiful with her flushed cheeks and glistening eyes. He saw in her gaze not the fear and anger of the moment before but a deep reflection and understanding of what they had meant to each other.

"Lori," he said again, lowering his arms and dropping the cloth to the floor.

Before he could react, Loralei lunged toward him. She pushed him with a force he hadn't known she possessed. The longing he felt for her was replaced with a sudden, grudging realization of her true strength of character and fierce love for her country. He looked deep into her eyes and grinned as he careened back and grabbed for the railing to stop his fall, but it slipped from his grasp.

"Ciao, bella," he said as he flipped over the railing and hurtled from the balcony to what he knew was his almost certain death on the hard, unforgiving earth far below.

***

"No!" Loralei screamed as Andre disappeared over the railing.

The anger that had surged through her and blinded her

with rage was replaced with horror at what she had done. She ran forward to look over the railing, knowing that Andre had no chance of surviving such a fall. She heard herself scream in echo in the same disembodied way she had heard herself scream at her grandfather's death and Mrs. Petrova's death before him. But this time, she screamed in agony and doubled over. She couldn't believe what she had done. She had killed her beloved Andre. She, who had devoted her life to saving others. She, who believed that life was sacred and knew the pain and grief caused by death. She, who had at one time given life to another. It was irreconcilable in her mind, even though Andre had killed her grandfather and probably Mrs. Petrova and even though he was a spy and an enemy of her country. It wasn't Andre who had done the killing this time. It was she who had killed someone.

Loralei clutched her stomach and moaned. The pain was unbearable. She screamed again as she felt a sudden gush of warmth run down her legs and realized what was happening. Her water had broken. The baby was coming. The baby was coming early.

She stumbled back into the lantern room when the pain lessened and headed for the stairwell, grasping for the railing to maintain her balance as she struggled to walk down the stairs. A contraction stabbed her with full force, and she sucked in a breath as she tripped on the top stair. She was well aware that a fall down the stairwell from the dizzying height of the lantern room would be fatal, and she clutched the railing in desperation, gritting her teeth through the pain. If she could get through the contraction, she would have some time to try to make it down the stairs.

The rain smashed into the glass panes of the lantern room behind her, and she realized the storm was upon them. She heard the wind howling around the lighthouse and rattling the windows. The foghorn sounded its low blasts in a haunting, sonorous rhythm with the pounding of the rain. Loralei suddenly realized, with a deep feeling of terror and loss, how alone she really was in a way she had never realized before. She was bringing a baby into the world, and there was no one to help her. Tears stung her eyes, but she blinked them away and concentrated on finding a way down the stairs. It was no use feeling sorry for herself. She had to make it down the stairs and ring the bell. It was her only option. She needed to alert the townspeople of an emergency so that someone would come out and help her.

She bent over and screamed again when the pain hit her with a force she hadn't known was possible. She leaned against the railing in agony until the pain receded, and she tried to catch a breath before starting down the stairs again. Somehow, she made it down several more before a contraction hit again. The pain was so strong that, for a moment, she wondered if her life was ending.

At least she had made sure the beacon was flashing before the storm hit. At least she had carried out her duties as a lighthouse keeper, and the sailors would see the beacon. At least she had done everything she could to bring her husband safely home.

She straightened when the pain mercifully let up and trudged down more stairs before pausing to breathe. She hoped Misha was okay by himself at her grandfather's cottage. She agonized with worry as she realized there was no way she could go to him. She hoped he would be okay by himself.

Loralei took a deep breath and continued down the stairs. She sighed with relief when she finally reached the floor and paused to breathe for a moment before shuffling through the kitchen to the lighthouse door. If she could only make it to the bell and ring it.

She fell back as the wind and rain pummeled her as she pushed open the door and stepped out into the storm. It was a bad one. As bad as she could remember. And it had gone on for so many days. She hoped the end was near.

She bent against the wind and sloshed toward the bell through the mud and water. She could feel another contraction coming on, but she didn't slow her pace. She had to get to the bell.

"Ahh," she screamed in agony as she felt the pain hit again. "Help me!" she screamed, knowing there was no one around to answer.

She gritted her teeth and pushed forward. She was almost to the bell when the wind gusted, and she slipped in the mud.

"Please, someone, help me," she cried, bending over and clutching her stomach.

There was nothing more she could do. She had given everything she had to help everyone in her life for her whole life, and she could do no more.

"God help me," she murmured before giving into the suffocating darkness that overcame her and falling to the ground.

***

Devon saw the rain in the distance. The storm had receded as they sailed farther west through Lake Superior toward Portstown, but it didn't look to him like it had moved on from the other side of the lake. It seemed to be in full force in front of them, and he imagined it was hitting Portstown at that very moment. He hoped Loralei was okay but could do nothing about it for now. He contemplated slowing the freighter and waiting for the storm to move out of the area, but he balanced that with the need to get the *Manitoulin* back to port before she split in half. The winches were holding the freighter together, but he didn't know for how long.

"We're sailing on through, men. We're taking the *Manitoulin* home now," he said to the crewmen on deck who were watching the storm in the distance with him.

Many of the crewmen nodded in agreement. They seemed to welcome him back as their captain, and he was glad to see that they seemed happy to follow his orders. Lanny had retired to the infirmary. The stress of the storm and the pummeling of the waves had seemed to take its toll on him, and he hadn't mentioned anything about reassuming command, which was fine with Devon. He was happy to be in charge again and happy to be instilled with the responsibility to sail the freighter safely home. He walked back into the pilothouse.

"Steady as she goes," he said.

"Steady on," the wheelsman said, calling out the compass heading as per protocol.

The storm battered the shore as they sailed toward the channel. He felt the wind pick up and suddenly realized the storm was turning and heading back out into the lake toward them.

"Damn this storm. Here it comes again!" he shouted to the helmsman. "What'll we do? We can't turn back at this point. The winches may not hold the ship together for much longer, and I don't think we could outrun the storm, anyway."

Devon pushed through the door of the pilothouse and ran out on deck. His head still throbbed from hitting it on the wall of the pilothouse, but he didn't have time to coddle himself right now.

"Stations, everyone. We're taking the *Manitoulin* home, one way or another. Batten down the hatches," he yelled.

He stood for a moment and watched the crewmen race to do his bidding before heading back to the helm to take the wheel. He wanted to sail the freighter himself. He turned the wheel to steer into the waves. *One more time.* He was going to win the battle with the storm and the lake for the *Manitoulin* one more time. But he wasn't sure how he was going to do it. The rain hit what was left of the shattered windows of the pilothouse, and Devon stared up at the turbulent, dark-grey clouds above him in the night sky. The blackness of the night obscured the light from the stars, and an inky darkness descended upon them. He could no longer see the shore through the black shroud of the storm and the torrents of rain that blasted through the shattered windows.

"Radar. We need radar," he yelled in desperation, even though he knew the radar antennae must have been lost when the freighter rolled.

If he could determine their position with the use of the radar, he could navigate through the storm. He didn't want to accept the possibility that the radar was useless. But he knew the answer before he heard it.

"Radar is no longer operational, Captain," a crewman shouted over the wind.

Devon grabbed his throbbing head with one hand, trying to think of how to navigate through the darkness. He looked up at the clouds and watched as they swirled into a familiar formation. For a moment, he was stunned at what he saw. He rubbed his head to try to stop the persistent throbbing.

Father, he said to himself, looking at the formation in the clouds.

He was sure he saw his father's image in the turbulent swirls of the clouds.

"Father, tell me what to do," Devon said, remembering saying the same thing when he'd seen his father's image in the painting Loralei had made of his father on the freighter in the storm that took his life.

He thought he heard an answer through the howling of the wind.

"Follow the light, Devon. The light of your life will bring you safely home," he heard his father say.

"Father," Devon called out, reaching for the sky. He choked back a sob as he watched the image disappear into the clouds. "Father, come back to me," Devon said.

Devon wrestled with the wheel as he gazed at the fading image. He had never felt more alone and lost in his entire life, even when he was battling the giant wave.

"Captain, the beacon is flashing off the port side. I can see it."

Devon heard, and he turned to see Lanny running into the pilothouse.

"I see the beacon shining from the lighthouse," Lanny said, pointing toward the flash.

Devon gripped the wheel. "I see it, too," he said, steering the freighter toward the beacon. "We're following the light home," Devon said. "We'll keep the light off the port side."

Loralei was waiting for him at the lighthouse with Misha, and he had to sail home to them.

CHAPTER 21

Loralei opened her eyes through a haze of pain and darkness to see her sister rushing to her side. The rain was splashing on her face and splattering up her nose, and Loralei gasped for air. She realized she was lying prone and soaked on the muddy ground underneath the emergency bell. She remembered running to ring the bell to call the townspeople for help but collapsing under the grip of an excruciating contraction instead. She didn't remember what had happened after that. She must have fainted.

"Marie. I'm so glad you're here. How did you know? How did you get here?" Loralei asked.

"I'm so glad I found you," Marie said. Loralei saw Marie drop down to her knees next to her. "It's the baby, isn't it? You're having the baby now, aren't you?"

"Misha," Loralei said, spitting out rainwater and gritting her teeth as she moaned through another pain. "Misha is at Grandpapa's cottage. You must go get him. I'm so worried," she said when she could talk again.

"No. Relax and breathe," Marie said. "Misha's with Finn in the lighthouse. He ran into town through the storm to get us. He said you were in danger and wanted us to save you, so we borrowed a car and drove out here," Marie said.

"Misha did that? In the storm he's so afraid of?" Loralei asked.

"Yes, he's fine. I'm worried about you now. It looks to me like the baby's almost here. We must get you inside," Marie said.

"I can't. I can't move. It hurts too much," Loralei said.

Loralei tried to breathe through another contraction but moaned instead. The cold wind was whipping rain in her face, making it difficult to see Marie.

"Put your arm around my shoulder. I'll help you stand," Marie said.

Loralei felt Marie put her hand on her arm. "No, the baby's coming. It hurts," Loralei said.

"Put your other arm around me."

Loralei heard a deep voice and peered through the deluge to see Finn at her side, extending his hand toward her. "You can do it, Loralei, if we both help you. We'll get you into the lighthouse out of the storm, where you can have the baby in peace. We'll fix the bed for you," he said.

Loralei nodded and tried to do as Finn asked. "All right," she said.

She gave a loud moan and let them help her up slowly. She stayed bent over against the biting wind and let them half-drag her through the muddy yard and into the lighthouse.

"Mama."

Loralei heard Misha call out to her when she stepped through the door. It was hard for her to talk, but she wanted to say something. She wanted to tell him how brave he was and how glad she was that, even at his young age, he was carrying on their family heritage of saving lives. But it was too much. She moaned instead.

"Your mother will be okay. You're a good boy," Finn said.

Loralei was glad to see Finn sign to Misha as she stumbled past him with Finn and Marie helping her. She gritted her teeth and held on to them until she reached the bed in the bedroom. Then she doubled over and screamed in pain.

"The baby's coming. I can feel the head," she said.

Loralei leaned over onto the bed and felt Finn and Marie help her in.

"Take Misha into the other room, Finn. I'll stay with Loralei," Marie said.

Loralei was relieved that Marie was taking charge. They had been through childbirth together before at the lighthouse. Marie had been at her side for Misha's birth. And before that, they had waited together as children for their mother to give birth to their siblings. It was something that had been done through generations of their family. But there were times in the past when the births had gone badly, and the babies had not survived their isolated forays into the world. She tried not to think about that now or about how the baby was coming early. She was in such excruciating pain that she couldn't think about anything anymore.

She heard the bedroom door shut. She watched as Marie poured some water from the cistern in the corner into a bowl on the dresser and grabbed some towels from the bathroom before hurrying to her side. Marie gently moved her onto the bed and put a pillow under her head.

"Okay. You can push, Loralei. You can push the baby out now," she said.

Loralei screamed in agony and relief that she could finally push and bore down hard through the contraction tormenting her. She hoped it wouldn't be much longer before the baby came. She didn't know if she could stand any more pain.

"I see the head," Marie said. "Hold up for a minute. I need to turn the baby's head," she said.

Loralei sucked in several quick breaths as she tried to stop pushing. "What's happening?" she yelled between breaths.

"I need to move the cord," Marie said.

Loralei groaned and held off pushing for as long as she could. Just when she thought she couldn't stand it anymore, she heard Marie call out to her again.

"Okay. You can push now. Push through the next contraction," Marie said.

Loralei didn't need to wait. She was ready to push. She pushed as hard as she could and felt the baby coming. She took a deep breath and screamed again as she bore down hard to push the baby out.

"It's a girl," Marie said.

Loralei heard Marie's words through a haze of pain and sudden relief.

"You did it, Loralei. You have a baby girl," she said.

***

Devon sighed with relief as he docked the *Manitoulin* in Portstown. Sailing the wounded freighter through the channel in the storm had been rough. But he and the crew, with help from the light of the beacon, had guided her safely into port.

Devon turned to see Lanny standing in the doorway of the pilothouse. "You did it, Captain. You brought the *Manitoulin* home. The crew and I are very grateful. You saved us all and our families from the trauma of another watery death," Lanny said.

Devon nodded.

"Welcome back as the captain of the *Manitoulin*. I'll make sure the coast guard and the shipping corporation know of your valor. I'm sure they'll reinstate you," Lanny said.

Devon turned away. The pain he'd felt at losing his command was still there, but he was glad to think he could get his command back.

"We need to check the winches on the crack in the hull and make sure they're holding. Have some men look into it. I'll be there shortly," Devon said.

Devon watched Lanny leave and looked off the starboard side of the freighter to see the coast guard and the harbor patrol racing toward them. He saw them pass a ship with a red flag on its mast, docking near the *Manitoulin*. He didn't know what was going on, but from the way he saw soldiers running down the dock toward it, Devon didn't think the ship would make it out of port anytime soon. It looked to him like the ship was being boarded and the crew arrested. He wondered, for a moment, if the situation had something to do with the war. Devon didn't know that it was the ship Andre Sorrento had contacted before he died and on which he'd planned to sail to Canada with Loralei and Misha. Devon turned his attention to the *Manitoulin* when he saw a coast guard cutter pull up next to them. Devon walked out on deck to talk to them.

"Do you need help, Captain? That's a nasty gash your freighter's got there," the captain of the cutter called to him through a megaphone.

"She's holding her own for now. But I sure could use some of your men to come onboard and help my crew. They've been through a lot," Devon called back.

"Aye, Captain," the coast guard captain called.

The cutter pulled ahead of them to dock as Devon walked to the bow to check on the crack. He saw the men gathered around inspecting it, and he gave orders to keep the winches tight and to follow the orders of the coast guard captain when he boarded.

"I'm going home now. God be with you all," Devon said, lowering his shoulders and giving in to the relief he felt at being safely back in Portstown.

The sailors waved at him as he left. Devon went back to his cabin and gathered his things. He walked down the gangplank to the dock and headed for town. The night sky looked clear, and the air smelled fresh and clean from the cleansing of the rain. It was hard for him to believe, after all he had been through, that he was alive and walking down the dock to go home.

A man ran toward him, and Devon realized, when he saw the worried face of Dan Paxton, that his feeling of safety and relief was short-lived.

"Devon, I'm so glad I found you. Come with me quickly. Something's wrong at the lighthouse. Loralei's in trouble," Dan said.

"What?" Devon asked.

"Finn and Marie borrowed Annie's car a few hours ago to drive out to the lighthouse. She told me. When I saw the freighter dock, I came over to drive you home right away. We have to hurry. Misha ran into town through the storm and told them Loralei was in danger," Dan said.

Devon ran with Dan to his car. He jumped in, threw his duffel in the back, and waited impatiently for Dan to get in the driver's seat. He couldn't imagine what could have happened. He needed to get home to Loralei right away and save her from danger, whatever it was. He hoped he would get there in time.

***

"Devon, where's Devon?" Loralei heard herself murmuring through the haze of nothingness that had overtaken her.

She wasn't sure how long she'd been lying there. She remembered Marie telling her she had a baby girl, but she had felt the darkness overtake her again after that. Her body felt sore and bruised and wet with sweat.

"I want Devon," Loralei said.

"He's on the lake, remember? He's on the *Manitoulin*," Marie said.

Loralei heard Marie's soft voice whispering to her through the darkness. "Oh, yes, I remember now. I wish he was here."

"I know. I washed and swaddled the baby while you were resting. Do you want to hold her now?" Marie asked.

Loralei relaxed at hearing Marie's soothing voice. "Yes, please," she said.

Loralei opened her eyes and smiled as she took the baby from Marie when she handed her to her. She snuggled her new baby and looked deep into her eyes. She breathed a deep sigh of relief to see the cornflower blue of her daughter's eyes, so like Devon's, gazing unfocused up at her. She had been so afraid she would see the piercing black of Jake's eyes staring back at her, but they were blue, definitely blue. There was no doubt in her mind now that the baby was Devon's daughter. Loralei heard the rain pounding against the window and the wind howling around the lighthouse, but she didn't look up. She was mesmerized by the miracle of holding her new baby in her arms. Loralei had been so afraid that the baby would not survive the fury of the storm and the trauma of being born more than a month early. But she had, and she was beautiful.

"Can I get you anything?" Marie asked.

Loralei looked up and gazed at Marie. "Only if you can get Devon," Loralei said. "I have everything I need right here in the lighthouse, except for Devon. I'm so afraid for him. I'm afraid the storm has taken him from me. I couldn't reach the *Manitoulin* through ship-to-shore communication today or yesterday. I think something's happened to him," Loralei said, feeling herself choke on a sob. "I'm sorry. I don't know what's the matter with me. I don't mean to cry," Loralei said.

Marie looked at her with undisguised compassion.

"You can cry, Loralei. There's nothing wrong with crying if you need to. You've been through so much, and you've survived it all. But I need to tell you something, and there's no good time to do it," Marie said.

"What is it?" Loralei asked.

Marie looked away for a moment and then back at her with tears in her eyes. "The sheriff came out and talked to Finn earlier. I'm so sorry to have to tell you this now, but Grandpapa was drowned in the storm. The sheriff and the harbor patrol found his body in the lake near his cottage. They think he may have slipped on the rocks and fallen in the water."

"Oh, no," Loralei said.

Even though Loralei already knew Edmund was dead, the

shock of it hit her again when Marie said it out loud.

"Go ahead and cry, Loralei. I've been crying, too. I'm here for you," Marie said.

Loralei did. She cried deep, wrenching sobs. She cried for her grandfather, her lost father and mother and for Mrs. Petrova. She cried for all the people lost in the war and the storms of the past. And she cried over her fear that she had lost Devon in the storm. She cried for Jake, remembering what they had shared before she realized who he was while treasuring the relief she felt at knowing her new daughter, with her cornflower blue eyes, could not be Jake's child. And all the while, she held her sleeping daughter, that she now knew was Devon's baby, in her arms, feeling grateful for the new life she'd been blessed to care for. After a while, Loralei felt her sobs subside, and she felt Marie pat her on the arm.

"It's okay. You needed to let it out," Marie said.

Loralei nodded. "She's so beautiful," Loralei said, gazing down at the baby.

"Yes, and so loved. She's a very blessed child," Marie said.

***

"Drive faster," Devon said to Dan, squinting to look through the rain splashing across the car windshield. Devon could hardly see anything. "Can't you make this thing go faster?" he asked.

"I'm doing the best I can. I don't want to drive off the road," Dan said.

Just then, a gust of wind hit the side of the car, and Devon felt the car careen off the road. It splashed into a rocky ditch that was filled with wide, rippling puddles of water.

"Damn it. I didn't come this far to drown on the side of the road. I have to get back to Loralei. Something's wrong. She needs me. I have to be there," Devon yelled.

"We'll get there. We have to. Come on. Help me push the car out. We can do it together. I'll drive, and you push. We'll get you home to the lighthouse to see Loralei," Dan said.

"God willing," Devon added, looking up at the turbulent clouds in the night sky.

He didn't know if he would make it home in time to save Loralei from whatever the danger was or not.

***

Loralei looked up at Marie later in the night when she heard a commotion in the other room.

"What is it? What's going on?" she asked.

"I'll find out," Marie said, heading for the bedroom door.

When Marie opened the door to the bedroom, Devon rushed in, panting and sweating. Loralei gasped to see the look of fear and worry in his eyes and his bedraggled appearance in soaking clothes and dripping wet hair.

"Loralei, are you okay? Are you hurt?" he asked.

"Devon, you're here. I'm okay. I was afraid you were lost in the storm. I'm so glad to see you. I'm so glad you're home," Loralei exclaimed, unable to believe he was standing in front of her.

"Yes, I'm home. I was worried about you, too," he said.

"Come over here. Be with me. See your new baby daughter," Loralei said.

The look of fear and worry in Devon's eyes transformed into a look of relief and obvious love, and she blinked back tears of joy as she realized that Devon really did care about her. She watched his expression turn to awe as he sat down next to her on the bed and gazed at the baby. Marie walked over with a towel and handed it to Devon.

"She has your hair," he said softly after a moment, patting his forehead with the towel.

"How can you tell?" Loralei asked.

"I can tell," he said.

"She has your eyes," she said.

"She does, doesn't she?" Devon responded, bending over to look at the baby more closely.

"Yes, she does," Loralei said, looking up at him. "She has your beautiful blue eyes."

Loralei watched Devon looking at the baby and felt a sudden, overwhelming love for him that she thought had been lost forever. She was so relieved that he had made it home safely through the storm to see their new daughter on the night of her birth.

"Would you like to hold her?" she asked, after a moment.

"Yes," he said.

"Here, you can put this on," Marie said, handing him a dry shirt before leaving the room.

Devon stood and put on the shirt before sitting back down on the bed. Loralei handed him the baby and watched his eyes soften as he held the baby and gazed down at her. She remembered how he had held Misha in the same way when he was born.

Loralei looked up when she heard a knock on the bedroom door. The door opened slightly, and Loralei saw Marie peek in.

"Misha's awake. He wants to see you. Is this a good time?" she asked.

"Yes, of course. Have him come in and see his new baby sister," Loralei said.

Marie opened the door further, and Misha padded through, looking disheveled in his cotton pajamas.

"Mama, Papa," Misha said, running over to them. As he approached the bed, he slowed and appeared to wonder what was going on.

"Come and meet your new little sister," Loralei signed to him, gesturing toward Devon, who was cradling the baby in his arms.

Misha moved closer and touched Devon's arm as he peered around him at the baby. "Baby. I love the baby," Misha signed.

Loralei smiled at the tender look on Misha's face. "She is

your new baby sister. You saved her. You saved me. You are very brave, like Papa and Grandpapa," Loralei signed.

Misha nodded and smiled.

"I wish my parents and your parents were here with us now to share in our joy. I know they would have been so happy to see the new baby," she said to Devon.

"I wish they were here, too," he replied.

"Perhaps they are looking down at us from heaven and smiling. I have to believe they are. I have to believe that, in some way, they are still here with us, welcoming our new daughter into the world," Loralei said.

"Perhaps they are," Devon said.

They all sat on the bed together as a family, talking deep into the night, until Devon left with Misha to allow Loralei to nurse the baby.

Later in the night, when Devon returned to her side, he told Loralei that Andre had been found dead on the ground beneath the lighthouse and that his death was being attributed to the fury of the storm, in the same way Edmund's death had been. It appeared he had been standing on the balcony to check the beacon or for some other reason and had fallen to his death, perhaps blown over the railing by a raging gust of wind. Loralei didn't have to pretend to cry when he told her. Even though she already knew Andre was gone, the tears poured out without ceasing for hours. Devon didn't know what had really happened to Andre, and she would never tell him. She would take the secret of Andre's death and her responsibility for it to her grave, just as she would take the secret of Jake's death to her grave.

Because of Andre's death and her responsibility for it, nothing would ever be the same for her. She had saved her country and her family, and her own life, and she would have done the same thing again. But she had taken the life of another, and she could never go back to the way she was before. Andre's death was something that would always be with her.

To Loralei's surprise, Devon held her and comforted her until the tears receded. She was finally able to come to terms with all she had lost and all that she had saved. She felt as though her whole life, as she knew it, had ended in the tumult of the night before and had begun again in the quiet of the peaceful morning as she and Devon welcomed their new baby into the world.

Loralei looked back down at her tiny daughter, a radiant new life in the midst of so much death. She looked so innocent and vulnerable to her, and she would do whatever it took to protect her. She was a child of their family, from generations of family before. A child of the light.

"I want to name her Marguerite," she said.

"Marguerite? Is it French?" Devon asked.

"Yes, it means 'child of light,'" she said.

Devon continued to gaze at the baby for a moment before looking up at Loralei and nodding.

"I like it. We'll call her Marguerite," he said.

Loralei noticed a drop of sunlight on the floor and asked Devon to pull open the curtains. She wanted to see the blue of the lake at dawn reflected in her newborn daughter's eyes. Devon opened the curtains, and Loralei smiled down at her daughter before gazing out at the wide expanse of shimmering water that was her life, reaching out to the horizon.

"This could be a new beginning for us. It could be a new beginning for our family," Devon said.

"Yes," Loralei said, gazing far out over the lake. "Yes, it could be," she said.

Loralei thought of all that had happened and of all who had come before, and she tried to remember what it was like to be innocent.

Terri Greening is a creative writer in the Great Lakes region. She enjoys yoga, gardening, nature parks, walking, and biking. She has a B.A. in journalism from Central Michigan University and an M.B.A. from Grand Valley State University.

www.ingramcontent.com/pod-product-compliance
Lightning Source LLC
Chambersburg PA
CBHW030120180626
46812CB00002B/501